Emmerdale: Their Finest Hour

Emmerdale:
Their Finest Hour

The Story of Beckindale
in World War II

GRANADA

Emmerdale is a Yorkshire Television Production

First published in Great Britain in 2001
by Granada Media, an imprint of André Deutsch Limited
20 Mortimer Street
London W1T 3JW

In association with Granada Media Group

Text copyright © Granada Media Group Limited 2001

A catalogue record for this book is available from
the British Library

ISBN 0 233 99919 1

Cover photograph property of Timepix.
Photo by Alfred Eisenstadt
Cover design by Nathan Skreslet

Typeset by Derek Doyle & Associates, Liverpool
Printed and bound in the UK by
Mackays of Chatham plc

10 8 6 4 2 1 3 5 7 9

Thanks to:

My wife, Cassandra May.

Karen Grimes, without whom this book wouldn't have been possible. Wendy Bloom, without whom *Emmerdale* wouldn't be possible.

Susanna Wadeson of Granada Commercial Ventures and Nicky Paris of André Deutsch, and my editor Hazel Orme.

I'm very grateful to Len Brattan for sharing his first-hand expertise of Yorkshire in wartime.

And to Mark Clapham, Mark Jones, Lisa Brattan and Nathan Skreslet.

And finally to Stan Richards, for some very kind words of encouragement. I'm gratified that Seth himself approves of the way he's been portrayed here!

CHAPTER ONE:

Don't You Know There's a War On?

The nights were darker than ever.

At the start of the last War, it was said that the lamps had gone out all over Europe. Annie Pearson hadn't been born then, but she could see what had been meant. Until the war, as the evening drew in, the first lights had come on – lanterns at the front of the Woolpack, guiding people in, lights on in every front room and kitchen as the men got home from work and their wives served them their dinner. For centuries past, if you'd stood where Annie was standing, on the path up to Emmerdale Farm overlooking the village of Beckindale, and looked down, you'd have seen the lines of Main Street, Church Street and Demdyke Row.

Tonight the village was all but invisible, just dark shapes huddling down into the hillside, hiding from the German bombers. You could hear them overhead most nights, now – either the Luftwaffe bombers or the RAF fighters sent up to stop them. Some of the young men could identify the planes by the noise their engines made, but to Annie they all sounded the same: a relentless drone, far away, but still managing to fill the night sky. It was the outside world forcing its problems on a small, peaceful village that had nothing to do with Czechoslovakia, Poland or all those other places.

1

Annie knew Beckindale had it lucky. Those German bombers were heading to the big cities – to Leeds, Manchester, Liverpool – perhaps even further afield. And the next morning, the villagers would hear about the destruction on the wireless, and they'd see the pictures in the paper. Every night, dozens were dying, or losing loved ones, treasured possessions or the roof over their heads. Annie couldn't begin to imagine what it must be like to be caught in an air-raid.

She counted her blessings. Life here hadn't changed all that much. There was rationing now, but in the country there weren't the acute shortages they had in the towns and cities. And, here in Yorkshire, people already knew everything they needed to about making do and mending. It said in the papers that women in London were getting used to stitching their own clothes, and darning socks, and not just throwing away a dress because its hemline changed from season to season. In the Dales, no one knew a different way of doing things.

Part of Annie treasured the simplicity of village life, the stoicism, the certainty, the way things never changed. But when she looked down the hill at Beckindale, and realised that if she held up her hand, just *so*, the whole village and everything in it disappeared from view, part of her wanted to run away to a place where she'd be expected to have new dresses every few weeks and there were theatres to be closed.

She sighed, and carried on up the hill, to Emmerdale Farm and Jacob Sugden.

'What the heck is that?' Betty cried, when the front door was half open.

'Pheasant,' Seth grunted, holding up the bird by its neck.

Betty recoiled. 'And what're you bringing it round here

for?' She looked back over her shoulder, clearly hoping no one else had seen.

'For you,' he said, unsure why he had to explain something so obvious. 'A treat. I caught it special.'

Betty hesitated. Seth took the opportunity to have a good look at her. She was a few years younger than him, but she was getting to be a fine woman. They'd grown up together in the village, and had known each other all their lives. They'd gone to school together, played together in the summer. But he'd never thought of her like *that*. Then, in the last year or so, she'd cut her hair short and Seth had decided she looked a lot like another Betty: Betty Grable. And she had the curves to match.

'Here, what are you staring at?' Betty scolded. She'd learned scolding from her mother.

Seth looked up quickly. 'Nowt. Look, do you want this or not? 'Cos there's plenty who will, and it's better than Woolton Pie.'

Betty frowned. 'Where did you get it?'

'Er . . . Verney's.'

'You poached it from Home Farm land,' she said. It wasn't a question, and every word was soaked in disapproval.

'Well, George Verney didn't just give it to me, did he?' Seth said, exasperated with the woman. 'Look, I can get sixpence for it in the Woolie if you don't want it. Come on, lass, it's getting cold out here.'

Betty looked at Seth, then at the pheasant, then back at Seth. 'I'll take it.'

'At last.'

'But I'll pay you for it.'

She disappeared into the house for her purse. Seth called after her that he didn't want her to pay for it, it was a present.

Betty's elder sister drifted past the front door, looking

down at Seth with contempt. She had none of her sister's charm – Seth had never liked her.

'Evening, Maggie,' he said.

'Margaret,' she replied coldly, before moving back inside the house. 'Betty, you can't leave the door open during blackout.'

Then Seth heard Betty's mother. He couldn't distinguish her words, but he didn't need to: he recognised the sound of disapproval.

'It's all right, Mother,' he heard Betty say. 'I'm getting rid of him.'

Betty emerged, purse in hand, and passed him a couple of coins. 'I don't want to owe you anything,' she told him, primly. 'Sixpence. Thank you very much, Mr Armstrong.' And she closed the door on him.

Seth looked down at the coins in his hand. If he added it to the cash in his pocket, there was enough to get him and Betty to the dance hall in Hotten. He'd been hoping for that, or at least the promise of it. Still, there was enough for a pint or two instead, so it wasn't a total loss. He headed across the road to the Woolpack.

Colin, the barman, was trying to get the blackout curtain to stay in place over the front door. He grumbled – this was the official material and they'd paid good money for it.

'You should get Ron to lend you a hand,' Seth joked.

Inside, Ron was there, as ever.

'Pint of Monk.'

Ron obliged. However many times Seth saw him pull a pint with only the one arm, he was still impressed. Ron had lost the other in the last war – amputated after a German sniper hit him. Seth's dad had been in the same regiment, and had dragged him to safety. Ron was Seth's godfather, and a good friend, and had always been concerned for his welfare.

4

'Seth, you're a young man, what do you waste your life in here for? You should be out and about in the evenings, not propping up a bar.'

'I'm young, there'll be plenty of time for that later,' Seth assured him, taking the pint.

Ron knew his customers well enough to tell when something was wrong – and, more times than not, precisely what the problem was. 'Betty Prendergast still playing hard to get?'

Seth looked up from his pint. 'She is.'

'She's a good-looking girl, it'll be worth the effort. And everyone knows she's sweet on you.'

'Her sister isn't, and her mother hates me.'

'You're not going after her sister or her mother, though, are you?'

Seth shivered. 'I'd need more than a pint before I did something like that.'

Ron chuckled. 'Faint heart never won fair lady, Seth.'

'So what do you think I should do?'

The landlord rubbed his chin. 'Aye, well, that's the question. You see enough of Betty, don't you? It's not like she avoids you, or anything. You talk to her.'

'Aye.'

'Find out what it is she's not so happy about. If you mend your ways, she's bound to think better of you.'

Seth supped his pint, then nodded thoughtfully.

'I hate this place. It's stupid,' said Joe.

'It'll be an adventure,' Adam said. 'That's what Mum and Dad said.'

'Staying at home would be an adventure – seeing bombs dropping, and our fighters shooting the Nazi bombers down.'

'But we never saw that, did we? We were down in the

shelters. We didn't hear anything. You've already forgotten what it was like.'

Little children did that, Adam knew. They only remembered the good things – Joe wanted to go home because he was missing his friends, and he'd forgotten all about the bullies. 'We couldn't do this back in town, could we?' Adam said.

'No,' Joe admitted, grudgingly.

They were playing in the woods. Beckindale was a tiny village, but it was surrounded by countryside. There was a stream, with bridges you could play under, there were fields and footpaths, and crags to climb. Best of all, at one end of the village, on the hill that led up to Home Farm, there was a huge wood – almost a forest.

They came up here a lot, especially when it was getting dark. There was nothing like this in Manchester, where they were from. Adam didn't think you could ever explore it all.

'We might see a deer again,' Joe said, getting back into the spirit of things.

They'd seen one the first week they'd been here. They hadn't known what it was at first – it was pale in the dark, but its eyes reflected, like a cat's. It had been too big to be a dog, too small to be a horse, and for just a few moments, the way it had been standing, it had looked like a forest spirit, or a ghost, not like an animal at all.

Then it must have seen them, or smelt them, because it turned and ran, leaping through the undergrowth and over the fallen trees as if they weren't even there.

'Shush,' Adam said. He'd just heard something moving. He couldn't see his brother's face, but he could tell Joe was excited.

Something was coming up the path. Adam knew he ought to be able to tell what it was from the sound of its footsteps on the hard ground, but he couldn't.

'Is it a deer?' Joe asked.

'If it is, you've probably just scared it off.'

They ducked out of sight, and stayed very quiet. They quickly realised that it hadn't heard them, and was still coming their way. But as it went past, and they sneaked a look, they were disappointed.

It was a woman.

'Who is it?' Joe whispered.

'I think it's Miss Pearson,' Adam said. He recognised her from around the village.

Joe slumped down. 'This isn't an adventure. It's a swiz.'

'I don't think deer walk along footpaths,' Adam said.

'What time is it?'

'It's only quarter to five.' They were meant to be in at half past, for their dinner but it was only a few minutes' walk back to the Sullivans', so they had plenty of time. However it was getting dark, and it was cold. They sat there for a moment.

More footsteps. This time, Adam could tell straight away that it was a man. Or men. Deer didn't wear heavy boots. As they got nearer, he could hear voices, not every word, but the handful they caught was enough.

'Luftwaffe.'

'Hamburg.'

'Düsseldorf.'

Adam and Joe looked at each other, eyes wide.

They saw one of them. A tall, handsome man, with Brycreemed black hair. He wore a flying jacket, but it was too dark to see the medals or any insignia.

Without needing to say anything, both Adam and Joe broke cover and started running. They knew the way back to the village so they didn't need to think about their route. And, while they would normally have tripped over roots, or been hurt by low branches, instinct seemed to protect them.

They were soon back on the proper footpath, but didn't slow down until they had run past the Woolpack. They almost demolished the door of the village shop as they pushed through it.

Mr Sullivan tried to slow them down. 'What is it? You look like you've seen a ghost.'

'Germans!' they shouted together. 'the Germans have invaded Beckindale!'

Annie almost walked straight past Jacob.

It was dark down in the village, but here it was pitch black, and she had found her way here because the path was so familiar. He was bent down, mending a wall about ten yards away from the front door of Emmerdale Farm. She could hear the clink of stone against stone.

'Jacob, can't that wait until morning?'

He looked round. 'I'll be with you in a moment.'

'Let me help you.'

Together, they eased the last stone into place.

'A job well done,' Jacob muttered.

Annie peered into the gloom. 'I'll take your word for it.'

'It's those girls,' he complained. 'They're meant to be helping with the harvest, but they make more work than they get done. They climb over the walls, rather than using the stiles, and they sit on them, too.'

Land Girls.

The Women's Land Army. It had been an idea they'd come up with during the last war. With virtually all the men who worked the farms called up to join the armed forces, and blockades meaning that food from abroad couldn't be guaranteed, women volunteers picked up the slack. It was a good idea – hard work never harmed anyone – but for the most part these were city girls. A couple billeted at Emmerdale Farm, Alyson and Rita, had claimed they had never even seen a cow before they'd come here, let alone milked one. They'd chosen to work on a farm rather than in a munitions factory, and who could blame them? But while he'd been setting them straight, it had meant far more work for Jacob Sugden, not less.

He stood up. He was a tall man, and broad. Whenever she was with him, Annie felt safe. 'Come here,' she said, and gave him a hug.

Jacob wasn't the sort to blurt out his feelings, but he needed a good hug from time to time, like everyone else. He risked a peck on her cheek, which became a proper kiss. They stood together for a couple of minutes, keeping each other warm, holding each other close.

'We don't want to give any of the girls ideas.' She giggled, breaking away. 'Come on, let's get inside.'

Jacob followed her over the doorstep. 'I doubt we could teach them anything. I've caught them talking, and—'

' "Caught them talking"!' Annie laughed. 'You sound like their schoolmaster. They're allowed to talk while they work, aren't they?'

'As long as they don't forget to do the work. This is graft,' Jacob said, 'hard graft. They don't want to lift hay bales in case their nails break.'

Annie bristled. 'Women can work just as hard as men,' she reminded him. 'Where are they at the moment?'

'They stay in their room, mostly.'

Annie put her bag down.

'You should leave your stuff here, you know. You shouldn't have to heft that bag up and down the hill every day,' Jacob said.

Annie smiled. 'People might talk.'

'Aren't they already?'

'Nora Prendergast is telling everyone what an outrage it is. I overheard her saying that we got up to terrible things. So I faced up to her: "It's true," I said, "I spend every night in Jacob Sugden's bed." '

Jacob blushed.

'And I told her that you sleep down here on the sofa. "Perhaps you'd like to go up there to chaperone those girls," I said. "Perhaps you'd put them up in your cottage. Or perhaps you should get some evacuee children in."'

Even Annie's father approved of the arrangement – it was a little out of the ordinary, but only a little, and these were extraordinary times. Jacob was uncomfortable living on his own with his dad and four young women. Not just embarrassed – although he was certainly that – but concerned that they should feel at ease sharing a roof with two men. Most of the other farmers were married – their wives or daughters could talk to the girls, make them feel more at ease. Even in peacetime Emmerdale Farm had been a place for men. Normally, Jacob and Joseph lived here with Jacob's younger brother, Edward, but he was in the navy now. On the *Solent*. It was a small world – the fiancé of one of the Land Girls was on the same ship. Jacob would have joined his brother, but his job was a reserved occupation. Despite having no women in the house, the three men could fend for themselves, do whatever cooking, mending and cleaning that was needed. But Jacob couldn't run a farm *and* cook and clean for four young women. Perhaps, when they were used to the farmwork, the girls would find the energy to cater for themselves. As it was, they were exhausted at the end of a long day, and they took it for granted that there would be a meal on the table for them.

So, for the last month or so, Annie had come here every evening, cooked dinner, organised whatever laundry was needed, then risen early to cook everyone breakfast before going home until the following evening. The cleaning . . . well, the others managed that task, just about.

Moving in with Jacob, sharing a roof, even if they weren't sharing a bed, that would have been . . . well, *wrong.* Scandalous, as far as some in the village would see it. Annie knew that. But she hadn't moved in. Not really.

She smiled. The idea of being scandalous appealed to her.

'Nora should put her own house in order,' Jacob told her.

'How do you mean?' Annie moved round the cupboards, started assembling the ingredients for tonight's casserole.

'Her Maggie.' Jacob paused. 'Haven't you heard?'

Annie laughed. 'I thought you were too busy to listen to gossip.'

Jacob wrapped his arms around her waist. 'That's right. Too busy causing gossip to listen to it.' They kissed again, held each other. Jacob pulled back a little. 'You don't mind what they say?'

'I know the truth. And I love you. Besides, we're engaged. We'd be married by now if there wasn't a war on.'

Jacob turned away again. 'I want Edward to be here. He'll be my best man.'

Annie took his hand. 'I know that. You're right. I love you, Jacob, I'll always love you. There's no rush.'

Brian Sullivan swept his torch around.

'There's no one here,' he grumbled. 'Come on, Jean 'as got our supper ready, we ought to be getting back.'

Adam tugged at his sleeve. 'We should call the police, or the army. They could send out a proper search party.'

How did you tell a pair of boys with active imaginations that he knew they were making it up? Life here couldn't be very interesting for them so of course they'd come up with games and stories to make village life more eventful.

'I'm sure they know about it already,' Brian assured them.

'How? We need to be vigilant, Mr Sullivan.'

Adam could be a real prig sometimes, he thought. 'There are no Germans here,' he told them. 'And we're going home.'

Adam opened his mouth to object, but soon changed his mind when he saw the look on Brian Sullivan's face.

CHAPTER TWO:

The Village Invaded

The manor house stood just outside Beckindale, as it had – or at least its oldest parts – since the eighteenth century. Over the years, it had acquired a number of names – it was the manor house of the Miffield Estate; on the Ordnance Survey map and in some of the guides and local history books it was called Miffield Hall; but the villagers knew it as Verney's, after the family who had owned it for as long as records went back, or, more usually, just Home Farm.

It was set in hundreds of acres of land. Once, long ago, that land had stretched over the horizon. Over the years, due to taxes and death duties – or to some other tricky financial situation – the estate had gradually shrunk. Only ten years ago Jacob Sugden had bought Emmerdale Farm and a large amount of land from the Verneys.

For centuries George Verney's ancestors, whose portraits hung beside the staircase and along hallways and corridors of the house, had ruled the estate, and by extension the surrounding villages and their residents. They'd been the law, judge and jury. But now, for the duration of the war, at least, George Verney wasn't even the master of his own home.

Squadron Leader Roland Pilgrim looked over the maps and notes that were laid out on the billiard table. A couple of his engineers, in tweed suits, puffing at pipes, were helping him to decipher them. They'd just been on a tour of the land, which had taken most of the day.

George Verney didn't resent their presence: he was an officer in the RAF himself and had been keen to volunteer the use of Home Farm. But it was an awkward situation.

'It's ideal,' one of the boffins said. 'The hills round it will provide natural cover and shelter. There's room for three runways.'

'And access?'

'There's a road . . . er, there – the main road to Hotten. I'm not sure any of the others will bear the traffic. They're only single-track lanes.'

Roland studied the map. 'Who owns that field?'

George leant over. 'West Field is part of Emmerdale Farm. Jacob Sugden.'

'You know him?'

'I sold him his farm. His father works as my estate manager.'

'So you get on well with him?'

George smiled. 'I didn't say that . . .'

Sam Pearson shifted the last bale into place and sat down on it, exhausted. 'This gets harder every year.'

Joseph Sugden slumped beside him. 'Aye.'

'It's not like we're old men. Well . . . I'm not.'

It was a running joke between them. Joseph had been old when he'd married, even older when he'd had his children. He was in his sixties now and years of labour meant he looked his age, at least, but he was still strong and sharp. And still Sam's boss.

'Your daughter's doing you proud,' Joseph said, passing over a flask.

'Annie's a good cook. She'll make Jacob an excellent wife.'

'Then we'll be family.'

The two laughed.

They'd been more than family for a long time. They'd served together in Flanders during the last war. Sam had been one of the youngest in the regiment, with Joseph one of the eldest. They'd kept each other sane. All around them . . . noise, machines, mud and death. It was the first time either of them had been abroad – the first time either had gone further than Leeds. At first the terrible churned landscape had been shocking because it was so unfamiliar, but as Sam had got used to it, what frightened him was how like home it was. Isolated farmhouses, tiny villages, country roads . . . and all lying in ruins, with trenches cut through the fields and new roads imposed on the landscape for the trucks and artillery pieces. It was a foreign country, but a few years before it hadn't been very different from Beckindale. The towns where they spent their leave, doing what soldiers did, had once been quiet market towns like Hotten.

But Joseph had been there to prove to Sam that the world hadn't gone mad. They'd both fought, they'd escaped injury. More than that, they'd escaped the madness that had afflicted so many of their fellows.

'There should be young men here to help us,' Joseph said. He'd been remembering Flanders, too.

'Aye. Next year, do you think?'

Joseph sighed. 'No, this one's a long haul. Longer than the last one.'

Sam winced. 'I thought *we* had it bad.'

'And I thought we were fighting so that our kids wouldn't have to.'

*

15

Adam and Joe were perched on a low stone wall, looking into the field where the Land Girls were working.

'Can we move on?' Joe asked. 'I'm fed up of looking at girls.'

Adam snorted. 'You'll understand when you're older.'

'You fancy one of them?' Joe, said.

Adam blushed. 'Well, what do you think about that dark-haired girl?'

'She's all right, I suppose,' Joe said. 'She looks Jewish, too.'

Adam looked over again. 'She does, doesn't she?'

'Doesn't mean she is.'

'No. But if I see her in the village, I'll ask her.'

Joe giggled. 'You fancy her. You think that because you're the only suitable boy around she's going to marry you.'

'I don't,' Adam insisted. But he did think it gave him an excuse to talk to her.

'Come on,' Joe said. 'We came up here to look for German spies, not girls.'

'All right.'

'I think we've got some admirers,' Louise said.

Alyson spun round to look. 'They're only little boys,' she complained. 'You got my hopes up, then.'

'What do you want from life?' Louise asked.

Alyson looked like she'd just been asked to do calculus. 'How do you mean?'

'Simple question.'

'Well, same as anyone. Meet a nice bloke, get married, have kids.'

Louise sighed.

'Go on, what do you want?' Rita challenged.

'Not to have to pick potatoes.'

'You asked the question, you ought to have a better answer than that. Don't you want to be swept off your

16

feet? See a man, fall for him, have him bring you flowers and chocolates?'

Louise laughed. 'If *I* want flowers and chocolates I'll go out to work and earn the money to buy them.'

'I don't think you've got a romantic bone in your body.'

'I think you're right,' Louise replied happily.

'That's sad.'

Louise shook her head. 'I think romance is a lie. I don't want a man to be on his best behaviour while he's courting me, I want to know what he's really like.'

'But you want to be courted?'

'I certainly don't want to be chaste.'

Rita and Alyson sniggered, and Louise joined in with the laughter.

'Mr Verney.'

Sam and Joseph doffed their caps.

'How's everything going?' Verney asked.

'Baling's done now. We were just going on to Miffield Rise.'

Verney glanced in that direction. 'No need for that. There's a wall come down between us and Emmerdale – all those damn Land Girls sitting on it, I'd have thought. Could you see to that instead?'

Sam and Joseph looked at each other, a little puzzled.

'Aye,' Joseph said finally.

George took an envelope from his pocket and handed it to Joseph. 'And could you give this to Jacob?'

Joseph slipped it into his pocket.

George smiled amiably at them, then strode away.

'What was all that about?' Sam said.

Joseph knew that Sam was always suspicious of anything new. No, more than that, *fearful* of it. The way he used the word 'new' seemed to cover everything from a recent invention or machine to a change of routine, like the one George Verney had just suggested. Joseph Sugden was hardly a man to bend to the whims of fashion – he liked things the way they were, the way they had always been – but compared with his friend, he was practically a revolutionary.

But it *was* a bit queer. George Verney had a keen interest in the running of the estate, knew every inch of it, but he rarely interfered with their work.

'Was he trying to keep us away from Miffield?' Joseph asked.

Sam frowned. 'Why would he do that?'

Two boys were running towards them.

'Hey!' Joseph shouted. But the boys showed no sign of stopping. Normally, when challenged, trespassers, particularly young boys, ran away from the man shouting at them. But these boys were heading fast towards Sam and Joseph.

Joseph recognised them now: they were the Jewish boys staying with the Sullivans at the village shop. He'd seen them around, and thought they were quiet, well-spoken boys, not like a lot of the evacuees they heard about – urchins from the slums who weren't even housetrained and had arrived in infested clothes that had to be burned. He'd seen these boys playing in the fields before, and they'd always stuck to the paths and behaved themselves.

'Mr Sugden! Mr Sugden!' they were both calling.

'Good grief,' Sam said, as they stopped in front of him, panting. 'What's so important?'

'You shouldn't be on this land,' Joseph told them.

'Germans,' the younger one blurted.

'We've seen a couple of German spies. We heard them talking.'

'And you speak German?' Sam asked sceptically.

'Our grandfather's German, sir, or he was. We know a few words. Enough to recognise it when we hear it.'

Sam and Joseph looked at each other.

'Stranger things have happened round here,' Sam concluded sagely.

Joseph couldn't think of any, but nodded. 'And you know where these Jerries are?'

The boys nodded.

'You'd better show us, then.'

Annie entered the village shop. It was a small, dark place, but it always seemed to have just about everything the villagers needed. And there were rarely the queues that town shops attracted.

Mr and Mrs Sullivan were stacking shelves. Brian Sullivan had lived in the village for almost all his forty years, except for a couple spent in Leeds just before the war. In that time he'd found his young wife Jean. They'd married at Hotten Register Office, because she was Jewish. Perhaps that was why she had never quite settled in. Or perhaps once you'd tasted city life, a village seemed staid, unglamorous. Annie wasn't sure why, but Jean rubbed her up the wrong way. She was always well dressed: she usually wore a little gold jewellery and even some perfume – she was the only woman in the world who still had any – however menial the job she was doing in the shop. To Annie it seemed as if Jean was saying, 'I'm better than you and this place.'

That had been a lot of people's reaction when she'd first come to the village. She was fifteen years younger than her husband and, unlike poor Brian, she was very attractive. A lot of the men had been rather jealous – a few of the women had been surprised by just how eager their spouses suddenly became to pop over to the shop at the slightest excuse. But she had been distant, almost uninterested in the village.

'Good morning,' Jean said, straightening up and coming over. 'What can I get for you?'

'Good morning. Tea, sugar . . .' Annie ran through the rest of the list. Jean listened intently, then, without needing to ask again, worked her way round the shop, pulling tins, barrels and packets down, piling them up on the counter, weighing out the tiny amounts of the rationed produce, like butter and tea.

'How are you, Mr Sullivan?' Annie called across the shop, while she waited.

'Oh, as well as can be expected.' he replied automatically.

His wife had assembled everything Annie had asked for, except marmalade, for which Annie hadn't held out any hope. She had made jam, and that would have to do. She counted out the money Jacob had given her, and handed it over with her ration book and the books she'd taken from the girls. Jean counted the coins again, while Annie put her shopping in the bag.

'How's Jacob?'

'Coping. It's difficult this year, with Edward away.'

'I thought he had all those Land Girls.'

'Oh he does, but they're city girls, they don't know anything about the country.' Even as she said it, Annie was aware that Jean might take that as a personal criticism. She did bridle a little, but Annie decided an apology would make it worse, so continued, 'And that means they don't know anything about farming. When we first heard about it, we thought they'd already be farmers. You know, that they'd be trained up before they were sent over. But no. They're learning.'

Joseph wondered if Sam felt as foolish as he did, sneaking round the estate like a couple of poachers. The boys were close behind, almost clinging to them.

As they turned the corner and saw Miffield Rise, their

suspicion was confirmed. A couple of men in tweed suits were surveying the field, one pacing it out with a length of rope, the other making notes in a tiny book. He was aware that there was a perfectly innocent explanation for their presence, but wasn't sure what it might be.

'Recognise them?' Joseph asked.

Sam shook his head.

'They're very bold Germans, out here during the daylight,' Joseph pointed out. 'And what are they doing with all that rope?'

'They're well turned out, though.'

Sam had a point – they weren't labourers, not dressed like that. They were professional men. Surveyors, maybe even architects.

'Look,' the older boy said. 'That one in the flight jacket.'

He seemed to be in charge. A young man – thirty, thirty-one, with black hair. 'That's an RAF jacket, son,' Joseph assured him.

'How do you know?'

'Mr Verney, the squire round here, wears one,' Sam explained.

'Is he selling off more land?' Joseph asked.

A little over ten years ago, when George's father had died, the estate had faced huge debts. Unpaid tax bills, all sorts of financial trouble. Verney had done the unthinkable – sold off some of his land to tenants. Joseph couldn't help but smile remembering it – his son, Jacob, had bought Emmerdale Farm, and got himself a good price into the bargain.

'Makes no sense,' Sam said.

And, again, Sam was right. Miffield Rise was right in the middle of the estate. It was difficult to see how it could be separated from the rest into a working farm.

'Well, Verney's not got the money to be building anything. And the bank would wait until the war's over,

wouldn't they, before they lent him anything?' That had
been Joseph's experience, anyway: the uncertainty the
war brought had made the banks wary of lending to pay
for anything but short term investments, especially with
prices rising so fast.

'So, what are they doing?'

'Whatever it is, Mr Verney knows about it, and he does-
n't want us to know about it.'

Sam clearly wasn't happy, but that was that, as far as
Joseph was concerned. 'OK, lads, I'll get you home,' he said.

Seth ran up to Betty. 'Hello there.'

Betty looked round. Seth had noticed that she always
did that when they met. He'd never worked out why, but
sometimes she'd talk to him, sometimes she'd make a
show of not talking to him. And it wasn't that she was
ashamed of him and would only talk if no one else was
around. Now she seemed almost pleased to see him. 'I've
got a letter from Wally,' she told him.

Wally Eagleton was a friend of theirs. He was in the
army.

'What's he doing?'

'He says he can't say because the letter might be inter-
cepted by the Germans and then they'd be able to work
out the British military plans.' Betty held the letter to her
chest. 'He's probably on undercover missions, deep in
enemy territory, busy undermining Nazi defences. Wally
always was brave.'

Seth studied the envelope. 'Postmark says
"Bridlington". And he's not so busy he can't write to you.
Everyone I know that signed up spends their time white-
washing walls and cleaning their boots. Square bashing.'

Betty narrowed her eyes. 'Private Eagleton is doing his
duty,' she told him, snatched back the envelope and
stormed off.

Seth watched her go. He'd never understand Betty and her moods.

Joseph could hear the commotion before he opened the door. Women's voices – girls' voices, really. It felt *wrong*. Since his Mary had died, a long time ago, there hadn't been a woman at Emmerdale Farm. Now they outnumbered the men by more than two to one, and only Annie counted as family.

The kitchen table was crowded, with Jacob at the head and four girls around it. Annie bustling around putting plates down.

Joseph took his place, squeezed between the two city girls, Alyson and Rita, who chuckled at him.

'You're late,' Annie said.

'I'm sorry,' Joseph replied. 'You know how it is, this time of the year.'

Beef stew. He tucked in. Whatever he thought of the women's intrusion, the quality of the food had gone up since Annie had moved in. She made the rations go a lot further.

He remembered the letter George Verney had given him, and passed it to Jacob.

The Land Girls were arguing and giggling among themselves. Joseph could just about remember which one was which by now.

'What the hell?'

They all turned to face Jacob, shocked.

'Ladies present,' Joseph said, indignant.

'What the hell?' Jacob repeated, oblivious to them. He stood up, so fast that the chair fell backwards. He was heading for the door, grabbing for his coat.

Annie was moments behind him. She hesitated on the doorstep – it was a cold night, but if she went back for her

23

coat she'd lose Jacob in the darkness. She pressed on.
'Jacob, what's the matter?' she called out, hurrying to
catch him up. But he was striding on ahead, and didn't
look back. She had to run to get level with him.

'Read that!' Jacob said, and flung the letter at her.

It was all Annie could do to catch it and it was far too
dark to read – too dark even to tell which side the writing
was on.

'I can't see it, Jacob, you'll have to tell me.'

'Compulsory purchase,' Jacob spat. 'Verney's buying
West Field back off me, and there's nothing I can do about
it. And he even got my own father to do his dirty work.'

'But . . .' Annie looked back at the farmhouse. As estate
manager at Home Farm Jacob's father would have
mentioned it if he'd known anything about it. George
Verney must have been keeping something from him.

'Jacob, wait a moment,' she called after him.

It didn't make him slow down. Jacob was striding
ahead, muttering to himself.

'Calm down, Jacob, or at least think about what you're
doing.'

She caught up with him again at the stream that separated Emmerdale from Home Farm land. It was tricky to
get across in the day, but at night, it required concentration.

'What are you going to say to him?'

'Follow me and you'll hear for yourself.'

Annie knew better than to argue. She wasn't sure she
wanted to. George Verney had sold Emmerdale Farm to
Jacob as a last resort, and at the sale Jacob had made his
glee more than obvious. She'd been a child at the time,
and Jacob not twenty, but for the last decade now, Jacob
had never failed to remind Verney of his victory.

Home Farm sat, as ever, at the top of the rise. Even
here, the blackout was strictly enforced, but they both
knew the way to the front door.

Sally, the maid, opened the door. 'Mr Sugden, Miss Pearson, good evening.'

Jacob pushed past her. He'd barely slowed down since leaving home.

'Mr Sugden!' she squealed.

Annie apologised for him, then followed her fiancé. It was a bit cold in the hall and she felt uneasy: they didn't belong here, and you couldn't just barge your way in. Although Jacob was doing a good job of it.

They found George Verney in the billiard room, in the middle of a game with a tall, square-jawed chap Annie didn't recognise. They were both in civvies, but Annie guessed this was one of Verney's RAF colleagues. They were about the same age and both had that distinctive military bearing – there was something about the way they stood, even when relaxed.

Jacob almost shoved the letter into Verney's mouth. 'What's this?'

'It's what it says it is,' Verney told him, leaning on his cue.

'Annie Pearson,' she said, holding out her hand to the other man. 'That's Jacob Sugden, my fiancé.'

The man had a wry smile, and seemed unconcerned by the intrusion. 'Roland Pilgrim. I'm a Squadron Leader in the RAF.'

'Good to meet you, Mr Pilgrim. Squadron Leader.'

'Good to meet you too, Miss Pearson.'

They turned their attention to Jacob and Verney.

'It's not me, it's the War Ministry,' Verney was telling him patiently.

'Oh, yes? Why are you hiding behind your military friends?'

Verney took a step back. 'If you'll calm down, I'll explain. The RAF want the field to provide an access road.'

25

'To Home Farm?'

'To RAF Emmerdale.'

'Eh?'

'They're building an airfield on Miffield Rise, and they need to connect it to the Hotten road.'

Jacob knew the lie of the land well enough to understand the implications straight away. Annie needed a little more time to picture it. Emmerdale was on the hillside on one side of the valley; almost opposite was Home Farm, with Beckindale village between them in the dale below. Miffield Rise was on the other side of Home Farm; it was a flat area in the next valley. It was fairly isolated and any new route linking it to the Hotten road would have to cut through seven fields.

'An RAF base?' she said.

'Who knows about this?' demanded Jacob.

'People who have to. Like you.'

'Don't you need a public meeting before you just build an airfield?'

'There's a war on, Jacob.'

'I don't need to be told that, I've got a brother in the navy.'

Squadron Leader Pilgrim stepped between them. 'The decision was only finalised a few days ago. It's at an early stage. You'll appreciate that we don't want the Germans to know where our airfields are before we've begun building them.'

Jacob grunted. He'd calmed down, Annie realised.

'And that's the end of it?'

'Yes.'

'And when the war's over, I get my field back?'

'That's the plan, yes.'

Jacob took a step back. 'Right. Well . . .'

'Do you want a drink, Jacob?'

'Was this really the best way to tell us? Does my dad know?'

'Not yet. I was going to tell him in the morning. And yours, Miss Pearson.'

'It seems terribly secretive. Can you blame Jacob for thinking that you were up to something underhand?' she asked.

'It's the way things are done, I'm afraid,' Roland Pilgrim said. 'People will understand, I'm sure.'

'What is your role, exactly?'

'I'm the senior officer of the squadron that will be stationed here. The most senior man who'll be getting into a plane – and I was at university with George here. I'll be making sure the airfield meets the demands of the pilots.'

'Making sure the mess halls are well furnished, that sort of thing?'

Roland laughed. 'No. The furniture, I imagine, will be rudimentary, unless you know where to find any. I'll be making sure the runways are constructed properly, that we've got good line of sight, that the crosswinds aren't too bad. That we build the airfield in a place where we can take off and land successfully. But it would certainly be nice if the place was well furnished, too.'

Annie laughed at her mistake.

Jacob had a glass of whisky but she turned down the offer of one for herself.

'Are you happy now, Jacob?' Verney asked.

Jacob glared at him, conscious of how the scene would have looked if anyone had come in now – a farmer in his wellington boots, contrite, with the lord of the manor looking benevolently at him.

'Aye,' he said reluctantly.

CHAPTER THREE:

Rumours Spread

News that an airfield would be built near the village spread quickly. No one could remember telling anyone, although they could remember being told, and who told *them*. Sam and Joseph had heard it from the horse's mouth: George Verney had told them. Brian Sullivan had heard it from Adam, who'd heard it from Seth Armstrong, who'd heard it from Betty Prendergast, who'd discussed it with Sally, the maid at Home Farm.

Like the common cold, gossip spreads quickly in such a small community. If one person hears something at nine in the morning, and tells two other people straight away – well, everyone in the village will know by ten past. And that was the way it was normally. People had their secrets, but only if they kept them to themselves – tell one other person, and it was as good as telling everyone in the village.

One of the last people to hear was Ron in the Woolpack. No one told him: he pieced it together from what his customers were saying.

'Did you know about this?' he asked Colin.

'Heard it from Jean Sullivan this morning,' he said.

'Did you?' Ron asked, trying not to sound put out. 'So what's there to know?'

'Well, no one's sure at the moment. Hang on, here's Sam, he'll tell you.'

Sam Pearson took his normal place at the bar. 'It's terrible,' he said. 'An airport in Beckindale. It's ridiculous.'

'An airport?' Ron asked.

'Airstrip, aerodrome, airfield, whatever they call it. They're going to be flying bombers from it. Dozens of them, all day and all night.'

Colin frowned. 'In the village?' he repeated.

'Who knows?' Sam said, throwing up his hands. 'Airfields are big places, aren't they?'

None of them knew. Ron had been to an air show once before the war, seen lots of planes doing aerobatic displays. He couldn't remember how big the airfield itself had been. 'There would have to be hangars,' he said, trying to sound knowledgeable. 'And a control tower. And runways.'

'Where are all those pilots going to sleep?' Colin asked. 'We got off lightly with evacuees – do you think they were leaving the extra space free for pilots?'

'You don't think they'd be billeted here in the village, do you?' Ron asked. 'It might be good for business, but you can't run a village like that.'

'They'd keep them all on the base, wouldn't they?' Seth said, joining them. 'Wally Eagleton's at some camp in Bridlington.'

There was general agreement that Seth must be right.

Finally, Ron shook his head. 'This isn't right – they can't just build it. There must be something we can do.'

Jean Sullivan was making a careful note of what the delivery boy had brought and what he hadn't. Every week something would be in short supply or missing. And every week it was a different item, usually something from abroad – they'd not seen an orange or banana for a while,

but it was often coffee or tea. And her customers saw
rationing as a guarantee: the government had promised
them four ounces of butter and two ounces of tea, and
they blamed the shopkeeper if the shelves were empty.
They seemed to blame Jean in particular – an old, dark
suspicion that had nothing to do with her personally. This
week, though, it looked as if just about everything had
come through.

The bell above the door tinkled.

'Be with you in a minute.' She put the last of the
Reckitt's Blue in place, and climbed down to face the
customer.

It was a young woman, one of the Land Girls. She was
dark, with hair cut in a bob that wasn't quite fashionable
any more. 'Hello,' she said, a little nervous. 'Could I have
a stamp?'

'Of course.' Jean moved behind the Post Office counter
and looked for the books. When she looked up the girl was
staring at her. 'Do you mind if I ask,' the girl said, 'but are
you Jewish?'

Jean frowned.

The girl held up her hands. I'm only asking because I
am. Look.' She handed over her letter. It was addressed to
a Mr M. Goldman, in Manchester. 'My father,' she
explained. 'I didn't think I'd find a Jewish quarter in
Beckindale,' she said.

'You won't.' Jean smiled at the thought. 'Just me, and
the two evacuee boys staying here, Adam and Joe.'

'I think I saw them yesterday. Your . . . husband, too?'

'A long story, but no. I'm Jean Sullivan.' She held out
her hand.

'Rita Goldman.' The girl's hand was small, the nails
broken through farm work, but it was warm, and the
handshake surprisingly firm.

They looked at each other again, then laughed.

'It's like meeting another explorer in the middle of the jungle, isn't it?' Rita said.

'I'll have to give you the address of the synagogue,' Jean said.

'There's not one in Beckindale?'

'No! It's in Hotten, a bus ride away. There's a couple of families living there.'

'And do you go often?'

'When I can.'

Rita reached out and touched her arm. 'It's all right, I'm not your father. I'm the same. I'd like to know where it is, though.'

'Just the other day, I thought I ought to go more often, and should be taking the boys. We'll go together,' Jean said.

George Verney couldn't remember the last time he'd visited Emmerdale Farm. His estate manager lived here, as Sugdens had for hundreds of years. But relations between the Verneys and the Sugdens had rarely been amicable, and George had only walked up the path that led almost straight from Home Farm to Emmerdale Farm once in the ten years since he'd sold it to Jacob Sugden.

As a boy, he'd played in these fields. He remembered messing around in the barn at the side of the farmhouse, being caught by Mary Sugden, Jacob's mother, who had shouted the most terrible threats of what she'd do if she found him there again. George had led a sheltered life, idyllic almost. His father hadn't been strict – if anything, he'd erred in the opposite direction, both in how he raised his son and how he conducted his own business. Those few minutes in the barn were almost the first time George had been scared. He remembered lying in the hay, hoping Mary wouldn't find him, knowing that she must.

Her death had been terrible for Joseph, George knew

31

all too well – he had lost his own wife, Milly, a year after Mary had gone. As people had mumbled the same condolences to him as they had to Joseph, George had understood what the other man had been through.

That had been the last time he'd been here, the wake for Mary Sugden. Four years ago now. He had stood in the front room, full of black suits and dresses, no one knowing what to say or when it would be decent to leave.

George knocked at the door. He doubted that the atmosphere would be any less fraught on this visit.

Annie opened the door, looking pale, and he was surprised to see her relax at the sight of him. She was a fine-looking woman, and seemed out of place here in her pinny.

'I saw the uniform and . . .' She didn't finish the sentence.

'Can I come in?' George asked.

'Of course.' She was deferential, more so than George was comfortable with. He stepped over the threshold, into the kitchen.

Joseph and Jacob were sitting at the table. None of the Land Girls were in evidence. He presumed they were all upstairs in their rooms, or perhaps they'd gone into the village.

'To what do we owe the pleasure?' Jacob asked, his tone making Annie and Joseph feel uneasy. George found the studied insolence a little childish.

'Is there a problem, Mr Verney?' Joseph asked.

'Not with the estate. I'm here because I want to apologise. The purchase of West Field is important, vital even, to the war effort, but I should have talked to you about it.'

The apology took a little of the wind out of Jacob's sails – as George had intended.

'Aye. Well, as you say, it was going to happen regardless.'

'And so is the airfield. We thought the village would accept it but they clearly don't. I've had people telephoning all day. Jacob, you've got influence here, can't you talk a few people round? Ron? The Sullivans? Even the vicar. They all look up to you.'

'They look up more to you.'

'With me they have to. With you they choose to.'

Jacob gave a lopsided smile that George Verney would have loved to smack off his face. 'I'm not sure I can help.'

'There must be something we can do,' George said.

'It's the secrecy people don't like,' Annie put in, making it obvious that she was one of the "people" she was talking about.

'But there's a war on,' George snapped. 'We have to make difficult choices. There isn't time for public meetings.'

'We're fighting this war to preserve our way of doing things,' Joseph said, 'and this sort of thing will destroy the village life.'

Annie was looking thoughtful. 'Why can't you call a public meeting?'

'Because it's not up for discussion. If the village don't like the idea, well, sorry, but it'll happen anyway.'

'But you have good reasons?'

'Of course we do.' George was offended that Annie had to ask.

'Then you've got nothing to worry about. Explain them. Whether people agree with you or not, at least they'll know why it's happening.'

'What we don't like are these big decisions being made as is we don't exist,' Jacob said.

Joseph was nodding, and George had always respected Jacob's father. 'A public meeting?' he mused aloud. 'In the village hall, presumably. How much notice would I need to give?'

Annie shrugged. 'Tomorrow night's a bit early. I imagine people will have made plans for a Friday night. How about Tuesday evening? You'd only need to put up notices in the church, the shop and the Woolpack. It doesn't take long for news to spread.'

George nodded. 'Tuesday it is.' He looked around the Sugdens' kitchen. 'Thank you,' he said. 'Thanks a lot.'

CHAPTER FOUR:

The Village Meeting

'I don't understand why we're going,' Virginia complained, as the group trudged down the hill. 'It's not our village.'

'You ought to come,' Annie told them. 'This concerns you, too.'

'It might be a good place to meet fellas,' Alyson said.

That seemed to be a more persuasive argument for Alyson's colleagues.

'There's quite a gang of us,' Sam said. He was right – four Land Girls, Annie, her father, her fiancé and his father.

'Will Lil be coming?' Joseph asked.

'She'll be there,' Sam replied.

'I think everyone will be,' Jacob said. 'No one in the village is talking about anything else.'

'So who's in charge of the meeting?' Louise asked. Annie always thought she was the sensible one of the girls. Girls! Louise was a year older than she was – but she seemed five years younger than Annie. You'd think city life, with all the attractions and dangers would make people grow up fast, but from what Annie could tell, it prolonged your childhood, gave it a new phase where you were young and without responsibilities.

'George,' Annie said. 'Verney,' she clarified, when the

four girls seemed none the wiser. 'He's the owner of Home Farm, the manor house.'

'Rich, then?' Alyson asked.

Jacob laughed.

'Richer than most,' Annie reminded him, 'but his family fell on hard times after the last war.'

'George Verney's father—' Jacob began gleefully.

'It's a long story,' Annie said, stopping him before he recounted the whole sorry saga.

'Is he handsome?' Rita asked.

No one answered.

'A question for you, Annie, I think,' Sam said.

Annie hesitated. 'He's very dashing,' she said finally. 'I've not really thought about it, but, yes, I suppose he is quite handsome.'

'Is he married?'

'No, Alyson. He was.'

'Out of your league, love,' Jacob assured Alyson, to much merriment.

Seth worked his way through the village hall. As soon as he found Betty, he squashed himself into the chair next to her. Her sister was on her other side, looking like she'd been sucking a lemon.

'Your mother not coming?' he said.

'She's got a chill.'

Seth smiled to himself. Good.

Margaret leant over. 'Perhaps I should sit between you two, make sure Seth keeps his hands to himself.'

'It's not like the pictures,' he said curtly. 'They won't be turning the lights down or owt.'

'And even if they did, I'd make sure Seth kept his hands well away from me,' Betty assured her sister.

Seth looked away, annoyed.

*

'Brian, this is Rita. I told you about her, remember?'

'Hello, yes.' Brian Sullivan wasn't what Rita had expected: he was short, and balding and, she guessed, fifteen or twenty years older than his wife.

'And these are Adam and Joe.' Two boys pushed forward and the eldest, who was thirteen or fourteen, held out his hand, which Rita shook. He blushed. He was at the gawky stage, already taller than either of his guardians. His brother was a couple of years younger.

Jean was dressed smartly, in a tailored suit, with a gold necklace and earrings. Rita felt scruffy by comparison, even though she and Jean were the same sort of height and build. She took heart from the fact that a lot of the women here were Land Girls, or farmers' wives, and dressed like her.

'Are you going to sit with us?' the older boy asked.

'The other girls have saved me a space – over there,' she told him.

Ron and Colin found themselves a couple of seats at the front. As with all meetings of the sort, the hall was filling up from the back – it had been the same at school assembly, Ron remembered.

'You were right to close the pub,' Colin said. 'Is there anyone who isn't here?'

Ron looked back over his shoulder. 'Not of our regulars. A few of the widows are missing, I think. And that couple from Mill Cottage.' A thought struck him. 'We should have been at the back, really.'

'What – to get a view of the crowd?'

'To get out sharpish at the end, and back to the Woolie. This is going to be thirsty work, and people will want to talk about it afterwards.'

*

Rita took her seat with Louise, Alyson and Virginia.

'Who were you talking to?'

'It's the family that run the shop, the Sullivans. Mrs Sullivan's Jewish, too.'

'Are you Jewish?' Alyson asked, clearly amazed.

Louise and Virginia rolled their eyes, and Rita laughed. They'd been sharing a room for months, now, and she hadn't kept it secret.

'Not many men, are there?' Alyson tried to change the subject.

There weren't – at least, not eligible ones. A man in a long dark coat with light brown hair stood at the back, keeping himself to himself, and there was Seth Armstrong, but he was hardly eligible. The rest were the usual mixture of pensioners and spotty youngsters.

That changed, though, as two men stepped on to the small stage. Both were about thirty and in RAF uniform. They recognised the first – George Verney, the lord of the manor. He cut a dashing figure, with a neat blond moustache. The other had black hair, slicked back, a square jaw and broad shoulders. He looked as if he'd stepped straight from a recruiting poster.

'That's the German. Well, he's not German. We thought he was,' Joe explained to Jean Sullivan, who seemed distracted.

'Very good,' she said, but it was obvious she wasn't listening.

'He's an RAF man,' Brian Sullivan said.

'I know that now,' Adam muttered. He didn't like being proved wrong.

Roland Pilgrim looked around the packed village hall from his new vantage point on the stage. Only about a

38

hundred and fifty people lived in the village, even fewer with the men called up, but a quick head count showed that virtually everyone was here tonight. Gatherings like this were banned in larger towns: if there was a raid, even a small bomb would wipe out the whole population. The thought of Hitler studying a map and deciding that the Luftwaffe should target Beckindale amused Roland. He suspected that this evening they would be safe.

Almost everyone here was a stranger to him, but there were a few familiar faces: Annie Pearson, of course, with her fiancé, her father, the young man Seth Armstrong . . . Brian Sullivan, who ran the shop. It brought home to him that the RAF was intruding here, imposing on a close-knit community. Roland could understand why the villagers were unhappy. This meeting wasn't a means to negotiate, just to inform everyone that the airfield would be built. The RAF had a job to do, but that job was going to be far more straightforward with the co-operation of the locals.

Most people were looking at him suspiciously. He and George were going to have a job to win them round.

He tried to judge the crowd. There were a lot of old men, and a fair few children, up after their bedtime by the look of it. Not many men of his age, of course. The few he could see must be farmers or vets, men in reserved occupations, who could do more for the war effort by carrying on with their normal work.

The vast majority of his audience were women, from little girls to their sour-faced grandmothers, and they seemed restless, anxious. There were plenty of young ones; Seth Armstrong had a pretty girl sitting next to him, and he had spotted the group of Land Girls, dressed identically in shapeless green jumpers. They were giggling together and passing cigarettes between them. One was looking straight at him, a striking redhead, and she smiled. Roland realised he was staring at her, and looked away, embarrassed. He had to keep his mind on the job . . . until the meeting was over, at least.

George Verney stood up, and the villagers settled down. Roland was impressed: he had had no idea that the feudal system was alive and well, but George was the squire, and that still meant something in a place like this.

'Thank you, everyone, for coming,' he began. 'Now, as you know, the Ministry of Defence is looking to improve the country's air strength, not only to defend us against the bombing but to take the fight to Germany itself. And, as part of a concerted effort, they are building a string of airfields around the country. One of the places they've chosen is Beckindale. Now, this is quite an honour, but we all appreciate that it will have an effect on such a small village, and I know a lot of you have questions. So we've called this meeting for you to air your concerns. Where shall we start? Ron?'

A middle-aged man stood up, a little awkwardly. Roland saw that he had lost an arm. In the city that usually meant a veteran. Here, it might mean an agricultural accident.

'Where precisely is this airfield, Sir?' he asked, 'I've heard it's going to be in the village itself.'

Roland chuckled, and George smiled benignly. 'The airfield will be built on Miffield Rise, almost a mile from the village, and on the other side of Creskeld Wood. You won't even be able to see it from here.'

The villagers looked at each other, relieved. But a few voices of dissent were raised.

'We'll be able to hear it – all day and night.'

'Does that mean we'll be targeted by the Hun?'

'All those army vehicles will have to come through the village.'

'We'll not get any sleep.'

There was uproar.

George Verney held up his hand. 'If we could just try to stay calm.'

Roland noticed that Seth Armstong had his hand up. 'Mr Armstrong?'

Seth looked nervous. 'Is it taking up the whole of Miffield Rise?'

'That's right, yes.'

Sam Pearson knew what the lad was thinking. 'But that means your airfield's going to be bigger than the village,' he blurted out.

'Well, it is quite a small village,' Roland said quietly.

More uproar.

'How many men will be stationed there?' an old woman asked.

'I can't answer that question for security reasons,' George replied.

Roland grasped just before the crowd did that that had been precisely the wrong thing to say. He added, 'But we don't think there are any German spies in the room,' which drew a chuckle or two.

'I'm Squadron Leader Roland Pilgrim,' he went on. 'I'm going to be in charge of overseeing construction of the airfield, and I'll be the commanding officer of the base when it's completed.'

A few grumbles.

He held up his hand. 'It will be built.'

'Beckindale's a long way from Berlin,' someone shouted.

Roland faced him. 'How far away, Mr Sullivan?' he asked.

The man shrugged. 'I don't know that, but it's going to be quicker if you go over the Channel.'

'The German coast is about four hundred miles away by bomber,' he told them. 'That might sound like a lot, but bombers fly at about a two hundred miles an hour on a good day, which means that we're about two hours away from Germany. That's about as long as it would take you to get to Leeds and back by train.' He let that sink in. 'Our bombers will fly out over the North Sea, the same sort of route that ferries from Hull take when they head for the continent. If they flew from Kent, they'd have to cross hundreds of miles of enemy territory. This way, there's just the North Sea between here and Hamburg.'

People looked at each other and Roland let them digest the information for a moment. The war had suddenly come closer to these people's homes.

'Why Beckindale?' Brian Sullivan asked.

'It's not just Beckindale. I don't know exactly how many airfields like this are being built around the country, but it's many dozens. This will be a significant part of the war effort, maybe even the decisive part. The bombers will be targeting German factories, munitions works and airfields. It's the only way we have of stopping their war machine.'

More discussion.

Annie stood up. 'Mr Pilgrim, from the sound of people here tonight, you must think Beckindale doesn't want to be part of the war effort.'

Clever girl. Suddenly, the room was full of people assuring him that that wasn't the case.

'Ladies and gentlemen,' he said, 'I look around this room and I can tell that a lot of people's husbands, fathers and sons have gone to war. Our bombers can make sure that the Germans have fewer tanks and planes, that their supply lines are cut. This airfield is going to be built. We're fighting this war to preserve the British way of life, and I don't want to disrupt that way of life any more than I have to. There will be sacrifices, you know that – we've all made sacrifices already. There will, I'm afraid, be an increase in noise, and in traffic. But for a very good reason.'

'Aye, to beat the Hun!' someone shouted.

'We're Englishmen, we're God's chosen people.'

'You're thinking of Yorkshiremen!' Jacob Sugden called out, to laughter.

'Dalesmen!' Seth countered.

Annie stood up. 'No. That's what Hitler and his lot think, isn't it? They think they're the master race. But Englishmen know we're nowt special, we're just people. It happens we're the front line. The Nazis have to be stopped. It's fallen to us. And there's no debate needed. We must do it. If Beckindale can help, it must.'

Silence.

Roland held his breath, not daring to smile down at Annie. Had she gone too far? It had been like a scene in one of those information films.

Then someone started clapping. Someone else joined in. And now the whole hall was applauding.

'Why's it called RAF Emmerdale?' someone asked. 'Why not RAF Beckindale?'

'Because it's on the wrong side of the hill,' George explained.

The rest of the evening was going to be easier, Roland thought. Now the villagers even wanted the place named after them! He glanced at George, who was carrying on with his answer and looking a lot more relaxed.

'The Woolpack will reopen in two minutes,' Ron declared, as the meeting ended and before most people had stood up. He dropped the keys into Colin's hand. 'Hurry up, lad, get the place open. I'll be with you as soon as I can.'

'You're missing an arm not a leg,' Colin reminded him.

'Will you just get going? I want to extend an invitation to Squadron Leader Pilgrim, let him know that he and his men are welcome in the Woolpack. Good custom there.'

'Yeah, all right.' Colin sauntered away.

One of the Land Girls, a bonnie redhead, was standing in Ron's path. 'Excuse me, love, I want to speak to Mr Pilgrim.'

She stepped out of the way, rejoining the group of her friends.

The Squadron Leader smiled down at him. 'Ron, isn't it? How can I help?'

Seth had walked Betty home. It was barely fifty yards from the village hall to the Prendergast house, but he took every opportunity to be with his sweetheart. Now, though, they'd reached the doorstep, an obstacle he'd never managed to get across, despite his best efforts. He wouldn't tonight, either, not with Margaret and Mrs Prendergast alongside them like a pair of prison warders.

'Well, good night, Betty, love.'

She looked at him, with more pity in her eyes than he liked to see. 'Why can't you be like those RAF men?'

'Eh?'

'I was looking at them this evening, and I thought they looked so smart. And you heard Squadron Leader Pilgrim – they fly over the sea, right into Germany. Don't you think that's brave?'

Seth didn't hesitate to agree.

'So why haven't you signed up?'

'You know the answer to that. I'm not old enough, yet.'

Did he want to join up? Seth didn't want to die. He didn't want to be shot at. Who did? But he'd have defended his country if he could. People were always asking why he hadn't signed up and he *was* too young, but he was tall for his age.

'You should have joined the Local Defence Volunteers.'

'The Home Guard? They were full up.'

'Full up?' she echoed, mocking him.

'Aye – they only have so many uniforms. Some even have to share a gun.'

'Perhaps if you'd been at the front of the queue instead of the back you'd have got in.'

Seth frowned. 'That's not fair, Betty.'

'Don't talk to me about fair, not until you do your fair share.'

And with that the Prendergast sisters swept inside, and the door closed firmly behind them.

'Jacob's in Annie's room,' Alyson whispered to the others. 'I heard him go in. He was waiting until he thought we'd all gone to bed.'

'I think it's good,' Rita said quietly. 'They're clearly in love.'

Louise snorted.

'She wears a balaclava in bed to stay warm. A real passion-killer.' Alyson laughed. 'Do you and your fiancé wear balaclavas in bed?'

Rita found herself blushing. She wasn't a prude – at least she didn't think so – but Alyson talked about nothing but men and what she planned to do with them on Saturday nights. She had had a different upbringing from Rita, who had always understood that there were some things one just didn't talk about. Louise never talked about her love life: the other day, she had said she didn't believe in love, but from what Rita gathered, she had had at least one boyfriend in the past. And Alyson knew Rita was embarrassed, of course, loved teasing her.

Rita would never admit it to the others, but she and Paul, her fiancé, had never slept together. That wasn't what it was about.

Rita and Alyson were opposites. Alyson's family was huge – she was one of nine, she had told Louise – and lived in a tiny terraced house in Hull. Rita had a brother and lived in a quiet suburb of Manchester. Her father was a businessman; rather well off, she realised.

'I bet they've never done it,' Alyson said, and Rita blushed all over again, until she remembered that Alyson was talking about Mr Sugden and Miss Pearson.

'Alyson,' she said reprovingly, 'when I said we shouldn't go down there, it was so that Mr Sugden and Miss Pearson can talk. Have some time together.'

'I bet they haven't, though,' Alyson persisted.

'Let's not talk about that,' Louise suggested.

'You can tell just by looking at her.'

'Can you?'

'Yeah.'

'So what about me?' Louise asked.

Alyson raised an eyebrow. 'You?'

Alyson and Rita had talked about Louise, tried to get her measure, but she was a dark horse. Alyson reckoned that she was still a virgin, but Rita wasn't so sure. Louise seemed more assured than the rest of them, even Alyson, who claimed she'd had half a dozen lovers. Alyson peered at Louise now, looked her up and down, as though she could calculate her answer from the length of her hair or the shape of her leg.

'You?' she snorted. 'You've not so much as held a man's hand. What would you know about it?' She giggled.

'What did you think of Squadron Leader Pilgrim and George Verney?' Louise asked.

'Gorgeous!' the other three said simultaneously.

'I liked Mr Pilgrim particularly,' Louise admitted.

'I don't think he'd ask a Land Girl out,' Virginia said glumly.

'Well, I'll have to ask him out, then,' Louise announced, and the other three roared with laughter.

'I've brought you your cocoa,' Jacob whispered.

Annie had stayed awake, waiting for him. Out in the

country, they didn't bother with the blackout upstairs, they just kept an oil lamp handy.

'There'll be frost tomorrow morning,' he said. 'Ground's already quite hard.'

She sat up, pulled off her balaclava and tucked it, rather ashamed, under her pillow. She reached over for the cocoa. Bitter, just as she liked it. Before the war she'd have taken sugar, but it was rationed now, and she'd found she preferred some things without it.

'You were right about the airfield. I *was* being selfish, thinking about getting one over on Verney,' Jacob said.

These were not words that came easily to her fiancé's lips, Annie knew. He was looking out towards Home Farm land now, probably picturing the planes taking off behind the next hill, flying over his farmhouse. 'It'll be noisy,' Annie said, 'especially at night.'

'Aye. Well, until Edward comes back I don't think I'll be sleeping much.'

'Still ... we should ask Mr Verney what time the planes will be coming and going.'

Jacob laughed. 'I don't think the RAF gives out timetables. That sort of thing has a way of getting back to Berlin.' He was smiling down at her. 'Can I come in?' he asked. 'It's very chilly.'

Annie lifted the corner of the sheet, and shifted over to give him room. 'You don't have to ask every night, you know,' she told him.

CHAPTER FIVE:

Louise Makes a New Friend

'Miss Pearson!' someone called. Annie turned.

It was George Verney, heading towards her on foot, his walking stick swinging wildly with every pace.

She'd always thought he was rather good-looking, not that she could ever say that in front of Jacob and that wasn't because he would be jealous. It was more complicated than that. The Sugdens and the Verneys could trace their family trees back to the Normans, and over all that time, as far as the records showed, the Sugdens had been farmers, the Verneys lords of the manor. So while George Verney was the same age as Jacob, he was almost a different species of man – smooth-skinned and soft-spoken.

He was wearing a tweed suit that looked a little fussy and old-fashioned. But, somehow, Annie doubted that the Verneys were making do and mending.

'Good morning, Miss Pearson,' he said, his accent untroubled by a thousand years of Yorkshire ancestry.

'I think it's safe for you to call me Annie, Mr Verney,' she told him, as he reached her.

He nodded. 'I just wanted to thank you for suggesting the meeting last night, and for winning the day.'

'The airfield was going to be built whatever was said

48

last week. We all know there's a war on and we accept that there will be . . . impositions on village life.'

'Quite. But it will all be a lot easier with the villagers' support. And that was quite a speech. So thank you.'

'You don't need to keep thanking me, Mr Verney.'

'George. And . . . well, I'm sorry to hear that! I wanted to invite you to Home Farm for dinner, to show my gratitude. You and Jacob, obviously.'

It was an honour, not as thrilling for Annie as for some in the village – after all, her father worked at Home Farm – but still an honour.

She accepted, her voice betraying something of her surprise.

George smiled. 'I'll see you at . . . seven?'

Seth Armstrong stood at the top of the hill, listening. Something was wrong. He'd spent his life around here, barely ventured out of the village, and at first he'd thought he might be imagining it. He wasn't in a good mood, and that always got in the way. He needed to be calm, let the countryside wash over him, tell him things. There was a knack to it, and it wasn't going to work if he spent his whole time thinking about Betty. He wasn't getting anywhere with her. She knew he was keen, and Seth thought she was too, at least a little – he wouldn't waste his time chasing her otherwise. It was her sister and her mother. If he could just get her away from her family for an hour or two . . .

Trucks, he realised. Then the vehicles turned the corner. They trundled along slowly, no end of them. Military trucks, painted blue, all covered in drab tarpaulins. He could see the black exhausts, and hear the low rumbling of their engines and the hissing of hydraulics.

He watched the convoy. It was fascinating, but a little sad, too. They were coming here to build on Miffield Rise.

It would never be the same again. For the duration of the war, there would be concrete posts, tin huts and fences up there. Every morning, when he went on his walk, he'd hear trucks. After the war . . . well, it would never quite go away, would it?

There was also an all too familiar sound: the puttering of an ancient motorbike. Seth knew who it was, and that he'd stop for a chat. Sure enough, once the motorcycle had come over the hill, and its rider had spotted him, it started to slow down. 'Seth,' the driver shouted. He wore a flyer's cap and goggles. Like the bike, they looked like they dated back to the last war.

'Morning, Laz,' Seth mumbled.

The man dismounted, leant the bike against the stone wall. 'You've got a face on you.'

'It's them trucks. It's not right.'

'Hey, you've not just had to get past them. There's enough men there to liberate Paris.' Laz paused. 'That's not the only thing, though, is it? What's the matter with you?'

'Nowt.'

Lazarus was always smiling, always jolly. With his big black beard and heavy coat he looked a lot like Father Christmas. A seedy, criminal Father Christmas, admittedly. 'It's that lass with the knockers, isn't it?'

'Her name's Betty.'

'Seth, my son, the solution's obvious.'

'It is?'

'Get yourself a job.'

Seth couldn't think of a thing to say. Lazarus had never done a day's work in his life. Even before the war he'd been a spiv, a black marketeer, a shyster, and rationing, shortages and the diversion of almost everything into the war effort didn't seem to have affected his supply routes. What it had done was increase the number of his customers.

'And will you be getting a job, too?'

Lazarus held up his hands. 'No, no. Don't worry, I've not gone soft. You can get yourself a job without getting yourself any work. Get something that sounds impressive but that's just a title. Like my old dad – whenever anyone asks him, he'll say, "I'm a coronation flag seller." That sort of thing.'

'That wouldn't fool Betty. She wants me to sign up.'

'Come on, Seth, think. There's a war on. Everyone's got their own little war job, now, haven't they? You see them in the *Courier*, running around Hotten in tin hats, thinking they're important.'

Seth's eyes lit up. 'ARP warden.'

'What do they do, then?'

'During air raids they make sure everyone's safe.'

'And does the village have one?'

'Ron's the warden, isn't he? Or he would be, if it was needed.'

'Ron's over sixty and he's only got one arm. Can we trust him? Don't we need more than him between us and the Hun?'

'Beckindale's only a dozen houses, a church and a pub. The Germans aren't going to—'

Lazarus tutted loudly, cutting Seth off mid-sentence. 'Complacency. It's attitudes like that that'll cost us this war. If I was you, I'd go to Ron, explain that there's this young lad keen to do his duty. Like as not, he'll be happy to hand over the job. Then show Betty your uniform, and she'll show you them kno— She'll show you some respect.'

Seth nodded thoughtfully. 'If it works, I'll owe you a pint.'

Lazarus Dingle got back on his bike. 'I'll hold you to that.'

Rita smiled at Jean Sullivan as she reached the counter.

'Not buying anything?'

'Oh . . . no. I just came to say hello. I can buy something if you want.'

'That's all right,' Jean said. 'Are you on your lunch hour?'

'That's right, but I don't think Mr Sugden likes us to take one.'

'Oh, ignore him, he can be a real grumpy so and so.'

'I know that.'

'Are you lonely, Rita?'

'Is it that obvious?'

'Missing your fiancé?'

She shook her head, then quickly corrected herself. 'No, I mean I do miss him, but that's—'

Jean took her hand and looked her in the eye. 'I understand,' she said. And the way she said it, Rita was sure that she did.

'Why hasn't Mr Sullivan been called up?' Rita asked.

'He's too old. Only just, but he's lucky – too young for the Great War, too old for this one.'

Rita grinned. 'Do you want to go to synagogue on Saturday? I've not been for a while, and . . . you know, the guilt's catching up a bit.'

'I know exactly what you mean. You get Saturday off, then?'

'Religious observation. The others go to church on Sunday, so it's only right.'

'I'm surprised Jacob Sugden doesn't have you working extra hard on Sunday – or perhaps he does. I don't believe him sometimes.'

'What time do you want me round?'

'Half eight?' Mrs Sullivan suggested. 'A bit early for me but . . .'

'I'll see you then. I'd better get back, the others will be missing me.'

*

'Hello there.'

Roland Pilgrim was sitting in a clearing in the wood, away from it all: out of sight of the house, the village, human beings, their wars and other troubles. It was just getting dark, and he was watching the sun set through the trees, although double summer time meant that that wouldn't happen for a while yet. At the bottom of the hill was a stream, the one that ran through the village.

Normally he would have been annoyed at the interruption to his peace, but he recognised the young woman who had intruded into his world. 'I saw you at the meeting last week,' he said.

'You remember?' she asked.

'It would be difficult to forget you.'

She was wearing a green jumper, as she had been that night – it was almost certainly the same one, he thought – and thick trousers, splattered with mud. But he could tell she had a nice figure. Her face . . . It was what men called handsome, rather than beautiful, but her long red hair softened that, made it rather striking.

She smiled. 'It's Roland, isn't it?'

'That's right. Squadron Leader Roland Pilgrim. You're in the Land Reserve, aren't you? Shouldn't you be toiling in the fields?'

'Shouldn't you be building an airfield?'

'Just finished for the day,' they said together, and laughed.

'I'm at Emmerdale Farm,' she told him. 'It's just on the other side of the woods.'

Roland decided he might as well try his luck. 'I hope you don't mind me asking, but are you free this evening?'

'Free?'

'Well, if you are, I could take you for a drink. At the pub.

I think it's called the Woolpack, isn't it? I was chatting to the landlord after the meeting.'

'I've got nothing planned this evening.'

'Is the pub open now?'

'I don't know.' She looked around, then back at him. 'It's very quiet here.'

'Yes.'

She was tall, athletic, and carried herself with confidence. Her accent was difficult to place – northern, he thought, but upper-class at the same time. She was quite a bit younger than him, and there was an air of innocence about her.

'Do you have a French letter?' She was untying her hair.

Roland stared at her. 'I beg your pardon?'

She rolled her eyes. 'You heard me.'

'Do you know what a . . . what one of those is?'

It was obvious from the look she gave him that she did. 'Why invite me for a drink? Where were you hoping it would lead?'

'Well, I wanted to get to know you. And then I could, I don't know, take you for a drive, find a dance-hall, go on dates.'

'And eventually where did you see all this courtship heading?' But before he could answer, she continued. 'On the first date we might accidentally touch hands, the second you'd risk a peck on the cheek. Then there'd be a few weeks or months of that, with you getting the occasional glimpse of leg, or a kiss and a cuddle. Then, maybe, just maybe, we'd go a bit further. And a bit further still? Unless you're a very unusual man indeed, you'd hope for a night alone together sooner or later. Well, we could do it that way, or we could be honest with each other. Cut to the chase, as the Americans say. There's a war on, so there's no time like the present.'

Roland gulped.

'So, have you?'

'I beg your pardon?' He remembered her earlier question. 'Well, yes.'

'Here?'

'No. In my room at Home Farm.'

She smiled at him. 'So what are we waiting for?'

Jacob looked up at Home so-called Farm. 'Why are we having dinner with the enemy?' he asked.

Annie sighed. She knew he was teasing her. 'George Verney isn't the enemy, Jacob, as well you know. You're going to be on your best behaviour tonight, aren't you?'

'Of course.'

'It's nice of him to invite us.'

'Didn't say it wasn't.'

'So keep it polite, and don't try to start a fight.'

'Would I do that?'

'Wait!' Roland warned, ducking out of sight behind a tree and pulling Louise with him. 'George Verney's ahead, talking to a couple.'

'Anyone you know?'

'The young woman who spoke at the meeting last week.'

'Annie Pearson?' Louise was horrified.

'I think that was her name. Do you know her?'

'I'm boarded with her – well, with her fiancé. She cooks for us and stays the night. It's a long story.'

'There's another way round,' Roland assured her.

Almost before Ron had finished unbolting the door, Seth Armstrong was pushing his way in.

'Seth, lad, you can't be that desperate for a drink. It's not healthy.'

'It's not that. I've got something to ask you.'

'Go on, then.' Ron made his way back into the bar, straightening a table, dishing out cork beermats. Colin was behind the bar, checking the optics.

'Well, you know you're the ARP warden?'

'Yes.'

'Can I take over?'

Ron looked at him. 'You're keen, I'll give you that. But you're too young. The ARP warden has to be someone people look up to.' He frowned at Colin, who was sniggering from behind the bar.

'I want to impress Betty,' Seth admitted. 'She thinks I should get a war job, but I'm too young to sign up. Perhaps I could help you out.'

Ron thought about it. 'Oh, why not? But we'll need to go into Hotten to sort it out. We'll head there first thing tomorrow morning.'

'Here we are,' Roland said, as they reached his bedroom door.

'This place is a palace. I thought my father was rich but . . .' She let the words trail away.

'What does he do?' Roland asked. He closed the bedroom door behind them, hoping they'd got into the house, up the stairs and into his room undetected.

She laughed, tugging her jumper over her head. 'I don't want to talk about Daddy,' she told him. 'Come on, help me.'

A good soldier, he followed her orders, and then they stood face to face. Beneath the jumper was a rough cotton shirt with a row of grey buttons. She put her hands behind her back, making it clear that the buttons were his responsibility. It was a man's shirt and they were on the wrong side, but this didn't fox him.

He parted the shirt, slipped it easily off her shoulders.

Her face and neck were red – she'd caught the sun, even in a Yorkshire autumn – but the rest of her skin was pale, freckled.

She reached up and unclipped her brassière, leaving him feeling a little cheated – he had wanted to do that. She lifted it away, revealing small breasts with little pink nipples.

He sank to his knees, and she peered down. 'Where are you going?'

'You're still wearing your boots,' he explained.

They proved tricky. They were tightly tied, and – she explained – slightly too small for her, especially with two pairs of thick socks on. But while she held on to his shoulder, they got the first one off, and the second was less of a challenge.

He rose a little, undid the top button of her trousers,.

'Nearly there,' she said.

He tugged trousers and knickers down in one go, a bold move that seemed take her by surprise. He held her hips, and kissed her thigh. Their first kiss, he realised.

She stepped back, out of the pile of clothes.

He stared up at her, realised he was staring, and that she wasn't even slightly self-conscious. He stood up and she turned round.

'That was certainly worth waiting so long for,' he said lightly.

She laughed, held out her arms, and he went to her, holding her tight to his chest, one hand flat against her backside. Her skin was so smooth, so soft. He felt her arms wrap around her neck and her breasts press into him. They kissed.

She was getting cold. This was a cold room. Where were his manners?

He lifted her up – she was so light! – and carried her over to the bed.

*

Jacob was pushing a potato around his plate, barely saying a word.

'Cook was called up, of course,' George was saying. 'The new chap says he's got ten years' experience at the Queens Hotel in Leeds. At Armley Gaol more like.'

'Aye, well, we've all had hardships,' Jacob said, deadpan. Annie glared at him across the table, but George hadn't noticed.

'It's very nice,' Annie assured him, although it was a little disappointing. The beef was stringy, with too much salt. She picked up her glass – a little wine would wash away the taste.

George followed suit. 'To the war effort.'

Jacob lifted his glass and grunted.

'Am I forgiven?' George ventured.

'You should have talked to me, Mr Verney, that's all. Do you think I would have argued?'

'Your father would have. Mr Pearson too, in your place.'

'I'm neither of them.'

'We're all our fathers' sons.'

'Then God help you, Verney.'

Annie and George stared at him. Jacob scowled. 'Oh, come on, what now? We all know what your father was like. You of all people know the trouble he caused. If he'd done a bit better for himself, then we wouldn't have had to have this conversation, because Emmerdale Farm would still be in your family.'

Annie couldn't believe what she was hearing. 'You don't speak ill of the dead, Jacob.'

Jacob gave a gruff laugh. 'I said the same when he was still with us. And I said it to his face.'

George looked down at his plate. 'Yes. And you're right, my father wasn't perfect. But none of us is, Jacob.'

'Not all of us are lord of the manor, though. Verneys have the money, they have the land, they have the power, and so folk expect them to live up to that. They want to look up to them.'

'You've never looked up to anyone in your life, Jacob Sugden,' Verney told him, and Jacob couldn't deny it.

Annie wasn't sure what to do – stand by her fiancé, or apologise for his terrible behaviour.

George sat up straight. 'Now, more than ever, this country needs leaders,' he said.

'People like you?'

'People born to lead.'

Jacob gave a long, low laugh. 'How about people who are good enough to lead? People who get there because they're qualified, rather than related?'

'I never took you for a socialist, Jacob. You're a landowner yourself, now. In your way.'

In polite circles, Annie felt sure, the women kept quiet through tirades like this one. But she couldn't just sit there meekly. 'Gentlemen,' she announced, 'try to keep it civil, please. I'm sure both your mothers, God rest them, told you that if you can't say anything nice about someone, then you don't say anything at all.'

Jacob stared at George Verney for a moment, then looked down at his plate, a smirk on his lips.

The rest of the meal passed in silence.

Afterwards, Louise laid her head on Roland's chest, which was smooth, the muscles defined. Whatever else the war had done, rationing had made people leaner, and all that toiling in fields and marching around was good exercise. In some of the city slums, she'd been told, food rationing had been a godsend: it was the first time the poor had been properly nourished.

Roland had been a little agitated when he thought

George Verney would see them getting into the house, but seemed more at ease, now. She was in the best possible place to judge that, with his chest under her cheek, rising and falling regularly, his heartbeat slow and steady.

Roland's room was large, with vast mahogany furniture – a dressing-table, a chest of drawers, a wardrobe the size of a standing stone. The decoration was a little old-fashioned – art deco – but good quality. It was luxurious, but more intimate, less impersonal than a hotel. The bed was a single, and the fresh sheets had been tucked in tightly. They hadn't made it under them.

Would servants come in and find them here, she wondered. The idea made her feel giddy.

His chest smelt of sweat – his and hers.

She really must get back to Emmerdale Farm.

'Did he die?' Roland asked softly, surprising her. She hadn't thought he was still awake.

'Who?'

'Your husband. Your fiancé. The man you've done that with before.'

'No.'

'Then he's in the forces? At war?'

Louise pulled away. Couldn't he tell she didn't want to talk about this? 'What sort of girl do you think I am?' She got off the bed, looked for her coat, and the cigarettes in its pocket.

'I'm sorry. I . . . didn't mean to offend. It's just that I don't know anything about you and I'd like to.'

She knelt down, retrieved the packet and the matchbox. 'If you were that interested in me, you would have asked my name.'

Roland went red – all over.

'Louise,' she supplied. 'As for your question, I can't answer it for security reasons.' She clambered back on to the bed, kissed his cheek, then huddled next to him for warmth, offering him a cigarette, which he lit, then used to light hers.

'I beg your pardon?'

'It's like your airfield – it's best if you don't know how many men.'

'Men?'

'Men,' she confirmed. Then, after a moment, 'Look, I've already said too much. There's more to me than . . .' she hesitated '. . . a sex life, but already you're coming to all sorts of conclusions about me – I'm a tart, or a good-time girl, or a posh girl who wants to shock her daddy, or getting over some tragic, doomed romance. The point is, I can't sum you up just by tallying up how many lovers you've had. It's quite obvious to me that I'm not your first. Why else would you have a packet of French letters?'

'Er . . . well, actually they're standard RAF issue.'

Louise laughed, but he wasn't joking. 'Anyway, because you're a man, a soldier, it's taken for granted that you go to bed with women, and there's not a stain on your character. The more women you have, the more of a man you are. But if a woman has had a lover, it says something profound about her. If she enjoys herself, why, it's a scandal.'

'Point taken,' he said. 'But I just want to know that you're not married or engaged. There's no one else at the moment?'

She frowned at him.

Roland blushed. 'It's the last thing I'll ask and I think it's a fair question. I just want to know what . . . what *this* is. All that holding hands, taking you for a drink, getting-to-know-you, I'd like to do that, too. But if you're spoken for, if that's not what this is for you . . . then I'll understand.'

'There's no one else, not any more,' she assured him. 'And *this*? This is good. Yes? That's the only thing we need to call it.'

'Yes. And will we be doing *this* again?'

Louise smiled. 'Not until you've finished that cigarette, we won't.' She checked her watch. 'After that, I really ought to be getting back.'

'You can wipe that smile off your face,' Annie told her fiancé.

'I enjoyed myself, that's all. Didn't think I would. Ow! That was hot.'

'I know it's hot, that's why I did it.'

Jacob lay in the tin bath in the middle of the kitchen, soap-grey water barely covering him to his waist. Annie, fully dressed, still in her best shoes and coat, brought hot water, a ladle at a time, from the kettle on the stove.

The bath was up to the level now. She put down the ladle, and knelt to scrub his back. Jacob was solid muscle, not an ounce of fat on him. His skin was rough, full of dirt, which came off him in streaks. To think he'd dined at Home Farm in this state. 'I could stay in this bath all night,' he told her.

'No, you can't – I want to use the water before it goes cold, although I'll probably end up dirtier than I am now.'

'Get in with me, if you want.'

'With your father and those girls upstairs? Any one of them might come down.'

They both knew there was little chance of that – Joseph was a notoriously heavy sleeper, and the girls would be worn out after their day in the fields.

'They'd find us like this. Might as well be hung for a sheep as a lamb.'

Annie shook her head. 'I could just about explain this away, but if I was in there with you . . .' She remembered something. 'And, besides, I'm not talking to you, after the way you behaved tonight.'

Jacob grinned.

There was a knock at the door.

They glanced at each other, startled. Jacob looked like a hare that had just seen a fox.

'They wouldn't come this late,' she assured him. 'They'd wait until the morning. Or they'd telephone, I'm sure they would.'

'Aye, but—'

'It's OK, I'll go.'

Annie hurried to the front door. It was Louise, her hands in her coat pockets, looking chilly. 'Where have you been?'

'I'm sorry, I didn't wake you, did I?'

Annie hesitated. 'Louise, it's nearly midnight. As it happens, it's OK. Mr Sugden and I have just come back from Home Farm. But . . . you know Mr Sugden's brother's in the navy – he's on the same ship as Rita's fiancé. When we get someone knocking on the door in the middle of the night like you just did . . . well, we think it's news.'

Louise looked horrified. 'I'm so sorry, I didn't think.'

'Where were you, anyway?'

'I was with a friend and we lost track of the time. I'm sorry.'

Annie nodded. Louise looked suitably repentant.

'Is Mr Sugden there? I'll apologise to him.'

'He's busy,' Annie said quickly.

'Oh. Well, I'll just get a glass of milk, if that's all right?'

Annie blocked her way. 'I'll get it. Mr Sugden's having a bath.'

A knowing look settled on Louise's face. Annie decided to wipe it off. 'I thought I saw you up at Home Farm.'

Louise looked away. 'I'm always telling Alyson and Rita off for gossiping.'

'Let she who is without sin cast the first stone.'

She looked up again, a little angry. 'I don't think it's a sin,' she said quickly.

'Neither do I, not if you're in love. But others certainly wouldn't understand. We understand each other, though, don't we?'

Louise was already skulking upstairs. 'I can do without the milk,' she muttered over her shoulder.

Annie went back into the kitchen. Jacob had towelled himself off and was in his pyjamas, waiting to receive visitors.

Annie shook her head.

He crossed the room, held her so tight she almost suffocated. 'I thought Edward . . .'

'I know.'

He held her like that for a few minutes, until she had to wriggle free. 'I need that bath,' she reminded him. 'Stay and talk to me, if you want.'

CHAPTER SIX:

Getting to Know You

'Hello, Annie, are you looking for your father?'
'I'm looking for you. I just wanted to apologise for Jacob's behaviour last night.'

'Jacob's behaviour?'

'You know very well he said things last night that he knew would upset you.'

'I do. I also know that's why he said it. We were born in the same week, Annie. We grew up . . . well, not together, but there's always been a connection, his father being my estate manager, Jacob buying the farm from my family. The Sugdens and the Verneys have been at each other's throats for as long as anyone can remember.'

'You don't get engaged to a Sugden without hearing all about it, believe you me.'

George smiled.

'I'm sorry,' Annie repeated. 'I was looking forward to my first dinner at Home Farm, but Jacob spoilt the mood.'

'Are you free tonight?'

'I . . . I really don't think Jacob would want to come.'

'Then come on your own.'

She looked at him. 'Are you sure?'

'Of course. I don't want to cause any trouble between you and Jacob, but if you feel able to come, then please do.'

'I have to make the meals.'

'Then come for a drink tomorrow afternoon. I'll show you round the house.'

Annie considered her answer. 'See you at . . . three?' she suggested.

'I'll look forward to it.'

'Armstrong, Seth, reporting for duty.'

The man behind the desk looked up from his ledger and eyed Seth suspiciously. 'Duty?'

Ron stepped between them. 'It's all right, Alf. This is the lad I were telling you about on the phone. The one who wants to be an ARP warden.'

'Oh, right. He's very young.'

'He'll be deputising for me. He's keen, and it's a shame to waste that.'

The man looked him up and down, then scribbled something on a pad. 'Wait here.' Five or six minutes later, he came back, and handed Seth a package wrapped in brown paper. 'Helmet and armband. You've still got the leaflets, haven't you, Ron?'

Ron nodded. 'I'll pass them on.'

'Is there not a uniform?' Seth asked.

'Just an armband and helmet at the moment,' Ron explained, as the man returned to his ledger.

'Er . . .' Seth said, worried to speak up. 'What about my training, like?'

The man gave a wry grin. 'Ron, you'll train him up, won't you?'

Ron nodded. 'Don't worry, Seth, you'll soon pick it up.'

Roland sat in the drawing room of Home Farm, the paper unread on the arm of his chair. He was thinking about Louise. Before she'd left him last night, she'd given him her phone number – the number of Emmerdale Farm, where she was billeted, or whatever it was called when you were in the Land Reserve.

It had just occurred to him that she hadn't told him her surname. He knew nothing about her that anyone passing her in the street wouldn't know, yet they had shared physical intimacy, and she knew things about him that precious few others did.

Louise had been right: she *was* a puzzle to him, and now, his mind was searching for answers, a rationale for her behaviour. Demure in public, wanton in the bedroom – which was she really? She was right that society operated a double standard, with men celebrated for the sort of behaviour that would have a woman hounded out of town. Men despised whores, but were almost expected to visit whorehouses, or at least to have had experience. Louise was hardly the first to comment on the hypocrisy. But what had led her to break those standards? How had she gained such confidence?

He tried to sketch in the details – an affair with an older man, perhaps? A passionate affair, ending in tragedy or betrayal? He even toyed with the idea that she was a German spy. Or perhaps it was simply the war.

The 'proper' way of going about things was changing in every walk of life, in every way that could be imagined and in countless others that no one would have thought of. As a child, Roland had always been taught it was impolite to gobble up every last thing on his plate. 'Always leave something for Mr Manners,' his mother had told him. Nowadays, thanks to shortages, children were told just the opposite: eat every scrap. Mr Manners had been interned for the duration.

With the theatres, cinemas and dance-halls needing special permission to stay open – and with the city streets so dangerous to pedestrians during the blackout – the nature of courtship had changed. With so many men going to war, and with women in the factories and on the farms, working and earning wages of their own, the delicate balance between the sexes had changed, Especially with the threat of death everywhere, from the battlefields of Africa, the U-boats in the North Atlantic, to the air-raids and the threat of a gas attack at home. A soldier's leave was rarely longer than a few days, and each time sweet-hearts met, there was the chance that it would be for the last time. Well, people were living for the moment. It was impossible to plan even a few months ahead, whatever your station in life – so arranging a wedding was almost impossible, let alone buying a house, rearing children.

And it was a permanent change, Roland already knew that. When the war was over, girls like Louise weren't going to go meekly back to housework and relying on their husband's salary. Louise was ahead of her time, and one day all women would be like her.

Roland smiled – worse things could happen. 'Penny for your thoughts?' George asked.

Roland allowed himself a wry smile. 'I'm just thinking how much I'm enjoying my time here in Beckindale.'

George grunted. 'It's a good place to live. Can I have the paper, old chap?'

Roland handed it to him.

'I'm afraid I won't be able to join you for your survey this afternoon, Roly. I've got a friend coming round.'

'And you wanted me out of the way last night. Are you courting?'

George blushed. 'No, not at all. It *is* a young lady, as it happens, but she's just a friend.'

Roland nodded. 'Rest assured, I'll find something to do with my afternoon.'

'You know the village so this is going to be easy,' Ron assured Seth. 'Once it's dark, you just do a quick tour, checking all the houses. You have to be thorough, but it's not that tricky – in a blackout, even the smallest chink of light's easy enough to spot.'

'And what do you mean when you say the village?'

'Well, Beckindale itself, obviously – all the buildings. Start at the ... Malt Shovel,' Ron found it hard even to say the name of the rival pub, 'then do a quick circuit – you pick the route you think is best. You do Demdyke Row, too, and don't forget to check the cricket pavilion. I know it's not the right time of year, but someone might have gone in there and left a light on during the day. It's easily done, you can't be too careful.'

Seth looked around. 'What about Home Farm?'

'No. That's way out of the village.'

Seth relaxed a bit. 'The Dingles'?'

'Look up the hill, and if you see a light on, go up there. Same goes for Emmerdale Farm. But neither of them will give you any trouble.'

'But if they've got a light on . . .'

'If any of the hill farms have got a light on, they're making themselves a target, aren't they? And not a very big one at that. The German bombs aren't very accurate – I read that in the paper. They only hit their target about once in ten times that they try. In a city, when a bomb misses, it hits something else. Here it'd just make a big hole in the ground.'

'So our bombers are better?'

'Must be, mustn't they? Mr Churchill wouldn't accept any different.'

Seth nodded thoughtfully. Then he said, 'I can't let Mr Churchill down,' 'so what do I do if I someone's not got the blackout up?'

'If you see a light, you knock on the door and ask them to sort it out. You stay polite, but if they won't do anything, there's a fair few things *you* can do. There's a three pound fine, if you want to take it that far. Check that book I gave you.'

Seth nodded.

'And that's it. Oh, check the back of the houses – people seem to think if you can't see it from the road German planes won't spot it either.'

'Really?'

'There's not much to it, Seth.' Ron stopped and looked around, then leant in conspiratorially. 'Truth to tell, Seth, there's not much chance of a raid on Beckindale. It's not like we've got any factories. There's the railway viaduct, I suppose, but it's not even a main line. ARP warden in Beckindale, it's hardly a job at all.'

Ron could have sworn he heard Seth chuckle.

'You scared them half out their wits when the telephone rang. I don't think they get many calls. Miss Pearson said that her father refuses to use the telephone as a matter of principle. Can you imagine that?'

'I've met Sam Pearson. I don't think he's very keen on the modern world.'

Louise had met Roland half-way between Emmerdale Farm and Home Farm. They'd agreed that they wanted to do a recce of the village, get to know their new home a bit better. But as soon as they got down to the village it had started to rain. So they'd found the tea-rooms. Perhaps before the war this place had prospered but now they were the only customers and the owner, a surly old woman, treated even them as an inconvenience. The tea was good, though, and the cake was better than the privations of rationing should have allowed.

'It's very cold,' Louise said, hardly needing to remind him, 'even in here. I should have brought my coat.'

She wore a light dress, below the knee, with full-length

sleeves, and a neckline verging on prim, but it couldn't have provided much warmth.

He took off his jacket, draped it over her shoulders. She slipped into it, gratefully. Even though they were the same height, the jacket swamped her.

'Do I look like an airman, now?'

'Just like one. Except that you need a big handlebar moustache.'

'You don't have one. I thought it was compulsory.'

'Only for the unlucky ones.'

Louise frowned.

'They often grow them to hide burns,' he explained.

Louise almost blushed at her *faux pas*. Almost.

The old woman was lurking in the corner now, just out of earshot, but clearly straining to listen. Louise and Roland had seen her, and the pair had an unspoken agenda to scandalise her.

'So you've been turfed out of Home Farm?'

'George Verney made it clear he wanted me out of the way. I think he was . . . entertaining a lady guest.'

'Like you entertained me yesterday?'

'I suspect so, yes.'

'Lucky George. Unlucky us.'

Louise glanced down. 'We could go outside. Find a tree.'

'You're shameless.'

'Is that a no?'

'You deserve better.'

She nodded, pretending to agree.

'Besides, we'd either bump into my colleagues or yours. Or both. And it's raining.'

Today, they were talking, nothing more.

In between the innuendo, Roland was finding out more about Louise. Her surname was Price, she was twenty-one, which was older than he had thought, her father owned a bicycle factory. She was from Lancashire, but assured him that the Wars of the Roses didn't concern her unduly, and she felt safe living in the heart of Yorkshire. 'What did you do before?' she asked him. No need to ask *before what?*

'I worked for Donneby's.'

'Racing cars? How marvellous.' She looked delighted. 'A racing driver?'

'No. Chief mechanic. I ran the team. I tested cars from time to time.'

'You've got a car of your own?'

'Oh, yes, a lovely little Bugatti. A type 35B.'

'Take me for a drive.'

'Not in this weather – you'd never see the view. And I'll have to save up some coupons. You know how it is with petrol rationing. Is our journey really necessary?'

'I've not seen the famous Yorkshire countryside yet.'

'You spend all day in it.'

Louise gave him a look. 'You know exactly what I mean. The Yorkshire dales are meant to be one of the most beautiful parts of the country. There's a fantastic view from where I work, but I don't get the chance to explore.'

'Saturday,' Roland promised, 'we'll go for a drive. You point to something, we'll drive there.'

'Can you arrange the leave or whatever?'

'It's the RAF, Louise. I'm not some squaddie stuck in a camp.'

'Is that why you signed up?'

Roland laughed. 'I saw the war coming in thirty-six, and signed up then. Get a head start for the good jobs, that was the view I took. Why the RAF? I didn't want to fight in the trenches. And if I go, I want it to be in a fair fight, not because some U-boat torpedoed the ship I happened to be on.'

'It's very dangerous in the RAF, isn't it?'

'Yes.' No use denying it. 'But it's a job that needs doing.'

'Have you flown missions?'

'Ops. Operations. Not what you'd call a mission, no. I've done training flights, obviously. And supply flights. I spent a month laying mines in the North Sea. But I've not seen action, been shot at.'

'But you will be.'

'Oh, yes.'

'It doesn't scare you?'

'It scares me. I'm a human being – of course it scares me. What do you think?'

'Me?' He'd caught her out: she hadn't an answer ready. For the first time, he saw her search for one. 'It's a reminder that there isn't equality,' she said finally. 'That women have the vote, and work, and help the war effort, but they don't have to put their lives on the line.'

'And you want to chain yourself to the railings to gain that right?'

Louise thought about it. 'I'm really not sure. Men and women should be equal. But I don't think I could do what you do. I don't think I could be a soldier, or a sailor, or an airman. You're very brave.'

'I'm an ordinary man, that's all.'

'Better than being a farm labourer. I feel so ugly. Look at those nails – I'll never get that dirt out. And you should see my feet.'

'I've seen your feet,' he reminded her.

'You saw the corns and the blisters, then, and how rough they were.'

'That wasn't what I was paying attention to at the time.'

She flashed her eyes at him. 'I remember. Your attention was in just the right places.'

He had meant to make her blush, but it was water off a duck's back to her, and he was the one who had to look away. Redheads had pale skin, they were notoriously quick to go red, but in their short acquaintance he'd never seen Louise embarrassed by anything they'd said or done.

'How long have you been here?' he asked.

'A few months.'

'And you share a place with . . .'

'I share a *room* with three other Land Girls,' she said. 'An attic room, with a tin bath and a little wood-burning stove that none of us can work properly.'

'That sounds like barracks all right. Be grateful you're not woken up at six by a sergeant major who wants to do a kit inspection.'

'No, we're up just before dawn to go out and pick potatoes. How about you? How long have you been here?'

'A couple of weeks. I was stationed at York, with George Verney. When we were looking for places to put our airfields, he volunteered his land. He invited me to stay at the house while construction's under way.'

'If he's a lieutenant and you're a squadron leader, don't you outrank him?'

'Technically. But he owns a lot of land and he's got friends in the services, and the Ministry. There's no doubt who's boss.'

'So you get thrown out whenever he wants?'

'I do,' Roland replied, smiling at her. 'But I really don't mind. I get to meet the locals.'

Seth bustled in. 'I'm sorry, Mrs Prendergast, but as the ARP warden, I insist on checking your blackout curtains.'

And, with one small step, Seth was inside Betty's house. It was exactly as he'd pictured it: neat and tidy, small, but clearly tended by more than one houseproud woman.

'There's nowt wrong with this house's precautions, not that it's dark yet.'

Seth remembered something from church, or school,

somewhere. He had stepped into a lion's den. Margaret and Mrs Prendergast circled him, as if he was a zebra, or a Christian thrown into the arena.

Seth tapped his tin helmet. 'I'm sure that's right, but I have to check. I'll start upstairs. Whose room is that above the door?'

'Elizabeth and Margaret share a room,' said Mrs Prendergast, suddenly sceptical. It took Seth a moment to realise she meant Betty. 'Elizabeth is not here this evening. She's helping out at the church.'

Seth tapped his helmet again, tried to hide his disappointment. 'I'm here on official business, this isn't a personal matter. Would you like to show me the way?'

'You stay where you are, Margaret. I'll show him.'

Seth gulped.

The stairs were narrow, and Mrs Prendergast had to lead the way.

So Betty shared a room with Maggie. He'd thought as much. Two beds, quite narrow, neatly made. The room smelt of lavender and cedarwood, of which the dressing-table was made. He made a show of checking the curtains, all the time trying to sneak a look round. One still had a few dolls beside her bed. There were two whole shelves of books, and the odd china ornament.

He saw which bed was Betty's: there was a stencilled letter on the headboard, an E that had been altered into a B. And on the pillow lay a nightshirt, neatly folded. White cotton. There was a neat pile of letters underneath a paperweight on the bedside table, from Wally Eagleton by the look of them. Seth imagined Betty, tucked up in bed, just a foot or so from where he was standing. He tried to calculate how long it would have been before he'd seen this place if he'd not been an ARP warden.

'Well?'

'Years,' Seth replied automatically.

'What?'

Seth snapped out of it. 'I'll . . . everything in here is in order. I won't need to check anything else.'

Mrs Prendergast was staring at him, distinctly unconvinced.

'You've done a good job, Mrs Prendergast,' Seth said. 'Now, I need to be on my way.'

He risked another quick look round before he went.

The rooms at Home Farm were large, but almost ordinary – there was no great banqueting hall, ballroom, or long gallery. The Verney family had always been Yorkshiremen, and appreciated thrift. It was a cosy place, a home, more than a stately home.

That said, Annie never thought she'd feel comfortable there. This wasn't just the manor house, it was where her father worked, another world almost from the village she was used to.

But the fire threw its warmth over her and George was the perfect host. He'd given her a short tour of the house, helped her to identify some of the items – gilt ornaments, little alabaster statues, exquisite glasswork. Most of it was old, she could tell that much, but some pieces looked strikingly modern – art deco objects, items made from Bakelite.

They'd ended up in the drawing room, facing the fireplace. He prodded at the fire with a poker until it flared up again. 'There,' he said.

Annie sniffed at her brandy before she took another sip.

'Still not convinced?' George asked.

'I'm getting a taste for it,' she told him. 'It certainly helps to keep you warm.'

He grinned, and sat next to her on the sofa.

In pride of place on the mantelpiece was a large photograph of a woman of Annie's age, with long blonde hair, in a ballgown, a beautiful woman from another age, untroubled by war.

'You must miss your wife.'

'Of course.' George shifted, a little uncomfortably.

'Gentlemen never like to discuss their feelings, or even admit they have them, do they?' Annie regretted it as soon as she said it, and wondered if it had been the brandy talking.

George closed his eyes and sighed. 'I miss the company. I miss having someone to talk to. I miss waking up next to someone – you know how it is.'

Annie blushed.

'Oh, I didn't mean to imply—' George was horrified.

She held her finger to her lips, amused to see him flounder. 'It's all right, George. As a matter of fact, I do know, yes.'

George sat back, relieved. Then her meaning sank in. 'You and Jacob? I'm sorry, I . . . you're engaged, I mean there's nothing wrong with that . . . Milly and I, well before we got married, we—'

This time she held a finger to his lips. They were facing each other, now. 'It's best if we both forget the subject came up. Has there been anyone since Milly?' Annie asked.

George gave a tiny shake of his head. 'No one. Before or since.'

She took his hand in hers. 'I don't know what I'd do without Jacob, not now.'

'How did you meet?'

Annie laughed. 'I don't know. We've known each other since we were children.'

'But he's a lot older than you,' George noted. 'Ten years, isn't it? You were young when Jacob and you started courting.'

Annie nodded. 'We had our first kiss when I was fifteen, but it was love even before that. The age difference never bothered us, and it didn't seem to worry our parents. We don't even think about it any more. Our families have always been close, what with Dad and Mr Sugden working together and serving together.'

'So it was fate?'

'There's never been anyone else,' she agreed.

'He's a very lucky man. I had Milly . . . but fate had other plans for me.'

George was trying to stop himself crying, Annie realised. Before she knew what she was doing, she'd reached up to wipe away a tear. He let her do that, and mirrored the movement, stroking her cheek with his fingers. They looked at each other, then leant in. Annie had closed her eyes, she could feel his breath, cool, a hint of brandy. Their lips brushed.

Then, as if they'd agreed to, they pulled back, shifted away from each other.

There was a moment where neither knew what to say.

Annie busied herself by brushing down her skirt. 'I'm sorry, George, I think it's the brandy.'

He nodded. 'You'd better be on your way. I'll walk you home.'

Annie felt odd. What they were saying sounded like lines from a play and didn't seem to have any connection with what she was thinking or feeling.

'No need for that,' she told him, getting up. 'I'll see you again, George.'

CHAPTER SEVEN:
Coming to Terms

Rita didn't know why she was so nervous. It wasn't the thought of synagogue – she felt a little guilty that she'd not been for a while, but she had a reasonable excuse for that. The last time she'd felt like this had been when she had first visited Paul's parents. She had wanted to make a good impression then and she did now. She told herself to stop being silly, and knocked at the back door.

Brian Sullivan opened the door. He was in shirtsleeves. Clearly he wasn't going, and Rita wouldn't have expected him to. He smiled and ushered her inside. The house was smart and shockingly modern after the low ceilings and stone floors of Emmerdale Farm. The whole of the downstairs was one large room, with a kitchen at one end, a living room at the other, and a dining area in the middle.

Adam and Joe sat stiffly on the sofa; Joe was reading a comic. They both wore suits, which made them look absurdly formal. Jean bustled in, still in her dressing-gown, a gorgeous black silk robe. 'I'm getting ready,' she said, although that much was obvious. She had already put up her hair and done her makeup.

To her credit, she seemed to sense that Rita felt a little awkward. 'Why don't you come up and help me choose a suit?' she suggested.

*

Seth hurried over to Betty, doffed his tin hat to her. 'Good morning, Betty, love.'

'You playing at wardens?' she said scathingly.

'Serious work is this.'

'You're really the new ARP warden?' Betty looked him up and down. Seth fancied he could see a hint of admiration in her eyes.

'Aye. Did your mother not say?'

Betty caught herself smiling. 'My mother doesn't talk about you, she makes a point of it. That helmet's quite good.'

'Thank you very much.'

'But odd on such a beanpole.'

Seth's face fell.

'You look too young for it.'

'I *am* too young for it,' Seth insisted. 'Usually you've got to be twenty-five. They made an exception, seeing as how I was so keen to be part of the war effort.'

Betty considered what he had said, struggling to find something to criticise.

It had been a while since Seth had seen her lost for words and he wondered what to say next. Ask her if she'd like to come to Hotten, and he'd give her an easy way out: she'd just say no.

'So, are you proud of me?'

Seth congratulated himself. What else could she have said but what she did: 'Aye. You're doing good work.'

There was a tiny statue of two almost naked women on the bedside table. It looked like they were having a race, their veils streaming delicately behind them.

'You look very smart,' Jean told Rita.

Rita looked away from the statue. 'Thank you. I like your robe.'

'It's Chinese silk, I've had it for years, but it still looks like new.'

Without warning, she shrugged it off. Rita was relieved to see that she was wearing a bra and bloomers underneath. 'Two teenage boys in the house,' Jean said, reading her mind. 'I don't want them to catch a glimpse of anything they shouldn't.'

Rita was hardly listening. Jean Sullivan was beautiful, with an hour-glass figure she envied. She was hit by a wave of feelings – jealousy mostly. Jean seemed to have it all worked out. She was only a few years older than Rita, but while Jean had a husband, a house, a business and a Chinese silk robe, Rita's life was confused. That Jean had a better figure, too, made her feel more than a little cross.

Jean was retrieving a petticoat from a drawer. As Rita watched, she pulled it on, then a vest. 'Not very glamorous, but it's cold out there,' Jean said, turning to look in the wardrobe. After a moment, she pulled out a blue woollen suit. 'What do you think?'

Rita nodded. 'It's nice.'

Louise lay on her side, with her back pressed to Roland. His arm was resting on her leg. The mid-morning sun fell over their bare skin. According to Roland's bedside clock, it wasn't even eleven yet. She could spend all day here, surrounded by borrowed luxury, in the arms of her nice squadron leader. Yet, as often happened to her after the euphoria faded, she felt ill at ease. A sense of sadness had caught up with her.

'Have you ever been in love?' she asked, as he nuzzled her neck.

'I thought questions like that were against the rules of engagement.'

'I haven't been,' she said quietly. 'Have you?'

'Oh, a couple of times,' Roland admitted.

'I envy you.'

'I envy *you*,' he said quickly. 'You've never had your heart broken, have you?'

She hadn't. Her relationships had been civilised, and they'd ended amicably. 'But when you see lovers together, like Miss Pearson and Mr Sugden, they seem so happy I get jealous.'

'We're happy, aren't we?'

'But we're not *lovers*.'

They went to bed together, but they weren't in love. Neither of them wanted, or pretended to want, a white wedding and a life together.

Roland searched for the right word. 'We're friends,' he concluded.

She laughed a little, then rolled over to face him. 'Yes,' she said. 'That's it. Like tennis partners.'

'But not a love match.'

She laughed so loud, he had to lean over and press his hand against her mouth. 'Someone will hear,' he said. Sooner or later, he always remembered that there was no lock on the door.

She struggled free, pulling his hand away from her face. 'Would you get court martialled for this?'

'I told George I was drawing up requisitions for concrete aggregates for the runways and I wasn't to be disturbed. He'd take a dim view of this.'

She burst into laughter, then stopped herself. 'I told Mr Sugden I was helping rearrange the chairs at the village hall.' She closed her eyes. 'This bed's much more comfortable than the one at the farm. And the company's better.'

'You can't stay here all day,' he reminded her.

'No?'

'You know you can't.' He checked his watch.

'Are you expecting someone else?' she asked.

'Do you seriously think I've got any strength left?'

'*You* hardly did a thing,' she said lightly. 'I'm worn out, though. I think I should just,' she wriggled into the sheets, 'rest here for a bit.'

He slapped her hip. 'Time to get up,' he told her.

She frowned at him. 'You're not joking.'

'I thought we could go for a drive.'

Louise sat up, the sheets falling away. 'Really?'

'Yes. I thought we'd do a tour of the county. I've got Cook to pull together a picnic.'

'In this weather?'

'It's a bit brisk, but you're used to that, aren't you?'

Louise had a wicked expression on her face. 'I want to drive.'

'*Can* you drive?'

Louise toyed with telling him the truth, but decided against it. 'Of course!'

'You don't have to cook breakfast,' Jacob objected.

'It's no problem,' Annie replied cheerfully.

'I usually do it,' Jacob reminded her. His efforts didn't smell as good as this, though. Annie was pushing around some generous rashers of bacon. One of the advantages of owning a farm in a time of rationing was that you could always find meat somewhere, and you didn't have to worry about coupons. They weren't sitting on a huge hoard of course.

'Are all the girls getting that, too?'

'Well, Rita won't want it, but if any of the others do, they can have some.'

She let the bacon sizzle for a moment or two, then went over to Jacob. 'I love you,' she told him, hugging him.

'What's brought this on?'

'What do you mean?'

Jacob shrugged. 'A cooked breakfast, hugging . . . It's all

very nice, but – oh. You're not . . .' he glanced down at her stomach.

Annie rolled her eyes. 'No, I'm not.'

Jacob wasn't sure whether he was relieved or disappointed. 'Oh, well,' he concluded. Annie went back to the pan, checked the bacon.

'How was last night?'

Annie cut some bread. 'It was nice,' she said.

'Nice? Doesn't sound like Verney.'

'He's not as bad as you paint him.'

Jacob chuckled. 'I know. But he's the one in the big house, not me. I'm not going to treat him like Lord God Almighty just because the King gave his great-great-granddad some land because he fought in some battle.'

Annie took the bacon out of the pan and dropped it onto a plate, then lowered in the slices of bread. The fat was hot, and the bread soon browned.

'Are you sure you're all right?' Jacob asked.

'Yes,' Annie insisted.

Jacob wasn't sure what was the matter with her, but the bacon and fried bread looked great, so he wasn't going to argue.

'This is madness!' Roland yelled. They had to shout to hear themselves over the engine and the wind.

But Louise just laughed. 'I thought you'd driven racing cars!'

'That's right. *I* drove them – I was never a passenger!'

Louise threw the car around a corner, crunching the gears. Roland peered ahead. These country lanes were single track, but there was good visibility, and they seemed to be the only vehicle on the road.

'Where did you learn to drive?' he asked.

'Haven't you guessed? That's just what I'm doing now!'

'Stop the car!'

He might have known that that would only encourage her to drive faster.

'This is much better than driving that tractor!'

'I would hope so,' Roland muttered.

'Oh, relax! You're insured, aren't you?'

'That doesn't inspire confidence.' He glanced at the speedo. They were only doing fifty, which was less than he would have managed. But he knew what he was doing.

He decided to sit back and try to enjoy the ride, rather than picture disaster. He looked across at Louise, who was leaning forward, both hands tight on the wheel. Her hair was trying to fly free of the headscarf. For some reason, even though it was October, she was wearing the same summery dress she had worn when they were in the tea-room. She wanted to look glamorous, he assumed. Normally, when she was with him, she wore her Land Reserve clothes, when she wore anything at all. Here was a chance to wear something more feminine, even some makeup. Roland smiled – however modern her attitudes, Louise was still prone to vanity.

He was almost thrown from his seat as she took a sharp left.

'You were meant to warn me when we got to the turn-ing!' she shouted.

They were on the main road, now. Two lanes, and almost straight from here all the way to York, their nomi-nal destination – if his RAC roadmap was anything to go by. 'I clearly didn't need to!' he shouted back.

There were no roadsigns. That had been some Ministry man's scheme to prevent invading Germans finding their way around. The result, of course, at a time when tens of thousands of people were being mobilised, stationed away from home or called up to work on projects like the airfield and the harvest effort, was confusion.

Roland looked around, tried to appreciate the Yorkshire countryside. It was autumn and the trees were losing their leaves. Another glance over at the speedo confirmed his theory that the countryside was travelling past him even faster than it had been before.

'It's easier to get up speed on the straight bits, isn't it?' Louise shouted.

Roland sighed.

The bus was about half full, but the engine was so old and rattled so hard that Rita and Jean could barely hear themselves think. The boys were upstairs, eager to get away from their guardians. Rita looked at Jean. 'Is it difficult out here, being like us?'

Jean looked bewildered. 'What?'

'Jewish.'

'Not at all. It can be odd. Just little things. I don't think the villagers have really accepted me. Some people are friendly, but—'

'I wouldn't worry about that,' Rita interrupted. 'I don't think Mr Sugden accepts Mr Verney, and his family have lived at Home Farm for a thousand years.'

Jean laughed. 'You could be right. They don't mind us being Jews, but we aren't Yorkshire born and bred and that's the problem. Do you smoke?' She offered Rita a cigarette.

'No thanks,' Rita said.

'Ever tried?'

'No. Paul says they're terribly bad for you.'

'Just the opposite, I think,' Jean said breezily. 'Clears the lungs, relaxes you.'

Rita took the cigarette, weighed it in her hand.

'You put it in your mouth.'

'Don't you light it first?'

Jean took the cigarette out of Rita's hand and pushed it

into her mouth. Then she lit it with an elegant gold lighter. Rita wasn't really sure what happened next. 'Breathe in,' Jean suggested.

The smoke wasn't warm, like Rita expected, and did seem quite relaxing. She was proud that she didn't end up in a coughing fit. But Jean made the process look far more refined.

'I started when I was ten,' Jean confessed. 'Odd, really, I was a late developer in other ways. I didn't have a boyfriend until I was eighteen.'

Rita blushed. 'Neither did I.'

'How old are you now?'

'Nineteen. Paul's my first.'

'What's he like?'

'Oh. He's difficult to describe. Dark. Handsome. Quite short.'

'He's in the navy, did you say?'

'Yes. And before the war he couldn't even swim. He's a radio operator.'

'How often do you see him?'

'Whenever he has leave. He's on the Atlantic convoys. It's safe, he says – as safe as anywhere is, these days.'

'Is that why he picked it?'

Rita bristled. 'No. He's brave.'

'I didn't say he wasn't. I just wonder why he picked the navy if he couldn't swim.'

CHAPTER EIGHT:
Home Truths

Annie was meant to be doing the washing, but her mind wasn't on the job.

She was alone in the farmhouse as the Land Girls were taking advantage of a day off, while Jacob and Joseph were off fixing walls and checking the hedgerows. The washing was hard work, and would probably take her all morning. It wasn't something she had to think about, though. Just put a tiny amount of soap in the water, stir the clothes with the dolly stick, rub them, take them out, rinse them, run them through the mangle.

She usually enjoyed an opportunity to let her mind wander, but today it wasn't wandering very far. Only up the path to Home Farm, and George, and what had happened on their afternoon alone.

She'd gone up there feeling so nervous, toured the big house as if it was a museum or a gallery, but by the end of the afternoon she'd been sharing drinks and intimacy, telling George things she wouldn't have shared with anyone but Jacob, and George had reciprocated.

It would be easy to blame the drink, but she knew that that would be an excuse, a way of brushing the real reason under the carpet.

Even Jacob had been able to see it, in his way. Annie

had tried to keep her mind on her life, her fiancé, and she'd ended up behaving in the most peculiar way this morning.

Ignore your feelings for George, she told herself. But that didn't help at all. She wasn't sure what her feelings for him were. He was the same age as Jacob and, like him, he'd always been a part of her life, part of the landscape. He was her father's boss, he was lord of the manor. Annie had always had more day-to-day contact with him than many of the rest of the villagers, simply because of her father and her fiancé. She and Jacob had grown together. Neither of them remembered it happening, but after years of knowing each other, they had realised eventually that they shared romantic feelings. Friendship had turned to love. They'd often wondered if there had been a moment when everything sparked into life for them, but couldn't think when it might have been – long before they kissed.

That was their secret, Annie thought. Jacob had never wooed her or declared undying love for her. They had both known that they were in love, they didn't need the grand gestures. They talked, they shared, they knew each other.

George moved in different circles. He had been to boarding school and had been at university when his father killed himself. Annie had always thought him dashing, and most of the girls and young women in the village had a crush on him. He drove cars and flew planes, lived in a mansion, and had inherited a fortune, even if it wasn't the same size as the fortune his father had inherited. In his late teens and early twenties, he'd been quite the eligible bachelor, but the women in his life were all heiresses themselves. Milly, the girl he'd married, had been the third daughter of some Scottish duke. She wasn't rich, at least not by the standards of the aristocracy, but she was beautiful. In the three years they were

married, the villagers had started to see a warmer side of
George.

And when Milly died, the clock was turned right back.
It must have been a lonely time for him. People died –
husbands, wives, children, parents, friends – and
normally the villagers pulled together, looked after you.
No one dared do that for the lord of the manor. Barring a
couple of servants, George had faced it alone.

It was only now that the full horror of that occurred to
Annie. Without her support, Jacob wouldn't have coped
with his mother's death, she knew that. Even with someone to hold, Jacob had spent the best part of a year
brooding and drinking. It had been a difficult time, but it
had brought out the worst in him. For several months,
Annie had worried that his grief would consume him, or
make him act foolishly. He was not a complex man, or a
stupid one, but he liked to act, rather than think: he did
things because they felt right, not because he was following a plan.

Like so many upper-class men, and others, too, George
behaved as if he didn't have feelings at all. Jacob said that
was because the likes of him hadn't earned their place in
society – hadn't worked for their land or their big houses.
They didn't want to seem like ordinary people, doing as
their emotions dictated. But Annie wasn't so sure.

She knew she needed to see George again, but he had
made no effort to contact her – and she'd have run for the
hills if he had. But they needed to talk, set things
straight.

Annie resolved to go up to Home Farm just as soon as
the washing was done.

That they'd got to a picnic spot without killing themselves, someone else, or pranging the car was a source of
amazement to Roland. He had absolutely no idea where

they were, but the mileometer informed him they'd travelled seventy miles. That was his petrol ration blown for a few weeks.

To her credit, if this was Louise's first time behind a wheel – and Roland had no doubt at all that she'd never had any driving lessons – then she was a quick learner. She'd 'had a go' on the Sugdens' tractor, apparently, and had gleaned the basics, but Roland doubted that she'd have got up to eighty miles an hour on it. 'You should be a pilot,' he told her, as they lifted the picnic basket out of the boot.

'Women can't be,' she told him.

'There are women in the Transport Auxiliary.'

'Really? What do they do? Not dogfight stuff?'

Roland laughed. 'No. But planes have to be delivered from the factories to the airfields or from base to base. A couple of women do that and there will be more as the war goes on. If you can drive a car, and you can, after a fashion, then you can fly a plane.'

He laid out the picnic rug. Louise was unpacking the food now.

'Are you offering me a job?'

'Not mine to offer. I'll put in a good word for you, though, if you want.'

As they settled down on the picnic rug, Louise seemed to be considering the idea.

'Is farm work really so disagreeable?' Roland asked.

'I thought I'd like it. I used to have a horse, and I'd groom it, and look after it. I thought farm work would be like that, not pulling up potatoes all the time.'

'That's man's work. I thought you liked behaving like a man.'

'What makes you say that?' She was puzzled, not denying it, just curious to hear more.

Roland had been thinking about it a lot, and had an

answer. 'I don't mean that you're a tomboy, it's more than that. Your attitude is very . . . male. You like being in control – you couldn't imagine being driven, you have to do the driving. That first time we . . . met, you wanted to *have* me.'

She smiled, and didn't deny it.

'You're impatient, you're assertive. You know what you want and you aren't afraid to go after it. You don't like waiting, you want it now. You said yourself that if you were a man no one would bat an eyelid at your behaviour. Your attitude would fit right in with my crewmen.'

'Roland, are you really saying that if a girl goes on top once in a while suddenly she's a man?'

She had said it conversationally, and there was no one around, but her frankness still shocked him. 'Not at all. I don't think you want to be a man. Far from it. I think you want to be treated equally . . . because if you were you'd get whatever you wanted because you'd be a better man than most. If you see what I mean.'

To his intense relief, she was grinning. 'I've never really thought of it like that. You're right.' She gave a wicked chuckle. 'What does that make you?'

'Your friend,' he reminded her. 'Your equal.'

They leant towards each other and kissed, taking their time.

Eventually Louise broke away. 'Famished,' she explained.

Roland smiled. 'Have a sandwich,' he said.

At home Betty never liked mentioning Seth. It didn't do her mother's blood pressure any good.

Afternoon tea was something of a ritual in the Prendergast household. At midday on the dot, Betty's mother would bring out the teapot and the cake stand. The war had done nothing to change this routine.

'I was talking to Mrs Eagleton,' her mother told her, as she poured Margaret a cup. 'Her Walter's doing very well for himself. He's busy in training at the moment, but always finds time to write. He's sweet on you, isn't he, Elizabeth?'

'He's written to you, hasn't he?' Margaret put in.

Betty didn't thank her sister for mentioning it. 'He has.'

'I'd like to read the letter,' her mother said.

There was nothing unsuitable in any of the letters that Wally had written, but Betty objected to the lack of privacy. Or would have objected, if she hadn't known it would make no difference. 'I'll show you tonight,' she mumbled.

Her mother nodded, satisfied.

'Seth Armstrong's an ARP warden,' Betty said. 'The youngest in the Dales, he says.'

'He's a layabout. You stay away from him.'

'Don't you think it's good that he's doing his bit?'

'Seth Armstrong only did it to look around other people's houses,' her mother said sagely.

Margaret tutted. 'He's a bad sort.'

Betty knew that her mother and sister would love nothing more than an excuse to go into other people's houses and have a good snoop. 'I think he's brave,' she said quietly.

'There's nothing brave about making sure people have their curtains drawn,' Margaret scolded.

'You stay away from Seth Armstrong,' her mother warned. 'He wants his wicked way with you.'

Betty shuddered. She didn't want that, but she was sure there was a happy medium. Couldn't they at least be friends?

The washing was done and she'd used the rinsing water to mop the floor. The kitchen had almost certainly never

93

been so clean. Annie looked around. She'd been extremely industrious. It was amazing what you could find to do to avoid making a difficult decision.

She had thought that her whole life was mapped out. She had thought that marriage to Jacob was inevitable. She could even picture the wedding, down to the tiniest detail. Her dress would be quite plain and modern, and there wouldn't be a veil. She could see the bouquet, and she'd chosen the hymns. Her father would lead her down the aisle. Jacob would be waiting for her, scrubbed up and smarter than he'd ever been, and his brother Edward, resplendent in his navy uniform.

Then, she'd be a farmer's wife, which was hard work, tied to the ancient rhythms of the seasons. The machinery might change, but the job wouldn't. People would always need food. To her dying day, she'd live in this farmhouse, bringing up the generations that would follow her. A simple life, but a fulfilling one.

But now Annie wasn't so sure. Now she could see herself falling asleep in George Verney's arms. It was a vivid image: rich red firelight falling over elegant wooden panels, warmth and luxury. By comparison, Emmerdale Farm was cold and damp.

Everyone dreamt of living in a palace. All the storybooks were about princesses and kings and castles, and girls who owned horses for riding, not pulling a plough. Annie had never yearned to be rich. She didn't see any moral worth in poverty, and Jacob was offering a comfortable future, a secure one. He had been promising *enough*. But George offered a whole new horizon.

She remembered looking down the hill at the village, covering it with her hand. That was the stage on which she could play out the rest of her life. Now, for the first time in her life, there might be more.

George had almost kissed her. She had almost kissed

George. They'd discussed their love lives. If Annie had been single, she'd have been in no doubt as to George's intentions. What would she have done? That was the question. Not knowing the answer was answer enough for her. She needed to see George again and talk to him, in the cold light of day, with fair warning. She had to go over to Home Farm before the girls and Jacob came back, looking for their dinner.

It had been a small synagogue, but the people there were friendly. The men didn't just scowl at the women, as had happened in some Rita had been to. They seemed pleased to welcome another four into the fold.

Afterwards, Jean saw someone she knew, and Rita was left standing outside with Adam and Joe. 'This will be a good place to meet girls,' she told Adam.

He blushed. Rita allowed herself to smile. 'Seriously,' she added. 'I met my fiancé at synagogue.'

'You're engaged?' Adam asked.

'Yes. His name's Paul. He's in the navy.'

'Is he tall?' Joe asked.

Rita chuckled. 'Not really.'

Adam, who was quite short for his age, seemed to glow with the comfort of that.

Jean had emerged. 'I think we should go shopping, don't you?'

The boys agreed enthusiastically.

'Adam, do you know your way around Hotten now?'

'Yes.'

'You could find your way back here for two o'clock?'

He nodded.

Jean passed them a few coins. 'Right. The pair of you can go and enjoy yourselves. Keep together.' As they hurried off, she smiled. 'Some time away from them.'

'It must be odd having children of their age.'

'I'll say. I'm twenty-five, and I've got a fourteen-year-old son. And there was me saying I was a late developer!'

'Do you want children of your own?'

Jean looked away.

'I don't mean to pry.'

'Oh, you're not. Well, you are, but I don't mind. Brian and I don't really have that sort of relationship.' She hesitated. 'I do my wifely duties ... occasionally. And it is a duty. For both of us, I think.'

Rita was shocked, and sorry that she'd raised the subject. 'Why did you marry him?'

'Because I love him, but I didn't know it was only as a friend until it was too late. Perhaps I thought the rest would happen with time. Who knows? It may.'

'I love Paul as a friend,' Rita admitted, realising it was true as she said it.

'What do your parents think?'

'Oh, they adore him. He'll be going to university once he's out of the army.'

'But you've not slept with him?'

Rita was crushingly embarrassed. 'No,' she said firmly. 'Not until we're married.'

'That's the mistake I made with Brian,' Jean said wryly. 'Rita, if that side of it doesn't work, the rest ... well, it withers away.'

'There's never been anyone else?'

'I didn't say that.'

'You said you didn't like ... sex.' The last word appeared in the sentence before Rita could stop herself. She looked around, but no one around had heard.

'I thought I might if I found the right person.'

'But then you married Brian.'

'I thought he'd sort me out. Set me right. And, for a while, I settled down.'

'Then?'

'Then I got bored with him. Luckily I was in Beckindale. I've spent the last three years away from temptation. The chances of meeting the right person are fairly low and the chances of them being Jewish . . .'

Jean smiled at Rita and took her hand.

Annie walked up the path to Home Farm, full of a sense of purpose but unwilling to put it into words. She wanted to talk to George, that was all.

Someone was coming down the path towards her.

It was late: she hadn't expected anyone else to be around. Her father, Jacob and his father were all safely back at Emmerdale Farm. But she had heard footsteps. Boots, not a woman's shoes.

'George?' she called. Had he had the same idea?

The footsteps stopped.

'George, is that you?'

She ducked out of sight, waited for the man to show himself or leave.

For a moment, there was nothing. Had she imagined it? No.

There they were again. Boots on the hard ground. Getting nearer, but at a regular pace.

Absurd thoughts occurred to Annie. This was a German paratrooper, part of an advance guard – the boys staying with the Sullivans had thought they'd heard German spies in the woods. Rita had told her that. Like everyone else, Annie had dismissed it as the sort of story some bored city boys would come up with. Even if it wasn't a German, it might be a murderer on the loose – an escaped prisoner, or prisoner-of-war. She could go for help – either at Emmerdale Farm or Verney's – but by the time she'd be back here, he'd be long gone.

'Miss Pearson!' a girl's voice called.

'Louise?'

The boots had been Louise's Land Girl issue ones. Annie felt foolish.

'I thought you were going to attack me.'

Louise laughed. 'Why?'

'I didn't know it was you. What are you doing out here?'

'I was . . . visiting a friend.'

'At Home Farm?' Annie asked.

Louise hesitated. 'Yes. What about you?'

'Oh, just going for a walk.'

There weren't many women at Home Farm, Annie thought. A few maids, but they would have gone home by now. She was about to ask who Louise had been visiting, when she saw that it needn't have been a woman at all. She looked at Louise. 'Was it a gentleman?' she asked.

Louise seemed caught out, but not embarrassed. 'Yes,' she admitted. 'Look, you won't tell anyone? We're trying to be discreet.'

'No,' Annie said, hoping she didn't sound disappointed. 'Why would I tell anyone?'

CHAPTER NINE:
An Invitation

George found Roland in the library, looking over some old maps. 'I've been thinking of how we can keep the village on our side,' he said. 'Now that construction is under way, we're starting to see disruption to the community. The best way is to keep them involved, make them feel they're part of the process.'

'What do you suggest? Getting them to put up one of the hangars?'

George laughed. 'No. I thought a get-together up here, maybe this weekend.'

'Ah. Some of the top brass will be here.'

'We'll invite them, too. It wasn't going to be just villagers – a lot of the local great and good will come, you know. By all means invite your crew along. It's a chance for the village to come together. We used to have this sort of gathering often at this time of year.'

'Warming up for Christmas?'

'Celebrating the harvest, giving ourselves something to do on a long winter evening. It's fallen by the wayside since the war began.'

'It's a good idea,' Roland agreed. 'It'll make the airfield seem like something that brings us all together, instead of making it us and them. So much of this war is propaganda, isn't it?'

George could sense the regret in his voice. 'Eager to get to the fight?'

'I joined the RAF to fly, not sit around waiting.'

'Not long now.'

'RAF Emmerdale should be operational before Christmas.'

'So soon?' George was surprised – Christmas was only a couple of months away and he had thought it would be much longer, somehow.

'It's only a small airfield. It won't be finished, but the tower will be up, and we'll have one runway and a couple of hangars.'

'And operations will start. . . ?'

'As soon as it's up and the crews know each other. My wing are all training together in Devon. They'll be shipping up here as soon as the runway's dry, I'd have thought.'

'When did you last see them?'

'The day before I came here.'

'If they're due some leave, a few might be able to come for the party we're planning.'

Roland beamed. 'It would be nice to see them again.'

'They could stay here, of course.'

'They can find themselves a guest-house. The one thing my lads don't have any difficulty with is finding a bed for the night.'

George chuckled. 'Monday night?'

Roland nodded. 'Consider them RSVPed.'

The moment he saw Betty, Seth made himself look busy. He found his notebook and started studying it. 'You're never out of that armband, these days,' she told him. 'Is it really a full-time job? I didn't realise there was that much danger of a raid.'

'You've got to be ever-vigilant,' Seth informed her.

'And it's hard work is it?' Betty asked, scrutinising him. 'What's that say in there? "Strider 5/2, Durham Grey 6/1". What's all that?'

'Code words,' Seth told her. 'You wouldn't understand. I use them out on my rounds.'

'Rounds?'

'Aye. That's what I have to do, you see. When it gets dark, I have to go round, check everyone's blackout curtains, put out any fires. Ron took me round, showed me the ropes. Said I was a quick learner. And I use them code words because if I put the real names and addresses down and this book fell into German hands . . . well, you can imagine the consequences.'

'And you've got to do that every night?'

'Can't let people get complacent,' Seth said, feigning wisdom.

Betty seemed fooled. 'I didn't realise there was so much to this job.'

Seth frowned at her.

'I have to admit,' she continued, 'that I always thought it were a bit of a skive.'

'A *skive*?' Seth said, mock-outraged.

'No offence.' Betty reached out, touched his sleeve. She didn't see Seth grin. 'It's just that Maggie and Mum both used to say that Ron didn't really do very much in the job.'

'Well, I'm sure my . . . colleagues in London and Leeds have it harder,' Seth admitted. 'They're real heroes, and a lot of ARP men and AFS men have died in the line of duty. I only hope that I won't flinch if I have to lay down my life for my country. But it's not just what you do during an air-raid, it's about making sure the Jerries don't get a sniff of us in the first place.'

Betty's eyes were full of admiration. 'Can I come with you one night?'

Seth had to bite his tongue to stop himself. This was the time to play it slowly and carefully. 'I'm not sure you can,' he said slyly.

Betty was obviously disappointed. 'Don't you want me along?'

Seth looked down at her. 'Of course I do, Betty, love, but it's official business, you see.' He pretended to consider the request. 'Once,' he told her. 'I'll let you come along just the once.' He made a show of checking his notebook. 'Next Wednesday, but you're not to tell anyone.'

Betty looked delighted.

But she wasn't as delighted as he was. Seth chuckled to himself.

'Annie!' she heard George call. She had been avoiding him for over a week. It wasn't that difficult, even in a place as small as Beckindale. She was angry with him, and knew she was being irrational. Since she'd met Louise coming back from Home Farm, she hadn't known what to think. At first, she'd felt a sense of loss. She'd spent all day working up the courage to go up to Home Farm to see George, and had finally talked herself into it, only to have her hopes dashed.

Then she'd got home to Jacob and the life she was used to, and it had seemed comfortable, easy by comparison. Within a few minutes, she'd decided it was all for the best. She was happy with Jacob, and had been a fool even to consider anything else. But that night, she'd found it difficult to sleep. She was jealous of Louise. Why should George end up with some Land Girl, however well-spoken she was?

Silly, childish thoughts, and Annie knew it. But it was like a change in the landscape. Had he courted Louise in the same room?

'Annie, we need to talk.'

'It was a lovely afternoon.'

'About what happened just before you left.' Annie looked away. George knew he had to press her. 'We kissed.'

'No.'

'Our lips touched. We kissed.'

'I didn't mean to.'

'No?'

Annie looked at him again. 'I'm engaged,' she reminded him.

George took a step back. 'Yes. Of course. I'm sorry.'

Annie nodded sternly. 'I think we must have had too much brandy.'

'That was probably it. They were very large glasses.'

He wasn't going to tell her about Louise, wasn't going to admit to it. Now that Annie was looking out for it, she knew Louise often sneaked off after work. She always claimed she was out for a walk, but Annie had seen her hurry away, always towards Home Farm, not the village.

'I want to invite you up to Home Farm. You and Jacob. We're having a party . . . well, more of a cheese and wine affair. Monday night.'

'We?'

'The RAF are paying for it. A way of saying thank you to the village. A fair few villagers will be there, the Oakwells, and some RAF brass. Squadron Leader Pilgrim has invited some of the flight crews who'll be stationed here to take a look at where they'll be billeted.'

'Oh. I see. I'm not sure if we can.'

George looked disappointed. 'Wouldn't you like to?'

Annie straightened up. She was being silly. 'We'll be there.'

'Good girl.'

The moment Annie told him about the do at Home Farm Jacob had a sinking feeling – he knew she'd want him to go, and he knew he would refuse, so they were bound to have an argument.

'No,' he stated firmly, right from the outset.

'Jacob, it's an honour to be invited,' she remonstrated.

'Says who?'

'Just look at all the other people who'll be there. The Oakwells are going, a lot of the landowners – and you're a landowner.'

Jacob laughed: that was a line of attack he hadn't seen coming. 'I'm not old money, though, am I?'

'I know you can trace your family tree back further than just about anyone else who'll be there.'

'So are you saying I'm better than them?'

Annie hesitated, wisely sensing a trap. 'Yes,' she concluded.

'Well, I don't want to mix with them that's lower than me, that's not how it's done. I'd better stay here. You can go,' he told her. 'It'll be a nice change of scene. Verney seems to like your company.'

Annie wasn't budging.

'Oh, come on,' Jacob said, 'you know I'd hate it. And also you know that if I go you won't be able to enjoy yourself.'

'And I know that deep down you want to go and you want to enjoy yourself, but you're too stubborn.'

Jacob grinned.

Annie rolled her eyes, a little melodramatically.

'Are you looking forward to the party?' Annie asked Louise, as she came through the door. 'At Home Farm,' she clarified, because Louise looked bewildered. 'Monday night.'

'I've not been invited.'

'You must have been. Mr Verney and Squadron Leader Pilgrim have invited all sorts of people.'

Louise hadn't made it past the doormat. She had started to take off her scarf, but had abandoned the operation. 'You and Mr Sugden?'

'Yes, although Jacob won't be going. I think they're inviting a lot of people. Anyone who's anyone. I'm sure he'll invite you the next time he sees you.'

Louise looked a little embarrassed and Annie felt jealous. Absurd, but that was how it was. 'I was just out for a walk with him,' Louise said, and blushed. 'That's to say I just passed him on the path.'

'Perhaps he forgot,' Annie said.

'That must be it. If you'll excuse me, I might be able to catch him up,' Louise replied.

Louise turned on her heel and left the farmhouse, walking briskly back towards the footpath. Roland had been in his clearing, by the brook. They'd not planned to meet, but she'd headed up there knowing there was a good chance that he would be there.

She was almost running, now. She used to be exhausted after a day in the fields, but now she took it in her stride. By the end of the war she'd be an Olympic athlete. Yes, and she'd look years older than she really was, and she'd never get the dirt out of her skin – but she'd be as fit as a fiddle.

Roland was still there, surprised to see her running towards him.

'Forgotten something?' he called over the brook.

Louise came to a halt, not stepping over. 'No. Have you?'

He frowned. 'I don't think so.'

'What about Monday night?'

'Ah . . . you've heard about that.'

'Don't I get an invite?'

'It's awkward,' Roland said.

'No, it's not. Invite me. You invited a lot of other people.'

'You can't go – you said yourself that we're just friends.'

'Yes. So what's wrong with me going as your friend? Annie Pearson's just Verney's friend, isn't she? She's going.'

'He feels he owes her a great deal. Look, I don't understand why you want to go at all.'

Louise pointed back the way she'd come. 'Because this
morning I hosed out a cowshed and this afternoon I
whitewashed it. And that's been the highlight of my
week so far. I want to enjoy myself, just once, while I'm
here.'

'We enjoy ourselves, don't we?' Roland asked, looking a
little hurt. 'When we're alone, I mean.'

'I could get that from any number of people,' she told
him flatly.

Roland chose not to say anything.

'As soon as it's over, you pack me off home so no one
sees us,' Louise reminded him.

'It's awkward,' Roland objected. 'I'm a guest of Verney's,
and I don't want to put either him or you in an embar-
rassing situation.'

'I just want to come to a party, Roland, as a friend. I
want to wear high heels and a good frock, drink something that wasn't fermented in a barn.'

'You can't. Not this time.'

'Fine.' She turned round and started walking back.

'Louise, what is this?' he asked. 'I didn't think you
wanted romance. You said you didn't.'

'I don't. But I want to be treated as your equal. That's
what friends do, they don't pull rank.'

'That's not what this is.'

'And I don't want any secrets.'

'That's rich – you've been so mysterious all the time,
keeping your cards close to your chest, not giving a hint of
all those past lovers you've been so careful to mention
every so often.'

Suddenly Louise was angry, and her expression must
have betrayed this because Roland went on, 'Ah! So, you
do have emotions? I can get under that skin of yours.'

'You shouldn't want to,' she told him. 'If you're ashamed of me, then—'

'I'm not ashamed of you.'

'But I'm not someone you want your friends to meet? Which is it? Are you worried I'll make it awkward when you meet the top brass, or that'll I'll go off and sleep with half of your squadron?'

'Louise!'

'No. Sorry, Roland, I thought we had an agreement. I thought you could be civilised about this. But you can't. Fine. You go to your party.'

She stalked off, ignoring Roland's calls.

CHAPTER TEN:

The Party at Home Farm

Blackout regulations weren't relaxed just because there was a gathering at Home Farm, and the villagers found themselves walking up the hill in darkness. Every so often a car would sweep past, its headlights obscured by cardboard so as not to fall foul of the blackout – and, of course, defeating the object of having headlights in the first place. Large as it was, it would have been easy to walk past Home Farm if it hadn't been such a clear night.

Some of the guests, those who'd travelled furthest to get here, had arrived an hour or so before the party was due to start and as the villagers came in, they found that most of the airmen, barring a few of the top brass who were motoring over from York, had already made themselves at home. The drive was full of cars, although – mindful of petrol rationing – a lot of people had cadged a ride or found another way to share a vehicle.

'You might as well come in,' Roland had said to Seth Armstrong.

Seth had been only too keen: it was the reason why he'd come up here in the first place. He made a show of checking the blackout, then accepted the invitation.

He'd already made the acquaintance of the RAF men by the time Betty, Margaret and their mother arrived. Betty was in her best frock, wearing makeup and had curled her hair. Seth introduced her and her sister to a few of the airmen. Her mother watched them like a hawk from the other side of the room, but Seth knew she wouldn't intervene: these were men in uniform, defenders of the country and all it stood for, and as long as Seth stood near them he basked in their reflected glory. It was like Dracula and sunlight, Seth thought: Betty's mother wouldn't be able to get close. He looked at her as she buried her sour face in a gin and tonic. She wasn't as amiable as Dracula.

There were plenty of people here, from all walks of life, and they were all mingling. Quite how Solomon Dingle and his wife had got in, Seth couldn't fathom, but they were chatting away to a chap in RAF dress uniform, an admiral or whatever the RAF called them, without anyone raising an eyebrow, and Ron was already boring a pair of aristocratic young ladies with his war stories.

The men outnumbered the women by at least two to one, but the lack of quantity was more than made up for by the quality. Apart from Betty, who looked lovely, there were several young things in elegant dresses, dripping with jewellery. Even Annie Pearson was dressed up to the nines.

They weren't bothering much with a lowly ARP warden, not when there were pilots and eligible landed gentry in the room, but Seth didn't mind: he only had eyes for Betty.

The most beautiful woman Roland had ever seen was looking at him. Every man in the room was sneaking a glance at her. She was tall, blonde, and had an hourglass figure that would have had fashion designers hurrying to their drawing boards. She walked over to him, impossibly gracefully. 'Hello there, were you just looking at me?'

'I was, actually,' Roland admitted.

She laughed politely. 'You're a squadron leader, aren't you?'

'That's right,' he assured her. 'And you are?'

She raised an eyebrow at the question. 'I'm staying here tonight,' she told him. 'A guest of Mr Verney.'

'I'm staying here, too.'

She smiled. 'Now, that raises some interesting opportunities.'

'What are you suggesting?' he asked, playing along.

She leant towards him and whispered.

Roland coloured and declined the offer, as gently as he could.

'If you change your mind . . .' she said, and drifted away.

'Who's that?' Roland asked, once he'd found George Verney.

'Lucy Oakwell. The eldest daughter of Lord Oakwell. Out of your league, Roland, I'm afraid.'

'That's not what she's just told me.'

'Good heavens – well, good luck, old chap.'

Roland looked at Lucy Oakwell. Interesting opportunities indeed.

Annie realised she was one of the last to arrive. Sally, the maid, had taken her coat, and hadn't commented as Annie changed her shoes. Walking in heels was tricky enough as it was but going downhill, crossing stepping stones, then climbing up the other side of the dale in them was out of the question.

George saw her and came straight over, much to her relief. She looked around. 'Is Louise here?' she asked.

He looked puzzled. 'Louise?'

Annie nodded. So, he was playing it like that. 'I saw her, and she hadn't had her invite, yet.' If Annie didn't know better, she'd have thought George had no idea what she was talking about. 'Louise Price?' she said again. 'One of the Land Girls billeted with us?'

'I don't think we invited any of the Land Girls. Do you think we should have?'

Before Annie could answer, a middle-aged man in a dinner jacket had attracted George's attention. He apologised, and drifted off with the new arrival.

Annie watched him go, confused. One thing George couldn't do was keep a secret. As Jacob would put it, the upper class seemed crippled by guilt and embarrassment and, consequently, were hopeless liars. Annie knew that if George was trying to hide something it would have been as obvious as if he was wearing a sandwich board.

So if he didn't know who Louise was, then what was going on?

'Pilgrim!' a familiar voice called.

His crew had assembled, for all the world like a rugger team in the changing rooms after a game, however smart and dignified their dress uniform was meant to make them look.

His men. They'd all signed up before the war and wherever possible they'd trained together. Roland had done his best to keep them together. Current plans were that these men would be stationed at RAF Emmerdale, that he'd be fighting shoulder to shoulder with them when the time came.

They hadn't changed: Pilot Officer Mark Johnson, 'Jonners', with his glasses, the navigator; Atto, or Flying Officer Simon Atkins, the flight engineer; Flight Sergeant Anthony Galway, the gunner; and the youngest, Flight Sergeant Glyn Jones, a nineteen-year-old from Cardiff, the smartest wireless operator Roland knew who, like every other Welshman in every military organisation the world had ever known, was nicknamed 'Taffy'.

He did the rounds, slapping shoulders and exchanging vigorous handshakes. It had been a good few months since he'd seen them.

'What's it like in the land of fog and sheep?' Anthony asked.

'Ask Taffy about that,' Roland joked. 'Here, it's marvellous.'

'He's got his end away,' Atto concluded. They all started scanning the room, as if they were looking for Messerschmitts. 'Which one is she, then, old boy?'

Roland held up his hands. 'No use looking,' he told them. 'She's not here.'

'Never mind, that means everyone here's fair game.'

'Hope for you yet, Taffy.'

Taffy took it on the chin, didn't curl up and blush, like a lot of young men his age would have.

'Uh-oh,' Jonners warned. The men all gave a sharp salute.

Roland turned. Half a dozen senior officers were lined up in front of him. He saluted.

'It's like a ruddy court martial,' he heard Galway mutter.

'A firing squad!' Taffy laughed.

'Could we have a word, Squadron Leader?'

Ron was starting to get into the swing of things. He wasn't used to being handed drinks, he was used to pouring them, but he had to say he preferred being here to another night at the Woolpack.

'A piano!' one of the airmen exclaimed. 'Anyone play?'

'The mark of a gentleman,' George Verney told them solemnly, 'is that a chap can play the piano but he doesn't.'

'Seth can play,' Ron told the crowd.

'I'm no gentleman,' Seth said cheerfully, lifting the lid and taking a seat. 'Any requests?'

He started to play. Where he'd learned, Ron didn't know, but he was very good. One of the airmen, impressed by what he heard, even gave his cap to the lad.

'What do you do, sir?' one of the airmen asked Ron, a young Welshman.

'I'm a publican,' Ron said, a little ashamed. These people were fighting for their country, and all he did was pull pints.

'You lose that in the last one?' another asked.

Ron felt a little embarrassed. 'I did.'

'Nothing to be ashamed of, old chap, just the opposite.'

'It's one of the perennial questions,' the Welsh lad said, his accent drawing out the words, 'but which arm is it best to lose? I mean, obviously, it's best to lose a leg if you get a choice.'

'Well, I'm right-handed,' Ron answered, 'so it would have been worse if I'd lost this one.'

'You compensate,' someone said. 'You get used to it. Seen it happen. Never mind that, though. You said something about a pub.'

'That's right, The Woolpack. Finest pub in the area.'

'There are others, then?'

Ron thought about mentioning the Malt Shovel, but decided against it. 'None worth the name,' he replied.

'And I suppose your place is closed tonight, with you here?'

'No. I've got a lad who helps me. Name of Colin. He's holding the fort.'

'We might head down there.'

'This party not good enough for you?'

The Welsh lad grinned. 'There's brass here – senior officers. It's like having your parents in the room.'

'And the birds here are out of our league.'

'Free drinks, though. You won't get them at the Woolpack.' He wanted to get that clear from the outset.

113

'We'll pay our way. How do you get there?'

'You can't lose yourself in Beckindale,' Ron reassured him. 'Just go down the hill to the village, you'll see it.'

The two men slapped him on the back and headed off.

Roland hoped he'd remember everything that was meant to be going in this report. They'd found a spare room – the billiards room. He always ended up here when he was discussing the airfield: his maps and charts were pinned up around the room.

He waited for them to settle. 'The construction of RAF Emmerdale is proceeding ahead of schedule,' he told them. 'So far, we've had none of the problems with terrain or climate encountered on previous sites.'

One of the senior group captains was ignoring him, looking at the map. 'This is one of the smaller ones, isn't it?'

'That's right, sir, two bomber squadrons. We're expecting Halifaxes, but of course we'd be ready for Lancasters if that's what we get.'

'And it's north of York, so they'll be part of Six Group?'

'Sir,' Roland agreed.

'Where are your crews at the moment – those that aren't here already, of course?'

'A lot are seconded to work on the south coast. We've got a few pilots training up more.'

The air vice marshal nodded. 'So, how's the great experiment going?'

'Sir?'

'Do you think you're doing useful work? A few of us weren't sure about taking a man out of the air to look after the ground. Think you should be training others.'

'Yes, sir, I believe I'm doing valuable work. RAF Emmerdale is not far from a small village –' so small he had trouble at first in finding Beckindale on the map

'– and they saw it as an intrusion. But I think, with Flight Lieutenant Verney's help, that we've smoothed the waters.'

'You're not here to mollycoddle the civilians,' an air commodore warned him.

'No, sir, but co-operation with the locals has made things a lot easier, and it means morale among those working on the base is high. As I said, we're well ahead of schedule.'

The air commodore opened his mouth to object, but the air vice marshal spoke first. 'Very important thing, morale,' he said, putting an end to any objection. 'What else have you done?'

'It's little things,' Roland said, 'things that the surveyors and planners don't always think through because they won't be working there. Like making sure there are enough latrines.'

There was a laugh of recognition from one or two officers who had seen service in the last war, and a couple of mumbled anecdotes passed around the room.

'Also,' Roland continued, 'I noticed that the planned briefing room wasn't big enough – whoever drew up the plans seemed to want the CO to brief every crewman individually.'

More laughs.

'Ah, yes – we've had that problem before,' someone said.

Roland knew better than to ask why no one had thought to remedy it, if they were aware of it.

'Err on the side of caution,' the AVM advised.

'Sir?'

'Well, you're building the place for twenty Halifaxes, but leave room for more.'

Roland looked back at the plans, his heart sinking a little. 'There will be more planes stationed here than anticipated?'

'Our experience is that all the airfields are operating above capacity. If we have another Driffield, we'll need the other bases to take up the slack.'

The Luftwaffe had raided the airfield at Driffield, bombing it, strafing it with machine-gun fire, even taking pot-shots at workers in nearby fields. It had put the place out of action for months, and had had a devastating effect on morale there. A lot of the lads saw the airfield as safety – the sanctuary to which you tried to return at the end of every mission. To see the buildings bombed, the planes attacked on the ground, some of the WAAFs killed or injured had been a rude awakening. Nowhere was safe. The Germans targeted the airfields, of course, just as the RAF targeted German runways. It was one of the reasons why they didn't tell anyone where they were building them.

Roland was starting to think of Beckindale as home. To imagine some of the villagers he knew gunned down, or to think that a stray bomb, or malicious gunner, might target Louise as she worked in the fields disturbed him. He found it remarkably easy to hold contradictory thoughts in his head: that the enemy must be defeated to prevent this happening, and that the war should end now, because nothing justified that sort of cost.

'Sir, if there are plans to increase the capacity of the airfield, we should discuss that now. It needs to be factored into the plans.'

The air vice marshal chortled. 'You're beginning to sound like an accountant, Squadron Leader.'

Roland took the hint. It was a tricky subject, the base would be overstretched, but the top brass weren't admitting that even to themselves just yet.

'Where's Annie?' Rita asked.

'She's at the Home Farm party,' Louise replied. 'We've agreed to cook tonight.'

'Why are you so grumpy?' Alyson asked, surprised by how tetchy Louise sounded.

'Did you not get an invite, Louise?' Jacob laughed. 'Don't worry, love – neither did I.'

He didn't suspect, Louise realised. 'Aren't you worried about your fiancée being up there all on her own?'

'She's not on her own,' Jacob said, 'she's with all those blue-bloods.'

'And no chaperone.' Alyson laughed.

'Annie doesn't need one,' Jacob told her.

'You're all behaving like you really expected an invite,' Virginia said.

'Do you know Mr Verney, then?' Alyson asked Louise. 'Does he not want to let on he's got a fancy woman?'

The girls laughed, and even Jacob smiled.

'It's not that,' Louise said, crossly.

Alyson looked at her rather mockingly. 'We know. We're only pulling your leg.'

Jacob was aware that work on dinner was going slowly. 'Come on, help peel these spuds.'

'You don't peel spuds,' Virginia and Alyson said in unison. 'It's a waste,' Alyson finished.

'I've never been able to cook,' Louise admitted.

'You won't make a very good wife if you can't cook,' Jacob said.

'I don't intend to get married.'

'Oooooh,' the other girls chorused.

'Are you one of them?' Jacob laughed.

'One of what?' Rita asked.

Louise straightened. She wasn't quite tall enough to look Jacob in the eye, but she wasn't far off. 'No. I just believe in treating people like equals.'

'Good for you,' Jacob replied.

'You agree?'

'Oh, yes. Just because I live in the country, Louise, doesn't mean I live in the last century. It's people like Verney who are backward-looking, who rely on history, not their own ability.'

'Are you a Bolshie, Mr Sugden?' Virginia giggled.

'Far from it. If a woman works as hard as a man, she should get the same rewards as a man.' Jacob gave a wicked grin. 'So, get working, Louise.'

Colin was rushed off his feet. Ron was always a lazy so-and-so, sloping off from barwork at the earliest opportunity. He was a mean devil, too – he'd not hire extra help, even for the busy nights or nights like this, when he was off enjoying himself.

Ron had assured Colin that most of the villagers would be at Home Farm, and he'd have a quiet night. Fat chance. There might have been a do on at Home Farm, but the people invited to it weren't Woolpack regulars. The Oakwells never popped in for a swift half, and the villagers up at Home Farm were the people like Dragon Prendergast and Annie Pearson, people like that wouldn't have been able to tell you what the inside of the Woolpack looked like.

Seth Armstrong was missing, but the way he nursed a pint meant that Colin's workload was hardly affected by that. It just meant there was more room for other punters.

Lazarus Dingle was at his usual place at the bar. 'Busy tonight, isn't it?' he asked unhelpfully, and Colin was about to agree when the doors opened again and two airmen walked in, in full dress uniform. 'The party's not over at Home Farm, is it?' Colin asked, his heart sinking. All he needed now was another rush – it was too much to hope that Ron would be back to help him.

'Not at all. Just a bit dull.'

Lazarus held out his hand. 'Lazarus Dingle, at your

service, gentlemen. I take it you've been, how do they put it? *Stationed* to our new airfield?'

'Not yet, but we will be,' said the elder of the new arrivals. 'Flight Sergeant Anthony Galway. What are you having?'

Lazarus raised an eyebrow. 'Pint of Monk.'

'We'll join you. Taffy, do the honours. One for the barman, too.'

The Welsh lad sighed, and put his hand in his pocket.

'We met the chap with one arm up at the party. He sent us down here.'

'How is he?'

'Good chap.'

'Is the party really that dull?' Colin asked, relishing the thought of Ron having a miserable time.

'It was all right, but you can't beat a pub, can you? We're doing a recce,' Anthony explained. 'What we've seen of the village so far meets with our approval.'

'So you'll be recommending us to your colleagues?'

'Certainly will.'

'How many of you are there? How long are they here for?'

'Couple of dozen chaps, here for three or four days.'

'How about we do a special night for you, the night after next? First drink free for the RAF.'

Lazarus held his hand up. 'Are you sure Ron will approve of that?'

Colin felt cocky. 'I'm in charge, so what I say goes. I'll see you and your friends here?'

The RAF men nodded enthusiastically.

George noticed that Annie was one of the few who hadn't drifted home or to wherever they were staying tonight. He looked around. A couple of Roland's RAF pals were dozing on the sofa, and unless he was mistaken, Roland himself had last been seen escorting Lucy Oakwell upstairs. The lucky dog.

Annie was talking to the Hart-Wilsons, and George headed over to her.

'I've never been to London,' he heard her confess.

Those around her looked flabbergasted.

'You must,' Penny Hart-Wilson told her. 'If you do, we'll treat you to dinner at the Salted Almond.'

Annie accepted the invitation graciously, knowing she would never take them up on it. Then the Hart-Wilsons drifted away.

'Have you been avoiding me?' George asked.

Annie looked a little uncomfortable. 'A little,' she admitted.

'Why, for heaven's sake? I thought we'd agreed that—'

A glare from her silenced him. *There are other people here*, she was telling him.

No one sober or within earshot, though, George wanted to reply. 'I don't understand what the matter is,' he explained quietly.

'You're seeing Louise Price,' she told him.

'I told you before, I'm not even sure I've heard her name.'

Annie seemed to believe him. 'You're not? But . . .'

She floundered for a moment, and George didn't want to interrupt.

'Why would it bother you?' he asked eventually. 'If I was seeing someone, why would it upset you?'

Annie's eyes met his.

'I'm seeing Mr Sugden in a whole new light,' Alyson confessed, as the girls settled down for the night.

'Alyson,' Louise said sternly, 'what is the matter with you? You seem to fall for every man you set eyes on.'

'I only mean he's funny. I thought he was . . . what's the word?'

'Dour?' Louise suggested.

'Dour. But he can tell jokes. Now I see what Annie sees in him.'

'He's spoken for.'

'Oh, I know. I wish I would get a man.'

'Don't worry, Alyson, I'm sure you will.'

George's mouth was firm against Annie's as they stood in the hall, holding each other close. She'd never kissed anyone but Jacob, but George was confident, his hand flat against the small of her back, a reassuring, steadying presence. She ought to have been worried that someone would come through, but she wasn't.

'Come upstairs,' he murmured.

'No.' She laughed.

He broke away, took her hand, almost pulled her. 'Come on.'

She snatched it away.

'No,' she repeated, more firmly.

The spell was broken.

'I'm . . . sorry,' George said.

'I like you,' Annie said slowly, 'but I'm engaged to Jacob. I love him. Do you understand?'

George was nodding almost theatrically. 'I do. I quite understand. I'm sorry if I . . .'

She pecked him on the cheek. 'I'd better be going.'

It had been a late night.

Roland was far from a novice at either drinking or late nights but his head throbbed. Virtually all the guests had drifted home or to their rooms, and somehow – he suspected it was George's work – he had found himself escorting Lucy Oakwell to hers.

She didn't seem to know where she was. The relative quiet and claustrophobia of the corridors seemed to have disoriented her, as though she didn't function properly without a crowd of admirers. She giggled as Roland opened her door for her. Then he found himself taking her over to her bed. She sat down and, at her gesture, he removed one of her shoes, handmade, Italian, with a needle-thin high heel. In his hand, it looked like a weapon, an exotic knife.

She giggled. 'I have cocaine in my bag,' she told him. Some in her bloodstream, too, he thought. All the U-boats in the world couldn't cut some supply lines to the country, not when there was a lucrative specialist market. To her sort, the war was a game: the Oakwell brothers, if she had any, would get their commissions and some cushy office job, if that's what they wanted. Or they would persuade a doctor to sign them off as unfit, if they fancied sitting this one out.

'You're spending the war doing what you always did,' he told her harshly.

She was too drunk to take offence. 'Not at all. I want to entertain the troops,' she told him, patting the bed.

'All of them?' Roland asked.

She gave a wide smile, exposing a row of perfect teeth, then lay back, propping herself up on her elbows, her legs dangling off the side of the bed. 'Only the bravest officers. Bomber pilots are the bravest of the lot, aren't they?'

A moment before, she had seemed confused, but this room had become her element. She was gorgeous, quite the most beautiful woman Roland had ever seen. He felt a bit guilty comparing her with Louise, who was attractive, and who in any other company would have stood head and shoulders above the competition. But Lucy was a work of art. She spent her days grooming herself, making herself beautiful, while Louise worked.

Lucy held her leg straight up, ostensibly to make it easier for him to remove her other shoe but actually to give Roland a glimpse of her stocking tops. He looked up to see her watching him, with a knowing smile.

'Are you looking up my skirt, Squadron Leader?'

He found himself imagining what she would be like. An extraordinary body, a life given over to decadence. He imagined her kissing him, and more. It surprised him that he didn't feel any desire, just curiosity. Somehow, he had the feeling that she'd be capable of any number of things that an ordinary lover couldn't manage.

It was a fantasy, of course, like a schoolgirl falling for a picture of Clark Gable or Errol Flynn. No doubt being a film star had its perks, but when it came down to it, they were only people, they had their limits. Louise had said it this morning: what Lucy was offering, he could get from any number of people. And now his imagination was back in his own room, with Louise.

He wondered what Louise would do – seize the moment, take pleasure and experience what she could, he thought.

He must have had a glint in his eye, because Lucy was facing him, now.

'Are you a brave officer?' she asked. But the words sounded ridiculous, almost insulting.

He imagined Louise in her place, taking him seriously, not treating it as a game, however much pleasure there was. Concentrating on making each moment special. Being a friend.

'I'm spoken for,' he told her.

'I won't tell if you don't.' She held out her arms for him, pouting.

'No,' Roland told her. He took a step back.

She didn't seem to accept that he meant he was going.

'Are you playing hard to get?' she asked.

As Roland closed the door behind him, he wondered how long it would be before she realised he wasn't.

CHAPTER ELEVEN:
Changed Landscape

Sam Pearson couldn't believe the transformation. In just over a month, Miffield Rise had changed. It had been green grazing land but now geometric shapes had been carved into it, whole areas had been staked out and the ground churned up by heavy machines. So ugly, he thought.

Dozens of chaps in uniforms were digging away. He'd never had to dig a trench during the last war. By the time he'd got to the continent, the great lines were long established, seemingly a permanent feature of the landscape, mazes stretching hundreds of miles. He'd never thought he'd see the same in Yorkshire, even back then. Then, on the worst nights, he'd thought that the war might go on for ever. But the whole point of last time was that the lines didn't move. For all the bombs and shells and bullets, they barely moved for the whole war, or if they did, they moved back again within a few weeks.

And now, twenty-five years later, they were launching their attacks from here. War had come home.

'Magnificent, isn't it?'

George Verney was behind him, and next to him was the RAF chap, Squadron Leader Pilgrim.

Sam didn't trust himself to answer. 'How long will it take?' he asked instead.

'The first runway should be ready for Christmas,' Pilgrim said. 'The base won't be fully operational for months after that, though.'

'And when the war's over, it'll go?' Sam asked. He already knew the answer. How could it? This was going to be a place of concrete and thick walls. A place you could drop a bomb on. If it was designed so you couldn't blow it up, how would they ever get rid of it?

Verney looked confused. 'It's only here for the duration, Sam. You don't think I'd want it permanently, do you?'

'It would make a nice private airfield,' Roland told him. 'Aviation's the future. There are a fair few companies who'd be interested.'

'Beckindale Airport?' Verney said sceptically.

'Well, no, you're too far away from Leeds for much passenger travel, but this would be a great area to conduct low-altitude test flights . . . You could run a flying club, or a gliding one. The hangars we're building will make nice workshops. After the war, this will be a great little place to work.'

Sam turned and walked away, unable to listen to any more.

In front of him, were unspoiled views. Rolling green fields, all neatly delineated by stone walls. Clear skies, clean rivers, with people taking only what they needed from the land, and only when it was ready for them, just as they had for centuries.

Annie made the breakfast, and smiled at Louise as she came in.

'Did you enjoy the party?' Louise asked.

'I did, thank you.'

'Do you need a hand?'

Louise stirred the porridge while Annie got the plates.

'Any gossip?' Alyson asked.

'Oh . . . I don't know,' Annie said.

'Go on,' Virginia prompted, 'there must be some scandal.'

'Seth Armstrong was sick in a plant pot, I think.' Annie had watched him.

'Is that all?'

'Well, how many other people do you know from the village? You get on well with the Sullivans, don't you, Rita? They were there.'

'How about those dashing airmen?'

'Mr Verney and Squadron Leader Pilgrim? Well, Mr Pilgrim caught the eye of a very pretty girl. Mr Verney was the host, he . . . didn't have time for any of that.'

'What girl?' Louise asked.

'Oh, one of the posh ones. Lucy Oakwell, I think. We were introduced. She was very beautiful. The women there spent the evening trying not to stand next to her in case they looked dowdy.'

Alyson's eyes were wide. 'And he . . .'

Annie hesitated. 'I really don't know.'

The girls giggled.

'He did help her up the stairs,' Annie admitted, 'and we didn't see him after that.'

When she turned round to serve, Annie was surprised to see Louise had gone.

'I'll have hers,' Jacob said, coming in from outside.

'You might as well,' Annie said.

'How was the party, then?'

Annie looked away. 'Very good.'

'Spent your time talking to toffs?'

'A lot of it, yes.'

Jacob grunted, all his suspicions confirmed.

'One couple invited me to London.'

Jacob was checking the post. 'Are you going?' he asked.

Annie paused. 'To London? No. You couldn't spare me, could you?'

Jacob grinned. 'We could cope for a night. We did yesterday, didn't we, girls?'

The remaining three nodded enthusiastically.

'I'm not going to London on my own.'

'Well, I'm sure Verney would take you,' Jacob said.

'Why do you say that?' Annie asked, trying to keep her voice steady.

'Well, he's always going on about London, isn't he? "My work means I have to go there a lot." That sort of rubbish. I'm sure he'd love to take you.'

'And you'd let me go with him?'

'God, yes.'

'You don't look well.'

Normally, the sound of Betty's voice would be enough to lift Seth's spirits. Today, it echoed around his skull as if the Luftwaffe were doing a bombing run in it. He heard himself groan.

'I saw all that ale you drank last night.'

Seth mumbled.

'What was that?'

'You looked very nice,' Seth repeated.

'I'm surprised you could see anything. How on earth did you get home?'

'Instinct,' he said proudly. 'I know the land like the back of my hand.'

Betty sniffed, unimpressed. 'I pity them cleaners at Home Farm this morning. Especially when they find that plant pot.'

'I wasn't the only one drinking, Betty, love.' In fact, Seth was a bit hazy on the details, but it seemed unlikely that he had been.

'No, but them RAF lads can hold their drink.'

'They gave me this cap,' he said, pulling it out of his pocket. It was nice and warm, a blue woollen thing. It got cold up in them planes.

'Just one look at them, and you can see that you're a boy and they're men. Do you really think that suits you?'

'Eh?' Seth didn't try to work that one out, he just stored it away to think about later. 'Are you still coming out with me on my rounds tomorrow?'

Betty let him sweat for a moment. 'There's a do on at the Woolpack.'

'Oh, so you'll want to go to that.'

'No. I'll come with you. Keep you on the straight and narrow.'

Louise found Roland Pilgrim in his clearing, studying a notebook. 'Hello there,' he called.

She wasn't in the mood. 'You slept with her.'

'If you mean Lucy Oakwell, I didn't. I made sure she got to her room, then I went back to mine.'

'Really?' She glared at him. 'Then you're a fool. I would have done.'

Roland didn't doubt her. 'Make up your mind,' he said. 'Either you care or you don't. Either you have this wonderful, liberated life where either of us can do as we please, or you get jealous.'

'I want friendship,' she told him. 'Someone I can trust, share things with. You can sleep with whoever you want, as long as you don't lie to me. But if you tell me one thing, then do another, if you don't trust me enough even to stand next to you at a party, then what's the point?'

She tried to storm away, but Roland wasn't about to give her the last word. 'You can trust me,' he said.

'Why bother?' she shot back, and left.

*

Mrs Prendergast poured the tea. 'The Woolpack are organising a night for the RAF men. You and Margaret should both go.'

Betty looked up. 'On our own?'

'I know I can trust you. And those RAF men seemed very good sorts. Just compare their behaviour last night with that Seth Armstrong's.'

Betty had already done that, of course. The RAF lads had been confident, assured. Seth had simply seen an opportunity to drink without worrying about spending money or using coupons. He hadn't acted disgracefully – got up on the table and started singing rude songs, or leering at her – but he hadn't been irreproachable either. He'd just become unsteady on his feet. He'd been quite amiable, really, making sure Betty was all right, telling some jokes to the RAF men. They'd quite liked him, but it wasn't a relationship of equals: they looked down on him. He was a country bumpkin, and whatever the airmen's backgrounds, they were men of the world, the front line. Seth . . . well, they were tolerant towards him, but Betty had the impression that they had treated him as they would the regimental mascot, if the RAF had such a thing.

'Anthony was a perfect gentleman,' Maggie said.

'He was,' their mother agreed. 'Well-spoken, too.'

'So I've got to go along to chaperone them?' Betty asked.

'No!' her mother cried, horrified. 'There won't be any need for that. You can find yourself your own airman, if you want.'

Betty looked at her mother. 'What are you suggesting?'

Mrs Prendergast frowned. 'That you behave yourself. Whatever else they might be, those airmen are men, and you have to be on your guard. But they've got good prospects, and they're very brave. You could do worse.'

Betty doubted it. She didn't fancy the idea of courting a bomber pilot – they might be brave men, physically fit, mentally alert, but there were safer prospects for a long, happy married life.

Margaret was frowning, now. At twenty-two, she was already starting to look like their mother. While Betty loved her mother, she hoped she wasn't condemned to the same fate.

'I don't understand what you're saying, Mother,' Margaret said.

'Those airmen deserve to see pretty faces,' she explained. 'You go to the Woolpack, I'll give you some money. You talk to them, remind them what they're fighting for. But don't let them take liberties.'

Alyson was surprised to see that Louise had been crying. 'What's the matter?' she asked.

Louise looked up, trying to regain her composure. 'I'm all right.'

'You're not. If you tell me, I might be able to help. A problem shared is a problem halved.'

Louise looked scornful. 'It's nothing.'

'You disappeared just before breakfast.'

'I know.'

'Where did you go?'

'Look, leave it, all right?'

'Was it a man? Did some man turn you down or something?'

Louise was silent.

'It is,' Alyson said.

'Leave it,' Rita warned. 'Can't you see she's upset?'

'This is Louise,' Alyson reminded her. 'She's Miss Men Don't Bother Me. Well, they do. See?'

Louise scowled. 'You really don't know what you're talking about.'

CHAPTER TWELVE:

Woolpack Nights

Jacob had tried to hide his delight. That morning, over breakfast, Alyson had asked permission for the Land Girls to go out for the evening. They didn't need his blessing, of course, but someone had to let them back in, and they were being polite.

Jacob was only too happy to get them out of the house. He and Annie had exchanged glances – this would be a chance for them to spend some time alone together, the first for a long time. His dad was already out for the night, with Sam at a regimental reunion dinner in Hotten.

The four girls were downstairs now, all dolled up, over-doing the makeup a little, trying to look older or more sophisticated than they were. Rita looked ill at ease, but Alyson and Louise were in their element. Virginia was fussing with her hair. They all wore dresses that were the latest fashions, or the nearest they could buy on their budget or make for themselves with only Hotten to shop in.

Annie observed them with the same fascination that children watched animals at the zoo. It was difficult to believe that she was the same age. City folk took longer to grow up, Jacob had said. In the country, there weren't the same opportunities or the luxury to decide what you wanted to be. He was always going to be a farmer, it was in his blood. Not everything was decided from the day he was born – he might have been a good farmer or a bad one. He might have been a tenant all his life, but he'd become the owner of his farm.

'Come on!' Alyson almost shouted.

And then the four were rushing out the door, and Jacob and Annie were alone.

They went over to the sofa, sat down together and let the silence wash over them. The only sound was of the wood crackling in the fireplace.

'It's like a broken tap,' Annie said at last.

'What?'

'Those girls here, all day and all night: drip, drip, drip, and you get used to it. Then you fix it and you realise how annoying it was, how quiet the house is.'

They sat there a little longer, not needing to say or do anything, just enjoying each other's company.

Then Annie leant in and kissed him. She was so soft. That was what he always thought – his hands and face were almost leathery. The Land Girls hadn't believed he was only thirty. When they'd been told, they had thought it was a joke. Annie was still young – she'd never worked on the farm, never raised children, she had all that to come.

'Are you happy?' he asked her.

Annie looked surprised. 'Of course. Why are you asking?'

'Not a little envious of them?'

It took a moment or two for Annie to understand who he was talking about. 'The girls?' she asked.

Jacob nodded. 'You don't want to be out there, having fun?'

'I'm here, aren't I?'

'Yes. But lots of things are changing because of the war.

132

People are thinking differently. You've heard those girls talk – live for the moment. None of them have any savings, you know.'

'And we've put the wedding on hold.'

'Only until Edward gets back.'

'Yes.'

'And nothing else has changed. The war hasn't affected us much. Even that airfield won't. It's just one less field to plough because of the new road.'

Annie chuckled. 'But it might. This time next year, who knows what will have happened?'

'The war will still be on, that's for certain. They've not even started the land war yet.'

'And when they do, it might come to Hull, or Bridlington.'

'Don't be daft.'

'I'm not. If they can drop bombs, they can drop soldiers with parachutes. I imagine young French couples were having this conversation a couple of years ago, deciding that there was never going to be a war, and that France's defences would be good enough to withstand anything.'

Jacob shook his head. 'This isn't the front line, Annie.'

'It is for the RAF. I don't think Nazi paratroopers are going to land in Beckindale, it's just —'

'You can't plan anything. Can't see the future.'

'No. What about babies?'

Jacob patted her stomach. 'Is there something you're not telling me?'

Annie blushed. 'No. Why do you keep asking that? But I want children. No one's having them any more.'

'Oh, they are.'

'Not as many. We're not the only people putting off a wedding. And normally – well, wouldn't the Sullivans have had a child or two by now? No one's risking it, not when their husbands could be called up at any moment.'

'I don't think Brian Sullivan's going to get called up just yet. When he does, that's when we'll know we're in trouble. So you want children?'

'Of course.'

'How many. Six, seven?'

Annie coughed. 'A couple of sons, to carry on with the farm, keep the Sugden name alive.'

'Sons? What are their names going to be, then?'

Annie laughed. 'I've not thought that far ahead. And I don't want them yet.'

Jacob grinned, stroked her face. 'No harm putting in a bit of practice, though, is there?' He tried to push her onto her back.

'There's no rush,' she reminded him, 'they won't be back until closing time. We've got hours.' But then she leant back anyway, until her head was resting on the cushions.

Jacob shifted round until he was alongside her. They kissed, held each other, wriggled a little to get comfortable.

'And you're happy?' Jacob asked.

'Of course.'

'You want to be a farmer's wife, till death do us part?'

'There's only ever been you, you know that.'

The airmen trudged down the hill to the Woolpack. They were all in uniform, all looking their best.

'Right,' Roland told them, 'I don't want mayhem.'

'Mayhem, Squadron Leader?' Atto asked innocently.

'I don't want anyone to abuse our hosts' hospitality.'

'You don't mean we've got to be ruddy monks, though,' Anthony asked, quickly adding, 'Sir.'

'Not a bit of it. Eat, drink and make merry. But bear in mind that this is a small village, and you're going to be posted here for the duration. Getting the locals to lock up their daughters before most of the crews arrive is not going to make us popular.'

134

'Wilco.'

'Look, I know what you chaps are like. Just err on the side of caution. Except you, Taffy. You can go for it.'

The others laughed.

Seth tried to look serious. He stood straight, tried to walk in the brisk, controlled way that military men did, as if they could fall into a march at any moment.

Betty was huddled inside a coat and scarf, but her arms were crossed over her chest. Seth wished it had been a bit warmer – under all that stuff she could have been anyone.

'Do you think there'll be a raid?' Betty asked.

'Not if we do things right.'

'I meant in Leeds. You can hear it sometimes, can't you?'

Leeds was fifty or sixty miles away, but there were nights when there were flashes on the horizon, a terrible orange glow, even sounds like distant thunder. There were people who said they could smell the burning, but Seth suspected that what they smelt was stubble, or people's chimneys.

'It's a terrible thing,' Seth said.

'Well, with that airfield in place, we'll be doing the same to the German cities.'

Seth looked south, to Leeds. It was quiet this evening, but it was still early. He wouldn't wish an air-raid on anyone. 'Everything looks in place tonight,' he said. 'There's not a problem at your house, look. The Woolpack's good – Ron's been having trouble with his blackout material but he's sorted it, now.'

'Can we go in, do you think? It's cold out here.'

Seth could think of nothing he'd rather do. But he decided against it. 'We'll have to complete the rest of our rounds. Mill Cottage next.'

Betty looked serious. 'You're right, of course. We can't shirk.'

Mill Cottage was at the end of Main Street, the largest house in the village. The owner was away at the moment, Seth knew. He owned a factory in Hotten and was at some meeting in London with Ministry types. Even so, he made Betty go round the outside and check that no lights were on.

'And if there are lights on, what can you do?'

'Well, I can ask for them to be put out.'

'And if they don't?'

'I report them, and they get a fine. But everyone puts the light out. People do what an ARP warden says. They respect this.' He tapped his tin helmet.

'I'm so proud of you,' Betty said. 'Come here.'

She gave him a hug. It was pretty much the first time she'd let him touch her. 'I'm seeing you in a whole new light this week,' she said.

The Woolpack was full of young men in uniform, with money in their pockets.

'Got our hands full tonight,' Ron said to Colin.

'All three of them,' Colin agreed.

'I can pull a pint faster than you,' Ron reminded him. He looked around. The locals were in their usual spots, defending them against the invaders. There were girls here, too, Land Girls as well as a few of the local girls. But the place was swarming with men in uniform. Ron hadn't kept up with the uniforms and badges, but he knew that there were pilots, a lot of engineering corps, and a fair few assorted RAF types.

'New customers,' Ron said. 'Do you think they'll be here every night?'

Colin shrugged. 'That's Squadron Leader Pilgrim, isn't it? The one in charge? Ask him.'

'I'll do that.' Ron opened up the bar and headed over, leaving Colin to fend for himself.

*

'Can I buy you a drink?' an airman asked Rita.

'I've got one, thanks.'

He slunk away.

'Rita,' Alyson said, 'he wanted you to talk to him.'

'I didn't fancy him.'

'Well,' Alyson said, 'you ought to be nice to them. Remind them what they're fighting for. What do you think, Louise?'

'They're certainly a healthy-looking bunch.'

'You've got to be really fit to be a pilot. Fit and bright.'

'Good breeding stock,' Louise agreed.

Alyson and Rita laughed. 'I wouldn't mind *breeding* with one or two of them,' Alyson said.

'That Squadron Leader's looking at you,' Virginia told Louise breathlessly.

'No, he isn't,' Louise said, before summoning over one of the other airmen.

'Would you like a drink, miss?' he asked.

'What's that accent?' Alyson asked.

'Welsh,' Louise supplied. 'I bet they call you Taffy, don't they?'

The lad nodded, blushing.

Alyson grabbed his hand. 'Keep off, Louise, he's buying me a drink.'

She got up and followed him to the bar.

'Are you all right, Rita?' Louise asked gently.

'I don't really feel comfortable at places like this. You know – dances, parties.'

'Look at some of the men,' Louise said, trying to reassure her. 'They seem just as nervous.'

'I've got a fiancé,' Rita reminded her.

'You don't have to get engaged to them. You don't have to do anything with them you don't want to do.'

137

'They're only after one thing.'

'And what's wrong with that?'

'You'd give yourself to one of these lads?'

Louise looked around, a wicked expression on her face. 'More than one of them.'

Rita couldn't meet Louise's eyes. 'I'm not like that.'

Louise stubbed out a cigarette. 'You should try it.'

'Don't you think it should be something special?'

'For some people. But it's nothing magical.'

'I wouldn't know.'

Louise rolled her eyes. 'Being a virgin's nothing special, either.'

Rita blushed. 'Keep your voice down. And I don't want to be a virgin.'

Louise watched as one of the local girls left the pub hand in hand with an officer. 'Well, you've come to the right place.'

'I want it to be special.'

'Wouldn't it be that with your fiancé?'

'I'm not sure.'

Louise giggled. 'It's one of those things you'll never know unless you try.'

'No,' Rita replied, sounding downcast. She looked around. 'Where's Alyson gone?'

Louise shrugged. 'Off with her new friend, I assume. Giving it a try. That was quick.'

Rita stared into her drink. 'I think I'll be going home soon.'

'I prefer Anthony.'

'And I prefer Margaret, but people tend to call me Maggie. You're really the one who fires the gun?'

'That's what a gunner does.'

Roland saw Louise with the other Land Girls, at one of

138

the tables in the middle of the room, with half of his crew buzzing around them, waiting for the signal that they could land. She looked up, saw him, and immediately turned her attention to an engineer who was hovering over her. She accepted his offer of a drink, looking straight at Roland as she did so.

Roland could take a hint. He would try to talk sense into her, but not here.

He was about to leave when he was collared by Ron. 'Mr Pilgrim – that is, Squadron Leader. Good to see you here. Good to see so many of your comrades.'

'RAF stands for Royal Air Force, Ron, not Red Army Fraction.'

'Ah. Of course. I was wondering what the base's policy was on leave.'

'Leave?'

'To put it bluntly, are your men going to be coming down here every night?'

'I see. Well . . . unless they're working a shift, they can. We don't leave them cooped up on the base. They know their curfew.'

'But you don't want them turning up drunk in the morning?'

'No. Look, Ron, they're young lads away from home, with money in their pockets, to work as ground crew, engineers. I'd appreciate it if you could look after them.'

'And the pilots? The last thing you want are drunk pilots.'

Roland took a deep breath. 'The pilots can drink what they want.'

Ron looked at him. 'I'm not sure I follow.'

'The bomber crews know that their life depends on their reflexes. They know that if they don't keep their wits about them when they're over Germany they'll get caught in searchlights and hit by tracer fire. Or they'll get lost over the sea, and crash into it when they run out of fuel. Or they'll not even get off the ground.'

'So they're bright enough to be sensible with alcohol.'

Roland grinned at him. 'And they also know when they need a stiff drink.'

Ron nodded. 'I'll look after them, Mr Pilgrim.'

'Good. Thank you.' He moved to leave.

'Going already?' Ron asked, surprised.

Roland nodded, not saying another word. With a final glance at Louise, he headed for the door.

'I don't think your sister's going to show up,' Anthony told Margaret.

'Where could she have got to?'

'You know the village better than I do.'

'We could go and have a look for her.'

Anthony grinned. 'Why don't we do that as soon as I've finished this drink?'

Alyson looked intently at Taffy. He leant over, his face close to hers. 'You're beautiful,' she told him. 'Handsome,' she corrected herself.

They kissed again. She'd kissed a man before, of course. A couple of times, she'd even kissed men she'd only just met at a dance or a party. But she'd never got quite so carried away, or run off so quickly into the woods alone with a man.

They'd kissed leaning against a tree, then they sat at the base of the tree kissing until they found themselves lying down. Taffy was underneath her, like a picnic blanket, or the groundsheet of a tent. He was very warm, and was keeping his arms carefully at his sides. She lay flat on him, her legs tightly together. She hardly dared move them. The little advice she'd been given about sex involved keeping her legs together at all times. She wasn't sure why.

At the same time, she felt a little detached. A part of her mind realised that she should have felt cold, ashamed, and worried that someone would walk by and see them, but she couldn't remember feeling so giddy and warm. He . . . his crotch was about level with her thigh, and was pressed into it. It felt like he had something hard in his pocket.

'I'm very drunk,' Alyson confessed.

'Don't worry, I'm not,' Taffy said.

They kissed again. And again. Taffy shifted a little, but she was just lying there. Was she meant to be doing something? They were still kissing, but the intensity of the moment seemed to be fading, when it ought to be getting more and more exciting.

'I'm a bit cold,' he admitted.

'I'm not really sure what happens next,' Alyson said.

Taffy hesitated. 'What do you mean?'

'Don't laugh, but I'm a virgin.'

Taffy hesitated. 'Oh,' he said.

'I mean, I know the theory,' she said. 'I work on a farm and it would be difficult to miss what the animals get up to.'

Taffy shifted uneasily. 'Your first time should be special,' he told her.

Alyson looked down at him.

'It should,' he insisted. 'Not out here, in the cold.'

Alyson smiled. 'You're a romantic, aren't you?'

'No, not really. But you'll always remember your first time.'

'Tell me about yours.'

Taffy had gone very shy. 'Nah . . . it wouldn't be right.'

Alyson leant over and kissed him, but Taffy pulled away. 'I'll walk you home.'

Seth glanced over at Betty. She was getting a little impatient now. They were up at the cricket pavilion. There were no lights on, but Seth thought he'd seen movement. As they reached it, he realised he was right.

Seth turned on his heel. 'Best not go any further,' he said, very quietly.

'Why not?' Betty asked, without lowering her voice.

'There's a couple sitting there. You know, courting.'

Betty's eyes lit up, and she tried to peer round him. 'Who?'

'I don't know,' Seth said, exasperated, 'but they deserve privacy, don't you think?'

'Depends who they are,' Betty said, and before Seth grasped what she was doing, she'd turned on the torch and swung it at the couple.

'ARP warden!' Betty called. 'ARP warden, official business.'

The pair recoiled. The beam picked out details – a man's hand on a woman's leg, an RAF jacket, a tweed coat. Enough to identify her at least.

'Maggie!' Betty said.

The spotlight fixed on Margaret's face. She was red as a beetroot. From what Seth could tell, nothing too scandalous had happened. Her coat was still buttoned up.

The two stood up, like guilty children, and the beam flitted over to the man, who had more of Margaret's lipstick on his face then she did. 'Who are you?' Betty asked, delighted to have caught out her sister.

'This is Anthony,' Margaret said weakly.

'And how long have you known each other?' Betty asked him. 'I didn't know Maggie was courting.' There was a streak of mischief in her question. She knew as well as anyone that they had only recently met. The RAF uniform was enough of a clue that this was one of the new lot from the airfield.

'There's a lot about me I don't tell you,' Margaret said.

'Oh, I can see that,' Betty said gleefully. 'Come on, Seth.'

Seth was surprised that she didn't want to prolong her sister's agony.

'I've had my fun,' Betty told him. 'This ARP run's great, isn't it? You learn all sorts.'

When Taffy made his way back to the Woolpack, the girl Alyson had been with, Louise, was waiting outside. 'Are my lot still in there?' he asked.

'The pub's closed, now. Most of your friends disappeared some time before that, with a girl on their arm. I thought you'd done that. Where's Alyson?' she asked mischievously.

'I walked her home.'

It was like she was looking straight through him. 'And what did you get up to before then?'

'Nothing. I was a gentleman.'

'I bet you were. I don't want you to take advantage of Alyson. She's very naïve.'

'And you're a woman of the world, are you?'

'I'm not a virgin, if that's what you mean.' Louise looked at him and Taffy almost heard the penny drop. 'You are, though, aren't you?'

'I'm not,' he said, irritated.

'It's nothing to be ashamed of. Do you even know what you're meant to do?'

Taffy was bright red. 'Of course I do.'

'Go on, then, describe it.'

'All right. I know . . . you know, some things, but not enough. And if she doesn't either then we could get it wrong.'

Louise giggled. 'You met a Land Girl in the pub, you got her drunk, you thought you'd go off into the woods with her. I know what you lot call us – "Army groundsheets". You thought Alyson would know what to do, but it scared you that she didn't.'

Taffy was surprised at how angry he felt. 'It's not that,' he said. 'I want it to be special for her. If it's her first time, I want it to be done right. She wasn't ready. I know what I was expecting, but she just wanted a kiss and a cuddle.'

Louise smiled. 'Aw, that's so sweet.'

'Shut up. I knew you'd laugh. You're the expert, I suppose?'

'Compared to you, yes I am. I'll show you, if you want.'

Taffy was caught out. 'What?'

'I'll teach you. I'll be your first. Don't look so shocked – it's how you were planning to spend the evening. You can still have what you were after.'

'You'd . . . you'd go all the way with me?'

Louise laughed. 'It's really not that far.'

'Alyson's your friend.'

'She's not. I live with her, but you know what that can mean. She's always taking the hot water, or the last potato. And she snores. It's very easy to come up with a list of her little faults.'

'So you're doing this because you're selfish?'

'I'll be helping her out, won't I? You won't be a disappointment.'

'That's not why you want to do it. Why are you doing this?'

'The real reason?' She seemed to have to work that out for herself before answering. 'I've never had a younger man before. They've always been older, and they always try to make things complicated. I just like the idea of showing someone the ropes. Then he can go off, and won't bother me again.'

Taffy looked at her. 'Is this a trick?'

'It's not a trick. Look, it's not a big deal. This isn't the start of a beautiful friendship. If you don't want to, then you don't have to. But this is a one-off, all right?'

'I do want to,' Taffy heard himself say. 'There's a quiet spot just in the woods there.'

'I'm not wearing the right shoes for that.'

'Then—'

Louise took him by the hand. 'Then we find a nice quiet corner.' She looked around. 'Like that one. Come on.'

Alyson lay in bed. Virginia and Rita were both asleep. Airmen had bought them drinks, but it had gone no further. She could have done it tonight. She had surprised herself, it had just seemed so right. Taffy was quite ordinary, not much to look at, but he was kind, and very gentle. A good kisser.

Alyson heard a commotion downstairs – Louise arriving, Miss Pearson letting her in, stern words. 'Bossy cow,' Alyson whispered to Rita.

'She thinks it's the navy,' Rita explained.

'All of them?'

'No,' Louise said, entering the room. 'She thinks it's someone bringing a telegram to tell her that Mr Sugden's brother's been killed or is missing. I . . . did it before, and I promised I wouldn't do it again.'

Alyson felt bad about that. At times it was difficult to believe that the Sugdens had a life of their own. To the girls, Mr Sugden was just their boss, not a man in his own right. If she'd met this Edward, she might think differently. 'So why are you so late?' she asked.

'I met a nice RAF man.' Louise took off her coat, hung it up on the back of the door.

'Was he as nice as Taffy?'

Louise was already down to her underwear. She considered the answer. 'Just as nice.'

'Could you two keep it down?' Rita grumbled.

Louise was in her nightshirt. She extinguished the lamp and clambered into bed.

'What did you do?'

Louise's silence said it all.

'That was fast!' Alyson said, full of admiration.

'Says you,' Virginia laughed.

Alyson blushed. 'We didn't do anything,' she admitted. 'We kissed and cuddled.'

'What about you, Louise? Just a kiss and a cuddle.'

'Hardly.'

'You really did it?'

'So? We had a good time. It's not like we're going to get married. We might not even see each other again. So what?'

Alyson couldn't imagine doing the same thing. She was surprised by how shocked she was. 'It doesn't sound very romantic.'

'There's no such thing as romance,' Louise told her. 'It's a trick. Men are men, women are women, and everyone's the same deep down. We dress some things up to try to disguise them, or to make them seem more valuable than they really are.'

'That's not right,' Rita said quietly. 'It's the other way round. It's romance that's the important thing.'

'But what if you see him around the village? Won't you be embarrassed?'

Louise laughed. 'I won't be. He might, but that's his problem.'

'What's his name?'

Louise hesitated.

'Come on,' Alyson prompted, 'you can tell me.'

'John Harrison,' she replied. 'He's a . . . sapper.'

'What did he look like?'

'Short, a bit skinny. Brown hair.'

'Sounds like Taffy.'

'Yes, he does, doesn't he?'

'Tell me what you did,' Alyson said.

'Did?'

'Yes. Go on. You met him, and then you—'

'Alyson . . . I can go into details, but there's not much to tell.'

'Tell me anyway.'

'All right . . .' Louise began.

Standing on the doorstep, Betty's face was almost level with his. She hesitated. The same thought had struck her. 'Good night, Seth. Thanks for a lovely evening.'

'Do you think Maggie's back yet?' Seth asked innocently.

Betty laughed. 'The expression on her face!'

'Are you going to tell your mother?'

There was an evil glint in Betty's eye. 'Where would be the fun in that?'

'Remind me never to get on the wrong side of you, Betty.'

Betty was grinning from ear to ear. 'Put your hands behind your back,' she told him. 'I want them kept there and all.'

Seth did as he was told. Betty leant forward and kissed his cheek. Then she let him do the same. She opened the door, stepped inside, then closed it behind her.

Seth stood there for a moment, just grinning.

CHAPTER THIRTEEN:
Out of Her Depth

'You're off to synagogue today, aren't you?' Jacob asked Rita.

'That's right.'

'No need to feel embarrassed,' he reassured her. 'I know you're pulling your weight. That goes for all you girls, you're really starting to know your jobs. Besides, Rita, I'll have things for you to do while we're all at church tomorrow morning.'

Rita wasn't embarrassed about that, she was feeling guilty about lying. Underneath her church clothes was a one-piece swimming costume that belonged to Jean Sullivan.

Yesterday, she and Jean had agreed to go swimming together, rather than to the synagogue. They'd take the boys, who had been keen on the idea, particularly when they realised it was meant as a guilty secret. Mr Sugden was very good to let her take every Saturday morning off to go to worship. He would almost certainly be less charitable if he knew she was off to the baths. So Rita sat there, not eating too much breakfast – you didn't eat before swimming, everyone knew that – and felt her swimming costume clinging to her.

The others didn't seem to suspect. 'I'd better get going,' she told them.

'How was the Woolpack?' their mother asked.

Margaret glanced nervously at Betty, who didn't answer at first: she'd decided to bide her time. She was wondering how to spend the three shillings her mother had given her that she'd had no need for. Perhaps she'd take Seth out to Hotten for a night on the town, or perhaps she'd buy something useful or decorative.

'We had a very nice evening,' Betty said. 'Margaret caught the eye of a nice gunner. A flight sergeant.'

'Did you?' mother said, impressed.

'Yes,' Margaret said, squirming with embarrassment.

'Talked about cricket,' Betty said.

'Cricket?' mother repeated. 'Do you know much about cricket, Margaret?'

'A little,' she said, softly.

Her mother nodded approvingly, and started gathering up the breakfast things. As soon as she'd gone through into the kitchen, Margaret rounded on Betty.

'What's all that about cricket? Is that meant to be some clever remark about finding me and him at the pavilion? You know we didn't do anything, don't you?'

But Betty had been expecting this. She let her sister finish, then said, very softly, 'Oh, no. Not this time. I've got you. We both know what I'd have seen if I'd turned up there five minutes later.'

Margaret blushed, but tried to stare her out.

'And he wasn't exactly making all the running, was he?' Betty continued, regardless. 'I know for a fact that you only met him at the Home Farm party, and you didn't go off with him then. So, stands to reason that he's not the first man you've "entertained".'

Margaret said nothing.

149

'Now, what that means is that you're not going to lecture me ever again,' Betty went on. 'It means that you don't spy on me any more.'

Her sister nodded meekly, and Betty smiled, triumphant.

'Louise.' Taffy was grinning from ear to ear.

'I'm working,' she said. She was putting a bale of straw in a metal feeder. Taffy looked around, but couldn't see any livestock.

'Look. I've been thinking about last night.'

'I'm sure you have.'

Taffy felt a bit embarrassed. He'd spent most of the morning remembering the night before. He didn't ever want to forget the smallest detail. 'Not like that. I mean I've been thinking about you and Alyson.'

Louise raised an eyebrow, but Taffy carried on oblivious. 'I prefer you to Alyson . . .'

Louise frowned. 'No,' she said firmly.

'. . . and I hoped we could—'

'No,' she repeated.

'Didn't you like—?'

A glare from Louise shut him up. 'I told you last night it was a one-off.'

'But I thought you might have changed your mind after we . . .' He didn't need to remind her of what they'd done.

Louise shook her head.

'Taffy!'

Alyson was bounding over. She looked so much younger than Louise, like a girl.

'Louise, this is Taffy. This is who I went into the woods with.'

Louise's mouth twitched. She seemed to be enjoying Taffy's discomfort.

'Don't worry about Louise,' Alyson said, thinking she

was reassuring him. 'We talked all about you last night. Didn't we, Louise?'

Louise didn't answer for a moment, and Taffy saw just a hint of cruelty on her face. 'Don't worry,' she said then. 'Your secret's safe with me.'

Alyson looked almost giddy with excitement. 'You came to see me.'

'Yes,' Taffy said, as Louise turned and left. 'I just wondered if you wanted to come out tonight.'

Alyson clapped her hands together. 'Of course I do.'

But Taffy barely heard her: he was watching Louise walk off without looking back.

The water was warmer than Rita had expected and she felt a little guilty – shouldn't the heating oil or coal or whatever it was have been put to better use for the war effort?

She pushed away from the end, managed a few lazy strokes. She was out of practice, but the work in the fields was good exercise, and she didn't have that sensation of early stiffness in her arms she often got. Another wave of guilt hit her as she imagined all the grime that had ground itself into her from those fields dissolving into the water, but at least she'd be clean afterwards.

Some children were in the pool, and a couple of serious swimmers, but there were far fewer people here than she had expected. Joe and Adam were splashing around at the far end, when they didn't think she was looking. Rita was nineteen and it was odd to think that they saw her as some sort of mother-figure. But then Jean was only six years older, and she'd adapted to the role well. Imagine having a fourteen-year-old boy at the age of twenty-five! Rita still felt far more like a schoolgirl than a mother.

She wondered how Jean saw her – as an equal, or as another waif and stray. Rita still got homesick, living in the country, and despite all the hard work, it still seemed like a school holiday, rather than a real job. And her fiancé, Paul, wasn't a real fiancé. Not the way Alyson, Virginia and Louise seemed to define the word.

Jean hadn't been wearing her costume underneath her clothes so she'd had to change. Rita had been in the water when she came out of the changing room. Rita envied her figure again. They wore the same size in clothes, but Jean's legs were longer, her stomach was flatter, and she looked healthier, even without her makeup.

She climbed down into the water, wincing a little. 'Cold,' she said.

'Warmer than working in a field,' Rita replied cheerfully.

'Much colder than working in a shop. Colder than that synagogue would have been.'

She pushed away from the side, and for the first time since they had met, Rita felt she had the upper hand. She'd been in the school swimming team, she was used to the water. Jean was more hesitant. She could swim, but not as well as Rita, who swam alongside her, keeping up effortlessly. Jean had to stop after two lengths, but Rita had hardly started.

No complications.

There were always complications, though, weren't there?

Louise walked down the path to Home Farm. If anyone had asked, she'd have said she was drifting, just heading where her feet were leading her. But she knew better than that. She just happened to be heading towards the clearing where she'd met Roland. The ground was rock hard today, and she'd been trying to dig potatoes out of it all morning.

When she arrived, Roland wasn't there. She sat down at the base of the tree under which she had found him.

Taffy had been a surprise. Very eager, a quick learner.

The novelty had excited him, but he had been nervous. And the look of surprise and joy on his face . . . Louise smiled.

Yet she regretted it. She didn't feel guilty about Alyson – she'd helped her, if anything. Taffy had been noticeably more confident this morning. And it wasn't guilt because she felt loyalty to Roland.

Louise was upset because she had taken Taffy as some stupid act of revenge – she'd been annoyed with Alyson, and angry with Roland. Poor Taffy: it hadn't been anything to do with him at all. It hadn't even been the challenge – what challenge had there been? She'd just wanted to do something outrageous. And when it came down to it, if Roland had done something wrong, what she'd done had been worse, far more calculating.

Louise knew she was better than that, and when she allowed herself to do so, she acknowledged she missed Roland. Last night at the Woolpack had been soul-destroying: a cattle market, where a man picked a woman, went off with her and had his way. She'd taken part in it all, sat there in makeup and a nice dress, doing everything that was expected of her.

The strength of her anger with Roland overwhelmed her. As she told anyone who asked, she normally didn't seem to *feel* in the same way the poems and novels and plays and songs and films told her she should. She didn't keep her emotions in check, she just didn't seem to have any. But she couldn't get Roland out of her head, and she wasn't acting rationally.

Louise stood up. She wanted to steer clear of him for a while, until she'd got her thoughts straight. She didn't love him, and she certainly didn't want him to turn up with flowers and an apology. So what did she want?

After about half an hour in the pool, Jean pulled herself upright, clutching her leg. Rita was a little ahead of her, still hardly out of breath. She heard the splashing, flipped over and swam towards her friend.

'Only cramp,' Jean told her. She'd struggled over to the side. 'In my foot.'

'Here.' Rita held out her hands. Jean lifted her leg and Rita set to work, kneading her foot with her thumbs. Jean kept herself steady by holding onto the side of the pool, bobbing up and down, a little inelegantly.

Rita squeezed hard. Jean cried out, then grinned and bore it. When Rita felt the muscle relax, she was tempted to keep hold of the foot.

'Thank you. I'm out of practice,' Jean said.

Rita smiled. 'If it's colder than you're used to, and you ate breakfast, it's only natural. Are you OK to carry on?'

Jean nodded. 'You're good with those fingers.'

'I used to be on the swimming team. You learn to fix a spot of cramp.'

A few minutes later, Adam also pulled up, clutching his leg.

Rita swam over. He was in the shallow end, hopping along the bottom. She took his leg in one hand, prodded the foot and calf, then looked up. She thought he was smiling, but it was just a grimace. A moment later he was wincing with pain again.

'I can't feel anything,' she said. His legs were hairier than she'd been expecting. She massaged the foot a little, then let him go. She'd done the trick, and he thanked her, then swam off, embarrassed that he'd let a girl touch him. Rita grinned, then returned to the deep end and Jean Sullivan.

Jacob let Ron in, surprised to see him. He couldn't remember the last time he'd paid a visit. 'I'm not stopping,' Ron said, looking around almost nervously.

'Who are you worried about meeting?' Jacob asked.

'Girls,' Ron said.

'Girls?'

'Those Land Girls.'

Jacob was a little taken aback.

'There was a gang of them in the Woolpack last night, not all of them yours – I'll be having words with the Wylies and the Toleys, too, but yours were among them.'

'And they caused trouble?'

'There was a gang of lads in from the airfield. Good business, I don't mind that, even if none were locals. If I do that well every night until the end of the war, then I might get on the phone to Mr Hitler and see if we can drag it out. But it's what happened by closing time.'

'Which was?' Jacob prompted.

'Just what you'd expect – the young women and the young men paired off. And . . . well . . . it's the sort of thing you'd expect to see in – in ancient Rome, or Leeds. They all disappeared in pairs, off into the woods or the alleys. I had complaints, Mr Sugden.'

'Drunk, were they?'

'Worse than that. I heard a pair of them right underneath my window, straight after closing time. It's disgusting. It's never happened before. But they weren't the only ones. They were all round the village. If it happens again, I might even lose my licence. But it's not that, it's the intrusion. They aren't even from around here. I don't go to their houses and disturb them.'

'I'll talk to them, Ron.'

But he didn't relish the idea.

Rita felt fantastic – clean, exercised, more alive than she had been when she'd gone into the water.

Jean was hobbling a little as she entered the changing rooms. Rather than find a cubicle, she went to the benches in the middle and peeled off her costume.

Rita was scandalised.

'There's no one else around,' Jean assured her. 'We were the only women in the pool, weren't we, apart from a few little girls?'

Rita took a deep breath, then followed suit.

They looked at each other. Rita wondered if she should say something, then looked away, found a place on the bench, and started to dry herself.

'You're a good-looking girl,' Jean whispered. 'You've got a great figure.'

Rita's first instinct was to draw up her knees, but that would have been silly. She looked down at herself. 'No, I haven't. I've got bandy legs. Louise and Alyson, even Miss Pearson, they're good-looking. If I was a man, I'd go out with them, not me.'

'Would you go out with me?' Jean asked, dabbing at her neck.

Rita giggled. 'No, you're married. And I'm engaged.'

'If we weren't?'

She looked up at Jean. 'You're being silly, now . . .'

CHAPTER FOURTEEN:

Casualties of War

Annie looked around, then telephoned Home Farm. One of the maids answered, but George came to the phone soon enough. 'Annie!' he exclaimed. 'Have you been avoiding me again?'

'Er . . . no.'

'Are you OK to speak?'

Annie looked around. Everyone else was still in the kitchen, and would be for a while. 'Yes.'

'I've been thinking about you.'

Annie blushed. 'Look. I have to see you.'

A hesitation. 'That sounds ominous.'

'Well . . . yes. I think I want to take up the Hart-Wilsons on their offer. To go to London. But not on my own.'

'Who were you thinking of going with?'

'You.' She'd said it.

She thought the line had gone dead.

'Ah.'

'I want to come up to see you.'

'Right. Straight away?'

'If that's all right with you.'

'I'll be waiting.'

They said goodbye, and Annie hung up the receiver. Right, that was settled. Off to London with George. It seemed too easy, somehow. She didn't feel guilty – she had nothing to feel guilty about. She wouldn't . . . she wouldn't kiss him again, just enjoy his company. They'd be with friends. And she was engaged to Jacob.

Later that day there was a knock at the back door.

'You girls,' Jacob complained, opening the door.

There was a man with a telegram. 'Joseph Sugden?' he asked.

Jacob stepped back.

Annie hurried over. 'This is Jacob, his son.'

'I'm sorry.' He handed Jacob an envelope.

'The *Solent*?' Jacob said.

Rita looked up. 'No!' she shouted, and ran over. 'My fiancé was on that ship. Paul Silver.'

'You're not next-of-kin?'

'His parents . . .'

'You should call them, Miss. I'm sorry.'

Rita fell back. It was all Louise could do to guide her to a chair.

Annie felt numb. She looked at Jacob. He wasn't reacting at all, he was barely moving.

She looked over to their visitor. What a terrible job to have. He must have seen every reaction humanly possible to the news that a loved one had died.

'Would you like to come in?' Annie offered. 'We can make you some tea?' Even as she said the words, she realised it was her way of coping: lose herself in domestic routine; make sure everyone else was all right, rather than acknowledge her own feelings.

'No, no,' the man said hurriedly. 'I'd better be going.'

Annie glanced down at the sheaf of envelopes resting on his clipboard.

'Is there no hope?' she asked, when he'd gone and the door was closed.

'Rescue ships?' Louise suggested.

'Did they recover his body?' Jacob asked, so quietly he could barely be heard.

'It doesn't say. It says he's missing.'

'Is my dad with yours?' Jacob asked.

Annie nodded. 'At the Woolpack, I think.'

Louise was standing up. 'And someone should tell George Verney.'

Jacob scowled. 'Why?'

Annie placed a hand on Jacob's arm. 'Let her go.' She had already forgotten that she had planned to head up there herself.

Rita was also going out the door. She'd been out of the room, on the phone to her fiancée's parents, Annie realised. There was no need to ask what they'd said.

'Where are you off to, Rita, love?'

'I need to . . . I have to go out.' She seemed dazed. It was almost as if she was drunk. Annie didn't want to let her go, but couldn't see the alternative – she saw the appeal of the cold night air and a change of scene.

'We should find Joseph,' Annie told Jacob.

Jacob let Annie lead the way.

Alyson leant against the tree. She'd expected it to be cold, but it wasn't. Taffy was kissing her neck. He was a lot taller than her and her head was buried in his chest.

'Mr Sugden says we're not to do anything lewd,' she said. 'He said that the landlord of the Woolpack complained. He said he heard a man and a woman *rutting* just outside.'

'Did he?' Taffy seemed upset.

'I think it was Louise,' Alyson said.

'Louise?'

'Yes. She met one of your friends. She said he looked a bit like you. Well . . . it could have been them. Do you know John Harrison?'

159

'I . . . no, I don't think so.'

'Well it was him. A flying officer, like you.'

'Must be on a different crew. We don't really mix with the other crews.'

'She told me all about it. Standing up against a wall outside a pub. That doesn't sound very romantic, does it?'

'No,' Taffy said quietly.

'You've gone all shy,' Alyson said.

'And . . . what else did she say?'

Alyson laughed. 'She said it was all over very quickly!'

Taffy looked uneasy.

'What was your first time like?' she asked. He was looking sheepish. 'It's OK, I won't be jealous.'

'She was . . . quite tall. A redhead. We met at a party. She made the first move – she was waiting for me afterwards, and we went somewhere quiet.'

'Weren't you worried you might get caught?'

'At first, but soon it was just the two of us.'

'Go on.'

'Well . . . I mean, I don't want you to think I think about it all the time. I've got you now, and she was a long time ago.'

Alyson wanted him to tell it all – she wanted to know what it was like, she wanted to know what you *did*. 'I know that,' she assured him.

'Well . . . we stood facing each other, and I thought she was the most beautiful woman in the world. Then we kissed, and it was like nothing else existed. And I thought I'd be shy, but she made it all so easy. She guided me and gave herself to me and we didn't even stop to lie down, it was just so . . . right . . .' his voice trailed away.

'You did it standing up?'

'Well, yes.'

'I didn't even know you could do it like that. But that's how Louise did it with your friend, too. And was it over very quickly, like it was with her?'

'No! I mean, I wasn't checking my watch. It felt like . . . like it lasted for ever. She knew what I would like, and she definitely knew what she wanted. It was like we were the only two people in the world, and there was nothing else.'

'That's so romantic. What was her name?'

'I don't want to tell you that. I want to protect her honour.'

She looked at him admiringly. 'And what happened then? Did you see her again?'

Taffy shifted uncomfortably. 'I wanted to see her again, but she was going away. I used to hope we'd get back together.'

Alyson stroked his face. 'You're romantic, aren't you?'

'I like you now,' he said. 'I really like you. I hope when we're ready, we'll—'

Alyson put her finger on his lips, shushing him.

George Verney was in the drawing room with Roland Pilgrim, waiting for the front-door bell to ring. When it did he stood up. 'That'll be for me,' he told Roland.

But the maid appeared at the door with one of Jacob Sugden's Land Girls. The pick of the crop, George thought, the tall redhead, the one Annie had thought he was having an affair with. He looked over at Roland, expecting to see a healthy appreciation of the new arrival. But his friend was bristling a little, as though this was some terrible intrusion.

'Come in,' George said, rising. 'You're at Emmerdale, aren't you? You're—'

'Louise Price,' she supplied.

'What brings you here?'

Roland looked like he was itching for a fight.

'I've got some bad news. Edward Sugden has been killed. His ship went down, with the loss of all hands.

161

Rita, one of the other Land Girls, well, she lost her fiancé on the same ship.'

There was only one reaction to news like that. For RAF men, such bad news was routine. Neither George nor Roland had been in the thick of it, yet, but they both knew a lot of colleagues who hadn't made it back.

'How are the Sugdens taking it?'

'We've only just had the news. They're looking for Jacob's father.'

George was sobered. A death like Edward's would impact on his friends, on the whole village. 'I appreciate you coming up here to tell us,' he said.

'I . . . Really I came to see Mr Pilgrim,' she said.

'We know each other,' Roland said, and George was left in no doubt that they were lovers. Or had been.

'Lucky dog,' he said, and instantly regretted it.

Louise smiled, even if Roland didn't. 'I think I need to talk to Roland alone,' she said.

George agreed. 'Make yourself at home.'

'We won't get in your way,' Roland added. He escorted Louise from the room, and a moment later George heard them climb the stairs.

'Lucky dog,' he repeated.

Annie Pearson didn't often come into the Woolpack, thought Ron. He was about to go over to say hello, but it was obvious that something was wrong. She was here with Jacob and they barely acknowledged their surroundings. 'What's going on there, Colin?' he asked.

Ron watched the scene play out: Annie and Jacob went to the table where Sam and Joseph were playing dominoes. They sat down, reached out to Joseph, and whispered something. Then Joseph Sugden, a man as stoic as anyone Ron knew, was crying.

'Edward,' Colin whispered.

Annie was coming over to the bar. 'We've had some bad news,' she said quietly. She hadn't been crying – it still hadn't sunk in, Ron realised. Grief took time to catch up with people. You could tell someone the most terrible thing, and they would hear it, understand it, but the words wouldn't connect in the brain straight away.

She explained about Edward.

'Would you like me to tell people?' Ron asked.

'Yes please. I don't think you'll be seeing much of us for the next few days.'

'Of course,' Ron said.

'Do you know about the funeral arrangements?' Colin asked.

'I didn't ask,' Annie admitted. 'I don't think there's a body. At least, I don't think it's been found. We weren't really listening.' She was sobbing now.

Ron remembered what it had been like to wake up and discover he'd lost his arm. The nurse explained what had happened, and he'd felt calm, serene. He'd thanked God he was still alive, and a part of him had even been a little glad, because there was no way he'd be going back to the trenches now. He'd understood the words. Then he'd tried to pick up a glass of water, because his throat was so dry, and it was only then that he understood what they *meant*.

Jacob, Joseph and Sam were all on their feet, ready to leave. Annie joined them. The four looked shell-shocked, Ron thought, and when he used that expression he knew what he was talking about.

In the sanctuary of his room, Roland and Louise agreed they had been fools, that life was too short to bear a grudge, that they couldn't bear the thought of the other one dying or imagine life without them. They'd kissed and caressed and undressed each other as they'd said this.

They wanted to prove that they were still alive, that life went on, even with thousands of people dying every day.

They were lying under the sheets, holding each other, all their differences forgotten, and Louise even thought of admitting to her brief liaison with Taffy, then thought better of it. That was irrelevant, now.

'You might die,' she said.

Roland was looking her straight in the eye. 'Yes. It's far more likely than if I was a sailor.'

She clung to him. She didn't think she'd ever be back here with him, and the thought that he might leave her for ever was almost unthinkably frightening. 'Don't say that.'

'It's the truth. It has to be faced. My tour will be thirty operations over enemy territory at night.'

'Thirty? What happens after that?'

'Who knows? I get a Distinguished Service Order, and in theory when I've done my tour I get transferred to a ground job. But they need all the pilots they can get, so in all likelihood I'll be needed for another thirty.'

'You seem so calm.'

'Well, I'm not. But what can I do? Panic? Run away? Dwell on the statistics? You have to live for the moment. None of the crewmen have any savings, you know, no investments. They drink, they find women, they know how to enjoy themselves.'

'They make the most of it?' It was like an incurable illness, Louise thought. Her grandfather had had an untreatable liver condition. The doctors had given him months to live, a year at most. In the end, it had only been three months – but what a three months he had had, cramming in everything that he'd ever wanted to do. He'd started smoking great fat Havana cigars. That was her memory of him now, that pungent smell. Living life to the full.

'I don't want you to die.'

'I'm doing a job. I'd rather die here than in some air-raid shelter. Or in a trench.' He shuddered, then looked back at her. 'Stay the night,' he said.

'But Mr Verney . . .'

'Won't mind. I was a fool to think he would.'

'I'm not sure.'

'What's the matter? Never slept with a man before?'

She gave a little shake of her head.

Roland frowned at her. 'You're having me on?'

'I've shared a bed, obviously. Dozed off. But I've never stayed the night, or he hasn't, if it was at my place.'

'My God,' Roland said, genuinely surprised. 'A first. Here's me thinking you knew every trick in the book. Hope you don't snore.'

Louise laughed. 'I'm sure Rita or the others would have told me if I do.'

'You've never slept with a man?' He was still not sure whether to believe her. 'Why ever not?'

'It's different, isn't it? People say they've slept together when all they mean is they've had sex. But sleeping together . . . letting your guard down like that, letting him see you first thing in the morning, before you've cleaned your teeth, even. It's something different. It's not living for the moment.'

Roland shifted away a little. 'If you don't want to, I'll understand. I can't promise you a life together, I can't even promise I'll be around next month.'

Louise shushed him, moved in, held him close.

'The kitchen light is still on,' Alyson said. 'I won't be waking anyone up.'

'There you go, safely delivered to the doorstep.'

'And we didn't do anything lewd at all.'

'No.' Taffy seemed relaxed about that. He wanted to take his time, too. Which suited Alyson. They would do it, she thought, but only when the time was right. Some time soon, though, Alyson found herself hoping.

She kissed him, conscious that someone from the house might be watching. Then he disappeared down the hill towards Home Farm.

When she stepped inside Alyson was still smiling.

Around the kitchen table were Jacob, Joseph, Sam and Annie, stony-faced, silent.

Alyson checked her watch. 'It's only nine-thirty,' she said quietly. 'I'm sorry if—'

Annie cleared her throat. 'Alyson, love, it's not that. The *Solent* was sunk this morning. Edward, Jacob's brother, is dead. So's Paul, Rita's fiancé.'

Alyson's feelings changed so quickly she almost felt dizzy. 'I'm so sorry,' she said, her words sounding empty. 'I . . . where's Rita?'

'At the Sullivans', I think.'

'And the others are upstairs?'

'Virginia is. Louise has gone up to Home Farm to tell people.'

'Home Farm?'

'Yes . . . Alyson, I'm afraid we're not really in the mood to chat.'

'I'll go upstairs. I'm . . . like I said, I'm really sorry.'

Rita dreamt she was in bed with Paul, but the details were confused. Everything was more lucid than reality and she knew she was dreaming. She also knew Paul was dead. So how could he be lying with his back to her? Why was she still in her uniform? How could she nuzzle his neck or run her hand up his leg?

She'd never done this, and now she never would. Rita hugged him, clutched him close, cried all over his bare shoulder. He was warm and reassuring but he wasn't really there, he was dead. But the dream was a good one.

*

Paul Silver's father had rung for Rita and Annie had told them that she was with friends. Mr Silver said the same things she'd heard in the Woolpack, but from someone who'd suffered the same loss, at the same time, the words took on new meaning.

Jacob had left the room several minutes before that call. Now Annie was worried, and went to find him. He was in Edward's room, sitting on the end of the bed, hunched. He looked squat, distorted. His face was twisted, and tears streamed down his cheeks. It was almost as if steam was rising from him. The room was cold – the window was open.

'He's dead,' Jacob said, so quietly that Annie wouldn't have heard if she hadn't already known what he would say.

She went over to him, tried to take his hand, but it was locked into a fist. She had to prise his fingers open. 'Come here,' she said, trying to get close. But Jacob was like a statue. She kissed his face, but he didn't respond, just sat there. Annie had never seen him like this, even when his mother had died.

'I want to help.'

'Just go,' Jacob told her.

CHAPTER FIFTEEN:

Period of Mourning

Jean Sullivan was sitting with Rita.

Before she had opened her eyes she was aware of her friend's presence, that the room was warm, and smelt of perfume. Then, in a rush, everything else fell into place, and she realised she hadn't dreamt it: Paul was dead.

She opened her eyes to see Jean holding a glass of water. 'You must be thirsty,' she said gently. 'You cried so much last night.'

Rita was still fully dressed. No shoes, of course, no jumper (they were both in a heap on the floor), but other than that she was in full Land Reserve get-up. 'You were with me?'

'Yes.' Jean looked away, a little embarrassed. 'You needed someone to hold. You needed company. You needed a cuddle.'

'Mr Sullivan?'

'Slept on the sofa. He didn't mind.'

'You couldn't have had much sleep,' Rita said, guilty.

'That doesn't matter.'

'How did I get here?'

'You don't remember?'

'No.'

'You turned up on the doorstep, really upset. It took us a few minutes to work out what had happened. I brought you upstairs.'

Rita sipped her water. She usually felt hungry first thing in the morning, but today she was numb.

'Are you going to sit *shiv'a*?' Jean asked.

'I . . . yes, I suppose so. But I need to telephone his parents.'

'You can do that from here, when you're ready. You seem calmer this morning.'

'I was hysterical last night, wasn't I?'

'You had every right to be. I wonder how the Sugdens are taking it.'

'I'm so selfish, I've not even thought about them.'

'You're not selfish . . . will Paul's family know, do you think?'

'I think so. They're his next of kin. I think they got the telegram at the same time the Sugdens did.'

'You can phone them from here.'

'Thanks.'

'Brian's taking the kids out. Do you want me to pour you a bath?'

'Give me a moment, then I'll do it.'

Seth and Betty sat on the bench by the bus stop. It was cold, still a bit damp from the frost this morning, but neither of them was taking any notice of that. They were looking down at the village.

'Isn't it terrible?' Betty said again.

'Edward Sugden was a gentleman,' Seth replied.

'It brings it home. The first casualty from Beckindale.'

'Won't be the last,' Seth said gloomily.

'Don't say that.'

'He won't be,' Seth insisted.

'I know, but don't say it out loud.' She took a deep

breath. 'Will you come to the pictures with me this afternoon? For the matinée?'

Seth turned to look at her, the change of subject confusing him. 'Well, yes.'

'You'll be back in time for your ARP rounds.'

'Oh. Right.'

'And Mother isn't to know.'

'Well, I weren't going to tell her, was I?'

'We'll get the two o'clock bus into Hotten, then?'

'I'll see you here.'

Rita felt a bit embarrassed. There was a shower contraption at the same end of the bath as the taps. It looked a lot like a telephone, and for the life of her, she couldn't get it to work.

When Jean came in she blushed. She had wrapped the largest towel around herself, but it was hardly the same as being dressed. Then she remembered that they had got changed together at the swimming-pool and, anyway, she was used to communal baths – the Land Girls poured a tin bath, then took turns to wash in it. Rita was always the last in – standing there in her nightshirt, while the others splashed about. It was like being in the army, she supposed. Or prison, as Louise had pointed out. This, though, was much pleasanter.

Jean pulled a lever, and the shower spluttered into life.

'Oh, thank you, I really needed to wash my hair.'

'I'll do it for you if you like. I'll just get the shampoo.'

Rita shed her towel and got into the bath.

Jean was rooting around in the cabinet. 'I hide it so Brian and the boys don't waste it.'

It smelt of jasmine and impossible luxury.

'I got it from Crabtree's in York three years ago, and I've still not used it all up. Like my perfume, I hoard it. Turn round.'

Jean took the shower head, wet Rita's hair, then

handed it to Rita. She dripped a blob of shampoo on to the girl's head, then her fingers were pushing deep into the mass of hair, kneading the shampoo in. Rita felt self-conscious, not because of the physical contact, which was surprisingly relaxing, but because her hair was matted and dirty. She apologised for its state, but Jean didn't seem to mind. 'I've not had my hair washed for me since my mum used to do it when I was a child. You don't do this for Adam, do you?' she joked.

'Oh, he'd enjoy that. Did you see the look on his face when you sorted out his swimming cramp?'

Rita went red. 'I didn't realise. He's still a boy.'

'He's a young man. Getting that way, anyway. Brian and I were discussing him a couple of days ago. Do we tell him the facts of life, and about girlfriends and things, or do we leave that to his parents?'

Rita giggled. 'I don't envy you.'

'There you go, a smile on your face. You'll feel better. It might not seem like it yet, but give it time.'

Rita leant forward so that Jean could rinse her hair. 'I should be getting back. There's a lot to do.'

Jean nodded, and helped Rita out of the bath.

Louise woke up next to Roland Pilgrim. She was acutely conscious that her armpits reeked of sweat, that her breath smelt, that she was dying for the loo, and that her hair must look a state – she put her hand to her head, which felt as if it had spent the night in a cowshed.

Sunlight was streaming through the window – they'd neglected the blackout last night but fortunately the Luftwaffe hadn't taken advantage of their lapse.

Roland lay on his back, snoring softly, looking younger and far sweeter in repose than he did when he was awake. A flap of his black hair was sticking up. He was wearing pyjama bottoms, she had on the top.

It was late, and her body was telling her she'd had a long lie-in because she was even hungrier than usual. But she didn't want to move.

Roland still didn't believe her, but it was the first time she'd spent the whole night with a man, or at least the first where that night had involved sleep. The fact that people usually called sex 'going to bed with', or 'sleeping with', or that a man who had sex with a woman had 'bedded' her just seemed so wrong. Sex and sleeping together were two different things. What she and Roland were doing now wasn't the same as she and Taffy had got up to behind the Woolpack.

And as soon as Roland had suggested she stay for the night, Louise had become timid, virginal. In the end, a night in Roland's bed had seemed a far better idea than returning to Emmerdale Farm, with the Sugdens and Rita mourning their dead. Selfish of her, but Louise knew she could offer them little support.

She doubted that work would have started on the farm yet, whatever time it was, and snuggled up to Roland.

It had been a long time since Seth had been to the Plaza picture house in Hotten but it was less of a novelty for Betty, who often went with her mother and sister. To be there without them *and* with a man – well, a boy, really – made it an adventure, though.

The matinée was popular: at night, there was always the risk that an air-raid might spoil everything. The authorities didn't like so many people together in a building. For some reason, they didn't mind pubs being opened, but theatres and cinemas all ran reduced programmes.

Today there was only one film on.

'Have you ever heard of him?' Seth asked.

'No. He's not exactly Errol Flynn, is he?'

They queued and bought tickets anyway. The foyer had

seen better days. Normally, the carpets and fittings would have been replaced as they wore out, but in wartime, that sort of luxury had been abandoned. The carpet had been trodden bare along the route to the sweet kiosk and the WCs. It was like following a path. Betty checked the tickets – they were in the stalls and she knew the way.

'Where are all the girls?' Joseph asked.

Annie handed him his cup of tea. Barely twelve hours after his younger son's death, Joseph Sugden was pale, weak. It was as if it had drained some of his own life. 'Virginia and Alyson are out milking,' she said. 'Louise didn't come back last night. Rita must still be at the Sullivans'.'

'The poor girl.'

'Yes.'

'I didn't think he'd die,' Joseph said.

'No. Neither did I.'

'I mean, it was a possibility. But I just thought ... I thought I'd see him again. Is it in the paper?'

Annie had already looked. 'No. Perhaps the news came too late for it to be in this edition.'

'Or perhaps they don't bad news. Do we know what we do if they can't find his body?'

'A memorial service, I think. I'll be going down into the village later. I'll pop into the vicarage see what Mr Summerfield says. I'm sure he'll know.'

'It must happen a lot. Never finding the bodies if they're lost at sea. It must be the same for the RAF when they're shot down. Even on land, during the Great War, sometimes the explosions were so big we never found anything.'

'How are you, Joseph?'

'Don't worry about me.'

'Your son just died.'

'Yes. Yes he did. And it doesn't matter what I feel, does it?'

'Jacob's still in Edward's room. He slept there last night.'

'It's hit him hard. You'll see him right, won't you?'

'I'll do what I can.'

'You're a good girl, Annie. I know you'll see him right.'

'Didn't think much of the picture,' Seth added. 'No wonder it's coming off this week.

'It was very long,' Betty agreed.

'And there wasn't a newsreel. I thought it were a newsreel at first, but it were just the film. No newsreel, no B-film. Nowt.'

'And it wasn't even in colour. You expect an American film to be in colour these days.'

'They're not all in colour, though,' Seth told her. Truth was, he'd never seen a colour film. They must be more expensive to make, he thought.

'Not much happened,' Betty said. 'I mean, how could it, really, when you knew the man was dead right at the beginning?'

'Not much of a surprise, was it?' Seth agreed. 'And they never explained what it meant.'

'Eh?'

'You know. Those men from the papers were trying to find out what he meant and—'

'It were the sledge!' Betty exclaimed. 'The whole point of the film was that it were the sledge! Did you not get that?'

The three or four dozen people queuing to watch the next performance all glared at her. 'Save your money,' Betty advised them, much to the annoyance of the manager, who was just about to let them in.

'Why was he thinking about the sledge?' Seth asked.

'I'll try to explain on the bus,' Betty told him, patting him on the arm.

Alyson was getting the hang of kissing. She and Taffy had got no further than that, but she didn't mind. Last night Louise and Virginia had agreed that a kiss was nothing, but they were wrong: when Taffy kissed her, she felt alive, and happy. When things got 'more serious', as the other girls assured her it would, she didn't believe it could be better than this.

And Louise had been wrong about something else: Taffy wasn't pressuring her, or making her do anything she didn't want to do. He was in no rush even though it was his last night of leave. He'd walked her home, but she couldn't bear to say goodbye, so they'd snuck into the barn.

And now they were hugging each other, running their hands slowly up and down each other's backs. He was quite a wiry lad.

'What the hell?' Jacob Sugden filled the doorway. 'I told you about this. I warned you girls.'

'Sir, I'm—'

'Get out, lad, I don't care who you are. Girl, you get back inside the house.'

Taffy turned to Alyson. 'Are you going to be all right?'

She nodded.

'Get out!' Jacob repeated.

'Goodbye, Alyson, I'll write to you!' and with that Taffy scurried away, swerving past Jacob.

'I'm sorry, Mr Sugden, but all we were doing was kissing. It was cold outside, and it was his last evening here and we wanted to . . .'

But Jacob Sugden was ignoring her. He had just walked to the centre of the barn, and was looking around, oblivious to her. Alyson decided Mr Sugden needed someone to talk to. He had sat down on a bale of hay, hunched up. She thought better of it, and hurried into the house.

Betty met her sister at the bus stop, as agreed.

'Did you have a good time?' Margaret asked.

'I did.'

Despite the disappointing film, Betty had had a whale of a time. Seth had been the perfect gentleman, really good company. She'd expected to have to fend him off, but he didn't make a move, he was just happy to be with her. She had spent the bus journey home trying to explain the intricacies of the plot, but once he grasped that most of the story had been shown in flashback, he'd pieced it together. He had walked her as far as his house, and they'd kissed again on the doorstep, then Betty had almost skipped over to the bus stop to meet her sister, who'd spent the evening with her RAF officer at some do he'd been invited to.

'So, how was Anthony?'

Margaret blushed a little. 'Oh, marvellous.'

Betty had all sorts of questions for her sister, but was too embarrassed to ask. How long had she been sneaking out for an evening with a boyfriend? Betty found herself trying to remember when her sister had gone out on her own for the evening. Their mother was very strict, and insisted on curfews, but Margaret had disappeared plenty of times for a couple of hours.

And what, exactly, had she been sneaking off to do? Not just dancing – that was obvious from what she and Anthony had been up to when Betty and Seth caught them. But had it been more than kissing and cuddling? And if so . . . well, how often and with whom? It wasn't good for a girl's reputation.

Betty had always liked to know what other people were doing. It was good to be community-minded. At times of trouble, the village could all pull together. She'd hate living in a town where you didn't know your neighbour. It would be like a film, when people were taken in by spivs and rogues. They'd have to judge by appearances and, like her mother said, appearances meant nowt. But Betty's nose for news had let her down. Margaret had a secret life of which her family had no idea.

She was rather surprised that the first thing that occurred to her was that it might mean she and Seth could see more of each other. If their mum was blind to Margaret's activities, then Betty ought to be able to get up to all sorts – not that she wanted that, but it was nice to have the option. And that thought pleased her.

Taffy had been surprised to see Louise heading out of Home Farm. 'Were you looking for me?' he asked.

'No.' She laughed, and didn't slow down. 'Why would I have been?'

Taffy ran after her. 'It's my last day here, and I thought . . . I thought you might think the same way about me. You might have realised . . . Louise, whenever I'm with Alyson I think about you. Alyson's . . . she's shy. Even when we kiss, she gets nervous.'

'Well, give it time.'

'You and me didn't need any time. You didn't get all shy on me.'

'It wasn't the same thing.'

'I love you. Louise.'

'You don't.' She stopped dead. 'Look, what we did had nothing to do with love.'

'We *made* love.'

'It's not the same thing. That's just a figure of speech. What happened was physical, that's all. It was just like . . . dancing together. Or tickling.'

'There was more to it than that.'

'No, there wasn't. People sometimes like to dress it up, but there wasn't. You made me happy.'

'You made *me* happy.'

'I'm well aware of that.' She laughed again – not a cruel laugh, a friendly one.

'I want to do it again.'

'You will. But not with me. And if that's all you want, then you and Alyson aren't right for each other.'

'And it meant nothing at all to you?'

Louise sat him down on the wall. 'What sort of girl do you think I am?'

'A beautiful one, a generous one, who—'

Louise put a finger to his lips, and looked at him with as serious an expression as she could muster. 'It meant something to me. It meant we enjoyed ourselves. I won't ever forget it. But I told you before we did it exactly what it was.'

'How can you be so . . . calculating?'

'How can you not be?' she countered, without meaning to sound quite so hard.

Taffy looked confused.

'It's not something that just happened,' Louise said. 'It's not something where we didn't know what we were doing. We knew exactly what it was.'

'I didn't.'

Louise sighed. 'There's something else you don't know.'

Taffy looked up at her, faint hope on his face.

'I'm sleeping with Roland Pilgrim. I was before our little adventure and I still am.'

Taffy went pale as what she said sank in. 'You're the Squadron Leader's girlfriend?'

'No, we don't call it that, not exactly. 'Yes,' she told him.

'And you let me?'

Louise shrugged.

'You won't tell him?' Taffy stuttered.

She laughed. 'No, I certainly will not.'

'I could tell him what we did.' But Taffy knew that wasn't a serious option.

'You could, and what do you think would happen if you did? Do you think Roland would believe you? If he did, do you think he'd blame me, or you?'

Taffy nodded. 'I understand.'

'Tell me, then.'

'We're never going to be together. I should go back to Alyson and forget about you.'

'That's right. Alyson's a lovely girl, she's much more your type than I am.'

'She's very pretty.'

'And she likes you, she really does. I can see you getting married.'

Taffy blushed. 'Come on, how can you say that?'

'Because I know you quite well, and I've shared a room with her for months. I can see you together. You're both romantics. I'm not. I'm horrible.'

'Are you saying that the Squadron Leader's horrible, too?'

'Oh, no. But he's not romantic. He's practical, like me.'

'You don't love each other?'

Louise hesitated. She wasn't sure how to answer that one. 'Neither of us wants to send Valentine cards, or have a big church wedding. We like each other.'

'I see.' And it was clear that he had recognised his commander in her description.

'Forget me, and treat Alyson properly.'

'I'll do that. Yes.' Taffy nodded.

Louise pecked him on the cheek. 'Good boy.'

CHAPTER SIXTEEN:
Plans for the Future

It was the day after the memorial service for Edward when Annie realised that his death had changed everything. Almost every day for some time, she had thought about her wedding. She wasn't impatient for it, but she knew it was coming, like Christmas or the end of the war. She had had a clear idea of what the day would be like. When she pictured it, it was almost a vivid memory rather than a daydream. And she remembered that Edward was to have been there, handing his older brother the ring, smiling at her as she came up the aisle towards them, on her father's arm. He would have looked comfortable in his uniform, far more at ease than Jacob in his morning suit. His best man's speech would have been a true reflection of how much he loved his brother and his brother's new wife. The war would be over, they'd all be a few years older, and a new era would dawn at Emmerdale Farm.

It wasn't going to happen like that.

Who on earth would Jacob have as his best man now? And when would the wedding take place? They had been waiting for Edward. Now he wouldn't be there, so would the wedding be sooner? Would it happen at all?

Annie's future had been set in stone. But now . . . now

anything might happen. She tried to imagine the wedding with Edward out of the picture. She couldn't.

Jacob had changed, too. He was barely talking to anyone. He just ate his food, allocated farmwork, did his bit. Then he sat in the front room until it was time to go to bed. He kissed Annie good morning, but it was a ritual, nothing more. There was no feeling in it. They'd not shared a bed since the night Edward had died, and he didn't seem in any hurry to change that.

'Betty, love, hello!'

'Wally?' She turned round, and it was. Wally Eagleton. He looked a lot older than the last time she'd seen him. It was the uniform – not the clothes but the bearing that went with them.

Walter Eagleton had always been her mother's favourite. Out of all Betty's male school friends, he was the one she had earmarked as husband material. Wally's dad was a policeman, the desk sergeant at Hotten, and Wally would have gone to university if it hadn't been for the war. Like a lot of military types, he'd grown a neatly groomed moustache. It made him look older, a man, not a boy like Seth.

'Are you on leave, then?' Betty asked.

'I got a three day pass,' Wally said proudly.

'And you want to spend it here?' Seth asked.

'Where else could I go?' he replied happily.

'It's good to see you,' Betty said. 'How's life in the army?'

'He's only in Bridlington,' Seth reminded her.

'It's like another life altogether,' Wally said. 'You get to meet people from all walks of life, but we're all doing the same job.'

'What's the army doing at the moment?' Seth asked. 'Sitting in camps, aren't they?'

Wally looked up at him. 'There's a bit more to it than that.' He noticed Seth's armband. 'You're an ARP warden? I thought they had to be twenty-five.'

'Aye, they made an exception for me because I were so keen.'

Wally nodded. 'I'm sure it's important work,' he said, unimpressed.

'Aye,' said Seth, bristling a little. 'It is. I'm doing some training later today. How to use a stirrup pump. Going into Hotten specially.'

'What are you up to, Betty?'

'I was going to help Mother with the washing.'

'I'll take you to the pictures if you want.'

'She's been,' Seth said firmly.

'I've seen what's on, is what Seth means. But I'd love to catch up with your news.'

'I'll come round at two.'

Betty nodded eagerly. 'I'll look forward to it.'

'You've heard about Edward Sugden?'

'It's one of the reasons I've come back,' he told her. 'A terrible thing, that. How are the family taking it?'

'They keep themselves to themselves. We've not seen much of them. Annie Pearson's moved in there.'

Wally wasn't very concerned about the living arrangements up at Emmerdale Farm. 'So, you and Seth, are you courting?' he asked.

Betty had been wondering that herself. 'No, not really,' she concluded. 'We're friends, you know, but that's all.'

'Good,' Wally said quietly. He looked so dashing, Betty thought.

They were in the tea-rooms. and Mrs Dillon brought over a couple of slices of some tart. Betty always felt a little reluctant to take Seth anywhere local. Hotten was all right, she wasn't likely to meet anyone she knew there, but in the village she'd rather have had a man in uniform for company.

'What's in that?' she asked.

'Rhubarb,' Mrs Dillon told her. 'Do you want it?'

They did.

'Life in the army must be rough,' Betty remarked.

'Oh, you get used to it,' Wally said. 'It's a routine – up at the same time every morning, same work to do.'

It sounded like the regime at home, Betty thought. Her mother was always careful to make sure she and Margaret did their fair share of chores in the house. There was always plenty of cooking, cleaning and mending to be done.

'But you've not done any fighting yet?' she asked.

'Not had to,' Wally replied. 'We're training, getting ready.'

'You've heard about the airfield?'

'Oh, is that what it is? I saw it from the train. I knew it had to be something like that. It didn't look like an army camp.'

'There's going to be hundreds of RAF men up there, they say. Bomber pilots. It sounds like we're going to start taking the fight to Mr Hitler.'

'There's already fighting in Africa. But I think you're right.'

'Do you think the Americans will join in?'

'They'd be on our side but I'm not sure they want to. Can you blame them?'

'Can you imagine what it must be like not having the war? I'm starting to forget what it was like before. We don't need the Americans, though, do we?'

'No,' Wally reassured her. 'Why should we?'

'Are you sure you don't mind, Brian?'

'Of course I don't. I'm getting used to the settee.'

'I'm so sorry,' Rita said. 'It's just that I don't want to be alone, and I don't want to be in the same room as Alyson, Louise and Virginia. They don't understand, but they think they do. They think by asking me if I'm all right all the time that it'll be OK. I just feel so lonely.'

'Come here.' Jean gave Rita a hug. She felt so warm and her perfume smelt so nice.

'It's been a week,' Rita said. 'The last day of *shiv'a* today. 'It's helped. It's ... I don't know, given me a timetable. A shape to it all. Reminded me there's light at the end of the tunnel.'

Seth was out on his rounds. He was already a bit bored of being a warden – it was the same every night. He'd found himself hoping that the Nazis would launch an attack on the village, not paratroopers, or tanks, or a full-scale invasion – even a single thousand-pounder bomb would be a bit excessive. Hit the village in the right place, and there wouldn't be much village left. But couldn't they drop a couple of incendiaries? He wanted to use the stirrup pump he'd been given this afternoon. Until now, Beckindale hadn't been seen as a priority for getting its own pump – not least because Ron couldn't have operated it on his own. But with the airfield nearing completion, there was more risk of an attack.

Seth had tried out the pump as soon as he'd got home. It was easy to use. It would be a help in the garden for watering the vegetables. But, just once, he'd like to use it to put out a fire.

This train of thought was interrupted by the appearance of Betty, walking down the hill with a spring in her step. When he stepped out in front of her, she almost jumped out of skin, and looked about as guilty as she could.

'Did you enjoy yourself with Wally?'

'We had a lovely time.' She'd already regained some dignity.

'Did you, now?'

'What's that supposed to mean?'

'He likes you.'

'Don't be so jealous. I told him we were courting.'

'Are we? I mean, did you?'

Betty looked him over critically. 'You'd do well to be more like Wally Eagleton,' she told him.

'How do you mean?'

'Look at you. Your shirt's hanging out, your shoulders are drooping. He's upright—'

'Upright!' Seth snorted. 'He's barely five foot tall.'

'But he carries himself well. That brisk walk soldiers have. And he's so smart. Don't you think that moustache suits him? You should grow one.'

While Seth was considering the idea, he realised Betty was heading off. 'Where are you going?' he called.

'I'm seeing Wally tonight,' she told him. 'You'll be out on your rounds, so he's coming round for dinner.'

'Your mum lets him in the house?'

'Of course she does. She thinks he's marvellous.'

Seth stopped in his tracks. He didn't like the sound of that all.

Rita lay in Jean's bed. Her friend was having a bath. She imagined her luxuriating in it, the door locked, the outside world kept at bay. What a contrast to the Sugdens' tin bath, full of grey water, with Alyson, Louise and Virginia all staring at her, making scathing comments.

She found herself wondering about Jean's relationship with her husband. She'd been married a few years but there didn't seem to be much going on. Rita couldn't remember seeing them kiss, or cuddle, or even hold hands.

And they had separate beds. That was quite fashionable, of course, really quite sophisticated, but it seemed odd.

Rita had never shared a bed with Paul, of course, but they would have done if they'd got married. She had looked forward to her wedding night. Alyson seemed to think that everything revolved around the courtship, that there was nothing to marriage except getting flowers, going to dances. Louise, from what Rita could tell, attached no significance to sex. Virginia . . . well, Virginia kept herself to herself, but she'd told them all she wasn't a virgin.

For a mad moment, Rita wondered if the Sullivans had ever done it. But they must have, and Jean was a sensual woman – she enjoyed her clothes, perfumes, jewellery.

There was a tap at the door.

'Come in,' Rita said. She was careful to tuck the sheet under her arms – she was only wearing a vest and knickers.

It was Adam, who blushed when he saw her in bed. 'Sorry,' he said.

'Were you looking for Mrs Sullivan?'

'I was looking for you. I didn't realise you were in bed. I wanted to see how you were.'

Jean was right: Adam did fancy her. It was obvious from his face, now she was looking out for it. How sweet.

'I've got a biscuit,' he said.

'Good for you, Adam.'

'No. It's left over. I don't really like them.' He held out a digestive, a rare commodity these days. He was staring at her, and it wasn't difficult to work out what he was thinking. He was seeing her there, bare shoulders, clearly half naked.

'Adam, shouldn't you be in bed?' Jean said sternly, behind him. She stood in the doorway, wrapped in her dressing gown.

Adam handed her the biscuit, then hurried out.

Jean held it up and raised an eyebrow.

'A gift,' Rita explained.

'Ah.' Jean closed the bedroom door and hung her dressing-gown on the back of it. She was wearing a nightshirt underneath it. She put the biscuit on the bedside table. 'He really ought to eat everything he's given. It's not as though we can give him a lot.'

'I'll give it him back if you—'

Jean had started to brush her hair. 'Don't be silly. If he wants to give you his biscuit, then let him.'

'It's probably a feast to him. There's a lot less food in the cities.'

'Less?' Jean could scarcely believe that was possible.

'All the farms have their quotas, but the Sugdens can always find a little more milk when they've got a field full of cows. And people like Seth Armstrong catch rabbits and pheasants.'

'And I know I shouldn't, but I put aside a little extra for the good customers, and for the boys. But I'm always hungry.'

'And tired,' Rita agreed. 'On edge. Always fearing the worst. In a way . . . well, in a way Paul dying is a weight off my mind. The worst that can happen has happened. But that sounds so bad.'

Jean smiled sympathetically. 'It's all right, I'm a friend, I'm not here to judge you. I think I know what you mean. Budge up.'

She climbed into bed and settled in. There wasn't much room for both of them.

'It's warmer this way, isn't it?' Jean said.

'I'm not used to it. I never did this with Paul.'

'Really?'

'No. Do you sleep with Brian?'

Suddenly Jean was a little coy. 'Sometimes. Not often.

On cold nights, mainly. He takes up a lot more room than you do.'

Rita leant over, and kissed Jean's cheek.

'What was that for?' Jean asked.

'You don't know?'

'No.'

'Then . . . it's to say thank you.' She took a deep breath. 'You know before, when you said about if you were a man and you weren't married? Well, yes. I would.'

Jean giggled. 'Night, Rita.' She rolled over.

George took Annie aside. 'Do you still want to go to London?'

'I don't think there's much chance of that. Jacob needs me now and—'

'But you want to?'

'I'd love to,' she said.

'I'm going down on the fifteenth. Meetings at the Ministry. Last-minute stuff about the requisitioning of the land, and exactly who has responsibility for what. Do you want to come?'

'I'm sorry?'

'I'd love some company, and if you're there for dinner with the Hart-Wilsons, I won't feel like such a gooseberry.' I'll pay for your hotel room.'

Annie, practical as ever, couldn't see how this would work.

'You come down on the train with me,' George explained. 'I'll book an extra room for you at the hotel, you see the sights while I have my meeting, then dinner with the Hart-Wilsons. Back up to Yorkshire the next morning.'

It all seemed so simple. 'The fifteenth and sixteenth?' she echoed.

'That's right.'

'I'd have to ask Jacob.'

'Of course. Break it to him gently that he's not invited.'

Annie looked at George. A night away with George Verney. That's what it looked like. That might even be what was on offer.

'I don't think he'd want to come, anyway,' George added.

'No. He's not doing anything at the moment – he's barely talking.'

'You need a break, Annie.'

She had to admit that she was excited at the prospect of going to London. And, truth be told, the idea of spending some time living the high life excited her, too. George moved in such circles all the time, although it was hard to imagine. She'd heard the expression 'how the other half lives', but she'd always assumed that life at Home Farm was like life at Emmerdale Farm, only with everything of better quality – a warmer house, more expensive cuts of meat, bigger beds. But the way George conducted himself, his priorities, the scale he operated on was different: he'd offered part of his land to help defeat the Germans, he'd joined the RAF, even though he needn't have, he had parties like this, and got invited to the same. Not long ago, Annie wouldn't have thought it possible that she could get used to it, but now her horizons had broadened. There was more to life than what happened in Beckindale. She decided not to share that idea with her father. But there were possibilities she hadn't considered before.

She stopped herself. She had a fiancé, the prospect of becoming a farmer's wife. Her life was mapped out for her . . . No, that was unfair: she had chosen it as a life that would be a good one and that suited her values.

She'd got engaged to Jacob two years ago, just before the war, but things had changed since then. She was twenty now, not eighteen. It wasn't a vast difference, in the scheme of things, but she felt a lot older. With the death of Jacob's mother, she'd had to grow up. Now she was practically the matriarch of the Sugden family.

The war had changed things, of course, as war always did. After the Great War, women had got the vote and there had been many other changes. A whole generation of young men – men like her father – had been shaped by their experiences. This war, if anything, would bring even greater changes in its wake. It was obvious to her that farming would change: there would be more machines, more emphasis on the volume of production, more interference from civil servants. Emmerdale Farm was already far more efficient than it had been. And the factories that were rolling out planes, tanks and bullets would be turned to other uses. All those women at work now would see that as the natural way to be.

The future was uncertain. Even assuming they would win the war – and, for heaven's sake, they had to assume *that* – it might not be possible to live a sheltered life.

The future could be anything she wanted it to be, she thought. Which wasn't comforting at all. In fact, it was daunting.

CHAPTER SEVENTEEN:
London

Is Your Journey Really Necessary?
There were signs like that all over Hotten station, but if the number of people on the platforms was anything to go by, there were plenty of necessary journeys to be made today. By the look of it, a lot of soldiers were returning to their regiments from leave, or they had just been called up. There were few civilians.

She and George had a suitcase each, and he insisted on carrying hers as well as his own when they couldn't find a porter. The train timetable was scrawled on a board by the cafeteria. Annie knew that rail travel was often disrupted by the war: the main stations made large, tempting targets for the bombers, and if a section of track was damaged, the whole line ground to a halt while it was repaired. Added to the fuel and manpower shortages, it was a wonder that there was any service at all.

The London train was waiting on the platform, already half full, a quarter of an hour before it was due to depart. They wove their way to it, through the crowds and the steam, until they reached their first class carriage. It was less congested than the cheaper ones, although there were still people standing in it. George found Annie a seat, slotted the cases onto the luggage rack, then went to stand in the corridor, where there was a little more room.

The seats here were more comfortable than the normal ones, and an antimacassar was draped over each. She and George would also be able to take advantage of the First Class dining car. But other than that, Annie wasn't impressed. She wondered why he'd bothered getting a First Class ticket – he could have saved himself a bit of money. Look after the pennies and the pounds look after themselves. And if you were going to stand anyway, you might as well stand in Second or Third Class.

There was a final flurry of activity outside, the doors were slammed, the guard blew his whistle, and the train was under way. It nosed out of Hotten, gradually picking up speed. Annie glanced at George, who was talking to a fellow passenger and smoking a cigarette. The other passengers in her compartment kept themselves to themselves, reading newspapers and books. There were a couple of elderly women, two anxious looking young soldiers and a middle-aged man who looked like a bank manager or lawyer. He was engrossed in a small pile of paperwork.

Annie was sitting by the window, and had thought that the view would be enough to occupy her, but it consisted of little but fields. Everyone was busy ploughing, as they were at Beckindale. Occasionally, the train passed through a town. Here, there was more of interest, barrage balloons reminding her of the war. In one town she saw a demolished church, with a crowd of people salvaging what they could from the rubble, but otherwise life seemed to be going on as normal. Annie had assumed that life was completely different for everyone now, that the war had encroached everywhere except isolated pockets like Beckindale. That was the impression she got from the newspaper. Her father, of course, had spent the last year or so telling her that the whole of the rest of the country had become a munitions production line, but that just didn't seem to be the case.

It wasn't an interesting journey. When she had looked at the map, Annie had thought there would be all sorts of highlights, but the train line avoided them. Early on they had diverted away from York and if they had passed through Sherwood Forest, she'd missed it. Lincoln and Cambridge remained hidden from view. She saw only ploughed fields and small market towns. If she hadn't been engaged to a farmer, she doubted that she'd have noticed the soil gradually changing, that the stone walls became hedgerows, that the breeds of horses pulling the ploughs were different from the ones at home.

It wasn't until they reached London that the view became more interesting. Suddenly there were football grounds and towers on hills, picture houses and long streets. The city stretched over the horizon, and in the quarter of an hour or so that the train took to wind its way to King's Cross, Annie saw more cars than she'd seen in the whole of the rest of her life.

George had popped back into the compartment from time to time to check that she was all right. Now he returned for good, and started to fish about on the luggage rack. 'Nearly there,' he told her.

Annie acknowledged him, but was spellbound by the view. This was another world, and the ravages of war were evident. Each street had at least one property bombed into rubble. They all looked like mouths that had had a few teeth knocked out in a fight. Everywhere there were sandbags, and men in ARP helmets and armbands, trying to impose order. It was a different landscape from the one Annie was used to, and she could have gazed at it all day.

King's Cross station was dirty, smelly and full of steam. Large railway stations all looked much the same because they'd been built around the same time. This wasn't as elegant as York but it was more impressive than Leeds, the other two main railway stations Annie had been to. The platforms were heaving with people, many in military uniform, as in Hotten, but here they were outnumbered by old men in the pinstripe uniform of the City. There were few women here. A porter helped them with their bags.

The noise and smells weren't as overwhelming as she had feared and she realised how silly she'd been. It was her father's influence rubbing off, she was sure – she'd inherited his fear of anything that wasn't from the Dales. Here the pace of life was different: everything seemed more urgent, vibrant, and that was before she'd even left the station.

They had reached the exit, and the porter hailed a taxi for them.

Annie looked around. There was a vast Gothic building to their right, a wide road with the occasional van, taxi or red bus driving along it. She didn't recognise any landmarks. She'd expected to see St Paul's Cathedral, Big Ben, Tower Bridge, Nelson's Column and Buckingham Palace all piled on top of each other.

'We'll register at the hotel before we do anything else,' George told her. 'The Metropolis,' he told the cab driver.

Now, at last, Annie saw some of the city, but still nothing she recognised, just rows of Victorian offices and terraces. It was exciting, though. The fog swirled around, obscuring anything more than thirty or forty yards away. 'We'll get a chance to see the sights, won't we?' she said.

'Oh, yes,' George assured her.

'This your first time in London, ma'am?' the cabby asked.

'It is.'

'You're from the north? Yorkshire?'

'That's right. How can you tell?'

'Your accent, ma'am.'

Annie was about to object that she didn't have one, before accepting that she might. After all, the cabby spoke like every Cockney in every film she'd seen.

'Is the fog always this bad?' she enquired.

'This is a good day.' He laughed.

The streets were almost empty – petrol rationing and the need to keep them clear for fire engines and ambulances, Annie assumed.

Within ten minutes they were getting out of the taxi. Annie had no idea which part of London this was, and concentrated on the hotel. It was huge, seven or eight storeys at least. That was the main difference here – the buildings just didn't stop while in Beckindale nothing got to three storeys, let alone seven. The Metropolis was as long as Main Street in the village, with a great, colourful canopy running along the front. Even the pavement was covered in thick carpet. George handed a coin to the driver, and told him to keep the change.

'I hope you and your wife have a lovely time,' the cabby said cheerfully.

If anything, the hotel lobby was more impressive than the outside, with thick red and black carpets, brass banisters and frames. Incredibly, there were signs that it had once been even more opulent – the vast mirrors all had tape over them, to prevent them shattering, and it was easy to imagine that the simple light fittings that hung from the ceilings had replaced delicate crystal chandeliers.

George seemed perfectly at home, and Annie gained confidence from that. In the village, she generally got her way, even with stubborn beggars like Jacob and her father. Here she felt a little out of her depth, her natural instinct was to ask if anyone wanted any tea, or help with the washing up. But she would play the part of a northern aristocrat. She tried to emulate George's rather haughty bearing, started to behave as if she owned the place. She was surprised at how easy it was to adopt airs and graces.

The concierge at the desk signed them in, under their own names, without a hint of the disapproval Annie had feared. 'Welcome back, Mr Verney,' he said. 'I hope you enjoy your first stay with us, Miss Pearson.'

Her *first* stay! The idea that this might become a regular occurrence!

She glanced at George, who was checking through a few messages that had already arrived for him. He was in his element here – more comfortable than when he was being lord of the manor. Perhaps back in Beckindale he was playing a role. At times he seemed stiff there, a little awkward, as though he didn't relish throwing his weight about. He hadn't chosen his life, Annie realised, he hadn't asked to take on the duties it entailed. Even Jacob had a choice – he would never walk away from farming, would die tilling the land his ancestors had farmed, but he *could* walk away.

'You've been here before?' she asked.

'I always stay here when I'm in London. I first came here on honeymoon.'

They walked to the lifts, which they shared with the porter and the bellboy. There was a sense of ritual here, formality: the regular ringing of the lift bell, the smell of polish, the whirring of the mechanism. Everything was in order.

The porter led them to their rooms. Annie detected in him a hint of a smirk, an assumption that they had two rooms for show, that they would use only one. He didn't seem shocked – if anything, he exuded a weary acceptance.

George had been here with Milly, his beautiful wife.

She thought of them waking up here together, on the morning after their wedding night, imagining that they'd grow old together, that they'd have children.

She must have been reading his mind, because suddenly he looked sad.

'I'll let you settle in, then we'll get a spot of lunch downstairs,' he told her.

Annie felt strange, as though she was in a film. Nothing was what she was used to: everything was elegant, opulent, expensive and stylish. She felt detached from it all, a little light-headed.

Her hotel room was huge, with a high ceiling. It was roughly rectangular, with a dressing-table against one wall, a vast bed opposite, and a table and two armchairs by the window. A big wardrobe took up some more space, and past that was a door, which led to the bathroom. There were oil paintings on the wall, delicate china ornaments on the shelves, even a lacquered folding screen to dress behind.

Annie took off her shoes, marvelling at the quality of the carpet beneath her feet. She walked around the room and found on the table a neatly typed list of instructions on with what to do during an air-raid. The hotel, it said, had extensive cellars, and reassured her that in the event of a raid, the shelter provided would meet her accustomed standards.

On the dressing-table there was a large, glossy cardboard box.

At first, Annie assumed that the previous occupant had left it behind, but when she checked the card, she saw it had her name on it. She opened it and inside found a full-length silk evening dress.

There was a knock at the door.

George Verney was standing there. 'I thought we might

197

get some lunch now,' he said. Then, seeing the box, 'Ah, it's here – excellent.'

'You bought this for me?'

'You'll need something like it where we're dining tonight. I had to guess at your size.'

'You shouldn't have. I can't wait to try it on.' She had to stop herself unbuttoning her blouse there and then. She glanced at the screen, thought about getting undressed behind it, with George standing on the other side.

He smiled. 'Well, I'm famished, and that's a bit formal for daytime.'

'It must have been very expensive.'

'It wasn't,' he said, but Annie knew otherwise. She wondered if the underwear she had brought would fit underneath it.

After a light lunch, George took Annie on a tour of London. It turned out that the Metropolis was within easy walking distance of the first few sights on her mental list. They saw Trafalgar Square, but Nelson was invisible in the fog. During the day, the streetlights were on – ironic, really: they would be switched off as it got dark and the blackout came into force.

After their tour, George hailed a taxi and sent Annie to Harrods while he went to Whitehall for his meetings. There, she met up with Penny Hart-Wilson, who treated her like one of her oldest friends. The department store was a labyrinth, a Christmas grotto. Annie had thought it was exclusively for the rich, but there were far more people like her, ordinary people marvelling at the quality and expense of the goods for sale. Penny was more at home, and adopted the role of a curator, pointing out items of interest, leading Annie to the prize exhibits. She asked Annie if she had a dress for the evening. Annie told her she had, but remembered she needed suitable underwear, whereupon Penny grabbed her hand and led her to the lingerie department.

Annie quickly selected a brassière that she thought would fit under the dress, then a matching pair of knickers. She'd brought a suspender belt with her, and thought that buying another would be an extravagance, but between them, Penny and the sales girl persuaded her to buy silk stockings. Even here, she had to use coupons. Penny offered a couple of hers – which wasn't allowed, although the assistant didn't seem to mind – but Annie had plenty saved up. As the assistant tore them out, Annie couldn't help working out that for seven coupons and the money she'd spent, she could have bought herself a new coat.

Then Penny announced that she had an afternoon engagement, and left Annie to her own devices. The underwear had exhausted Annie's spending money, but she told herself that it had been an essential purchase. George had given her a card from the hotel its address, so she knew where it was. She asked a policeman which buses she needed, and he was happy to tell her. The buses were frequent, she thought, although Londoners in the queues complained to each other as they waited.

When she got back to the hotel and closed the door of her room, she realised she'd not thought once of Beckindale, the farm or even Jacob. It was as though they didn't exist. London was so compelling – the mix of buildings she'd seen so often in newspapers and newsreels and the fog made it seem like a dream. And the possibilities here . . . In Beckindale, whatever you did ended up as grist to the mill of village gossip. Here, you could do as you pleased, shop for whatever you wanted, and nobody would know. Even in Hotten, most of the faces were familiar. She'd never before thought it was possible to lose yourself in a crowd but in London everyone was a stranger, and that was the natural state of affairs.

Affairs.

While they'd been on their tour, and George had been pointing out the Houses of Parliament she had gazed at him. If she could do anything, then what would she do tonight? The answer to that made her blush.

But there would be consequences. She would always know what had happened, even if no one in the village did.

Annie was wearing her evening dress. It was of quite a daring cut, but it fitted her and, more than that, suited her figure.

There was a knock at the door, which she recognised as George's. She let him in and he looked at her, admiringly. 'Perfect.' He was smart himself, in dinner-jacket and bow-tie. 'Our carriage awaits.'

'Carriage?'

'Taxi,' he amended.

It didn't take them far, to a restaurant in Piccadilly, down a flight of stairs.

It was like stepping into another world. Everywhere was so bright, and the *smells* – perfume, thick cigars, a haze of wine and liqueurs you'd never be able to buy at the Woolpack. It was as though it had been preserved from before the war, and the decoration underlined the impression, owing more to the 1920s than the forties.

Near to them, an admiral entertained a pretty young woman in a gown that made Annie's seem almost frumpy. In the distance, a band played swing, and a pair of women danced together on a tiny stage. Waiters in spotless black dinner-jackets and bow ties wove their way between the tables.

'The war hasn't touched this place. It's a hundred feet down, with its own generator. We wouldn't even know if there was an air-raid,' George observed.

Annie hesitated. Outside, people were suffering, dying. Here, the rich and privileged could close their eyes to that. She was torn. She felt out of place here, awkward in her silk gown with her funny accent. But at the same time she wanted the war to go away, just for an evening.

The head waiter welcomed them and led them to their table. Heads turned, watching the new arrivals. Again, it was as if she was playing a part. She didn't sense disapproval – rather, she fancied there were some admiring glances from some of the men.

'Verney!'

'Reed!'

Reed was tall, with a neat moustache. He was in army uniform, but the most striking thing about him was his companion, an African woman in a uniform identical to his. Her skin was pitch black, her body like a sportswoman's. She had flecks of grey hair, which threw Annie, who was trying to guess her age.

'Have you never seen a black person before?' the woman asked, in an accent Annie had no chance of placing.

'No,' Annie said. 'Have you ever met anyone from Yorkshire?'

The woman gave a wide grin, revealing impossibly white teeth. 'I haven't,' she admitted.

George had finished his brief discussion with Reed. Now he took Annie's hand. 'Our table is over there,' he said, and led her away from Reed and his exotic companion.

'Who were they?'

'He does hush-hush work at the War Office. I've known him for years. I was at university with him.'

'And the . . . negress?'

'A colleague.'

'More than a colleague, I think.'

201

George looked back over his shoulder. 'How can you tell?'

'A nose for gossip, honed over years in the Yorkshire Dales.'

George smiled, they took their seats, and the waiter passed them the menus.

The food was rich: the restaurant seemed untouched by rationing and the other privations of war. And they were alone. The Hart-Wilsons had phoned through to apologise – they couldn't make it, after all. Something about a prior engagement.

'I've not eaten like that for a long time,' George said.

'I don't think I've ever eaten like that.' Annie had lost count of the courses – there had been six or seven, she thought, and she'd found she was pacing herself, which she normally only did with Christmas dinner.

When George ordered a second bottle of wine, Annie realised she must have been responsible for at least half of the first. 'Are you trying to get me drunk?' she asked lightly.

'I was about to ask you the same question.'

George remained oblivious, she thought, but now she knew the shape of the rest of the evening. From there, it was a simple sequence of events.

They finished their meal, danced together, but only for a few minutes, because they'd eaten too much. But in those minutes, George had put his hand on her waist and they'd held each other close.

They stepped outside, into the cold night. The fog was thick, it was pitch black, and they were both a little drunk, but luckily, they'd rung for a taxi. The journey back was slow, as the driver inched his way through the darkness. There hadn't been an air-raid tonight, he told them, though they were hardly listening, and there hadn't been much bombing since the summer, he added.

The cab was cold, and Annie and George edged together. He put his arm round her shoulder, kept her warm.

They entered the hotel, laughing, and ended up outside his room. Annie knew that although hers was next door, she wouldn't see it again until the morning. 'George,' she said, 'would you happen to have a bottle of brandy in your room?'

'I do.'

'Might I have some? I think it helps me sleep.'

George opened the door. 'Come in.'

And now there were more uncertainties. She could spend the night in his arms, as they were now, in their evening-wear. She could sleep on the bed, with him in one of the chairs, perhaps wearing his pyjama top or a spare shirt.

She'd kiss him, Annie decided, either on the cheek or the mouth – she'd play that by ear. They'd kiss, then fall asleep in each other's arms. They'd eaten too much to do anything more. She felt warm, contented. They'd kissed before, and that hadn't led any further.

George found a table lamp, and switched it on. If she hadn't known, she would have thought this was her room: it was identical, even down to the pictures on the wall.

His hand had brushed her rear as he guided her into the room. 'Take a seat,' he suggested, pointing to a pair of armchairs. He was fishing around in the drinks cabinet – which her own room was missing, unless she had just failed to find it. His room didn't have a screen. It was funny the things you noticed.

They sat in facing armchairs, sipping their brandy.

Annie knew it was going to her head. Before that, there had been the wine at the restaurant. She felt absurdly overdressed now, but George's dinner-jacket looked just right on him.

George was having difficulty replacing the top on the brandy bottle. Annie stood up , stepped over and took the bottle and its cap from him, fitting one easily to the other. She put his glass on the table. 'We're not in the village, now,' she said. 'No one will see us, and nothing we do will get back there. We can do whatever we want.'

'So what do you want?'

She leant towards him and gave him a kiss, on his mouth. It lasted longer than she had planned, so long that she ended up sitting in his lap. She felt his hand on her shoulder, and helped push off the strap, then found the switch of the table lamp.

Then there was nothing, just them and the darkness. She felt his hand grasp hers. Somehow, they were both standing up. They held each other, swayed, as if they were dancing again. Then she helped guide them down until they were kneeling, then sitting on the floor. She couldn't see George, only hear his breathing, feel his warmth, smell his cologne. She could feel the carpet under her hand and through her stockings.

She shifted around and leant back until she was resting against him. George's hand found her shoulder, then her face, her hair. They held each other, and then lay down.

George was solid and real and warm beside her. His hand was on her leg, moving slowly up and down. Annie's mouth was dry. The brandy had gone to her head and she felt giddy, slightly apart from the world. But she was still in control. She helped him to find what he was after.

George's hand slid beneath her skirt, over her thigh, her stocking top. And all the time, they were kissing now: quick, stabbing kisses, finding each other's cheeks and lips and noses, even an eyelid. He was leaning over her, becoming more urgent.

So was she, Annie realised.

She helped him push her skirt up round her waist, and

shifted her legs a little. She could hear him hurrying to undo his belt and his flies.

She helped him with that, too.

CHAPTER EIGHTEEN:
The Morning After

It was finished, Roland saw. It was almost an anti-climax. Of course there were still the finishing touches to do, a lick of paint, a few signs, and when it was opened, teething problems would mean that some things would change – that was always the way. As the crews arrived, personal touches would spring up, jokey signs, nicknames for certain rooms. New furniture would appear in the mess halls, equipment would be installed in the control towers.

But for the moment the work was done.

He looked down on the site. A few months ago, this had been a series of flat green fields. Now there were three long strips of hardened concrete, as though a giant child had drawn a careless grey triangle on the grass, but let the lines run on a little too far, so the ends of the runways poked out.

To one side of the triangle, the control tower, an oblong brick building, painted in camouflage colours, three storeys high, stuck out like a sore thumb, with aerials bristling all over the roof. Dotted around it were mobile floodlights, radar trucks, a couple of artillery pieces and fire engines. There, at the far end from where Roland stood, were the great hangars, covered with earth, the tin mess halls and billets, the brick admin buildings – the briefing room, the chapel and the telephone exchange. Last-minute work was still being done there – mattresses were being moved in, an electrician and his mate were working on some fuse-box or other. A glazier was fitting new panels of glass, and as soon as they were in, a couple of squaddies were taping them up to prevent them shattering in the event of an explosion.

He looked back up the hill, but trees obscured the view. Otherwise it might have been possible to stand at the brow and look down at the village of Beckindale on one side and RAF Emmerdale on the other. The two were about the same size, he guessed, but the numbers at the airfield would exceed the population of the village. In the months the airfield had taken to build, he had sensed a change in the mood of the villagers: they had come to accept the inconvenience and many now saw it as an honour to have the base so close.

He had phone calls to make. RAF Emmerdale would be operational in days, and the crews would be flying their first missions almost as soon as they arrived. Roland took a deep breath. This wasn't the end of anything: the completion of the airfield meant they had reached the beginning.

The hotel room was still pitch black – not even a chink of light had made it through the blackout curtains – Annie knew it must be morning. She was an early riser, and had slept soundly. She wasn't hung over, which surprised her. Perhaps the quality of the wine had saved her from that.

George was fast asleep beside her. When she and Jacob shared a bed, he took up most of it, his weight making a dip in the mattress. He was warm, solid muscle, broad-shouldered. George was hardly there at all.

Annie found she was wearing her new knickers. She

couldn't remember retrieving them, and they were all she had on, but if she had been completely naked she would have felt far more awkward.

He hadn't seen her last night, and he wouldn't be able to see her now, if he was awake. Her eyes were accustomed to the dark now, and she could just about see his outline, where he started and the darkness ended. Just like last night.

She lay there for a moment. Last night she'd assumed she would have regrets, at the very least, in the morning. Now was the time to be honest with herself – and she didn't. It wasn't a surprise that she had ended up here. She had understood the situation and even helped to engineer it. Agreeing to come down here, the wine, the dancing . . . it had all bee contrived, so that they could do what they had done. It was not why it had happened.

She slipped out of bed, and padded invisibly across the thick carpet, then went into the bathroom, closed and locked the door.

There was a mirror above the basin, and the pull-cord for the electric light hung alongside it, she remembered. After a moment's searching, she rediscovered it.

She blinked. The light was harsh, and she expected to be faced with the sight of a Yorkshire farmer's wife, a plain woman, but she looked radiant. Her skin was glowing, her eyes were bright and alert, her hair looked lustrous. She straightened her back, turned this way and that.

It wasn't George's . . . attentions, she thought, seeing her reflection blush. It was London, vast, anonymous. That was it, she thought. No one here would be gossiping about her behaviour, she could lose herself, eat in a different restaurant every night, taste a different wine with every meal. It was all so different from Beckindale. There, they hadn't succumbed.

And once they were back in the village they couldn't do this again. She knew that already, and thought George did too. Last night had been their one chance, and they had taken it.

But one thing had been the same. George was lighter than Jacob, with an athlete's body, but Jacob, if anything, was the gentler. What she and George had done – the sequence of events, the sensations she felt, the pleasures – had been familiar. She'd expected the end of the evening to be as novel and extraordinary as the rest of her day. Not *better*, she thought, but different, somehow.

She decided to get dressed before he awoke.

Rita was dimly aware that Jean was getting back into bed next to her. 'Are you all right?' she asked.

'A bit nauseous, that's all.'

'You're sick?'

'I – I think I'm expecting,' she said quietly.

Rita looked at her. 'But you said you and Brian didn't—'

'I didn't say that.'

'I remember you telling me. We were in Hotten.'

'I said we didn't very often. We don't. But we are husband and wife.'

Rita felt angry. 'How long?'

'I don't know. I don't know for certain. But I'm very late. And I know. Don't ask me how I know, but I can tell.'

'Weeks?' Rita said softly. She imagined Brian looming over Jean, the two of them sweating and grunting. He was so fat, so hairy. But if it had only been weeks, then it had happened after she met Jean. 'Which bed?' she asked.

Jean looked exasperated. 'Why on earth does that matter?'

'Which bed?'

'His. Probably. That one. What's the matter?'

So, she'd gone to him, he hadn't gone to her.

'How often?'

'Rita, this doesn't help – it doesn't change anything . . . All right, all right. Once, maybe twice a month. That's all. We're married, Rita, you make it sound like I've committed some terrible crime.'

She went to him, she enjoyed it.

'I thought . . .'

Jean frowned. 'You thought what?'

'That you and I . . .'

Jean pulled away. 'We what?'

'That we were friends. You know? Good friends.'

Jean looked baffled. 'We are. I've told you about this before I told Brian.'

Rita managed to keep her voice level. 'Do you want a baby?'

'We weren't trying for one. But I love Brian.'

'You said he was boring.'

Jean looked away, a little embarrassed. 'Well, he is. But I can rely on him.'

'But the war, the uncertainty.'

'Brian's too old, he won't be called up. And . . . well, we know we can cope with Joe and Adam. Don't tell Brian yet, I'm not sure that I am pregnant. You're the only person who knows.'

Rita smiled weakly. 'Congratulations.'

Jean grinned and hugged her. 'Thank you.'

'I ought to move back in with the Sugdens.'

Annie had wanted to avoid embarrassment, and had thought that meeting in the dining room for breakfast would be easier, more *normal*, than she and George waking, washing and dressing together.

She had been wrong.

She had forgotten she only had her evening dress to

put on. Her room was next door to George's, but she'd had to get back into her gown, which smelt terribly of cigarette smoke, and sneak out of one dark hotel room into another. No one had seen her, but she'd burned with guilt at the thought that a maid or cleaner, let alone another guest, might have done.

Ever since she'd come downstairs, she'd felt so self-conscious. Surely every one of the waitresses could *tell*? Every clink of cutlery against crockery seemed like Morse code to her, tapping out her guilty secrets.

The contrast between the liberated young woman who had enjoyed the night before, the thrill of waking up in a strange bed, and the coy, cowering creature she'd now become was not lost on her. She hadn't thought it would be so difficult. But, of course, it was precisely 'what other people would think' that was the problem.

She'd already been through all this, she reminded herself. Things must have happened behind closed doors in this hotel that made her own escapade pale into nothing. This was London, where millionaires, politicians and royalty lived. Even if the staff here knew – and how could they? – they wouldn't care.

George had just come in, and was coming over to her. He'd dressed and shaved, and looked very smart. He smiled as he sat down opposite her. 'Good morning. Did you sleep well?'

He said it just as if he didn't know the answer. But not everyone would have discreeyly passed her her engagement ring.

'I did,' Annie replied, before she slipped it on. 'I overslept a little.'

'You had a late night.'

'I've ordered a pot of tea.'

'Good.'

An awkward silence followed.

'I can hardly bring myself to go back to Yorkshire after what we did last night,' she told him.

He looked down. 'No?'

'No. Spending money on two hotel rooms and only using the one. My mother would have been horrified.'

George chuckled. 'Thank you,' he said. 'Thank you for last night. I'm so grateful.'

Annie looked away. 'Don't say it like that. You make it sound like it was a duty for me.'

'Jacob's very lucky.'

Annie couldn't meet his eyes. 'Yes. And you know that last night was . . . special.'

George nodded. 'You have a fiancé, a future.'

'I know that now. I didn't last night, but since I left your room,' George looked around, worried they'd been over-heard, but Annie didn't care any more, 'I've been thinking. I should be with Jacob.'

'This life isn't for you?'

Annie smiled. 'Oh, it could be – I'm not hungry, I had a good night's sleep for the first time in ages. Months? Years, probably. It's like I've had a wonderful holiday. It's ridiculous – this time yesterday we'd barely left the village. It seems so long ago, so far away. But it also seems like reality. This . . . this is a dream.'

Annie could see herself married to Jacob. She couldn't picture the day any more, but that didn't matter. She could see how she would lead her life with him, their children. 'I also have a good friend,' she told George, 'one who I can share a secret with.'

George nodded, accepting the decision. He looked a little sad. 'We don't have to vacate our rooms until noon. We could . . .'

Annie considered the idea, but already knew what her answer would be. The idea of putting a do-not-disturb sign on the door of one of their rooms, of George undressing again, making love, this time in the daylight. One last fling.

'No,' she said. 'Let's leave it at last night.'

George smiled. She saw the same mixed emotions on his face that she felt. And the same sense that she was right. Last night hadn't been a calculated act. Press either of them, and they'd admit it had always been a possibility, ever since the prospect of a trip to London had arisen, but they hadn't planned it that way.

He stood up, pecked her on the cheek and walked out.

Annie watched him go.

Seth was watching Betty Prendergast's house as if it was an enemy base.

'What are you doing, Seth?' Adam asked him.

Seth didn't take his eyes off the front door. 'ARP duties,' he told him.

'Isn't that where Betty Prendergast lives?' Adam asked.

'Aye.' Seth looked down. 'Are you settling in, lad?'

'Oh. Yes.' Adam was a little surprised that Seth called him 'lad'. He was only a few years older than Adam, after all. Seth had started to grow a moustache, but a few boys at school did that, and usually looked younger, not older, as though they were dressing up as adults. It was still a little early to see the effect it would have on Seth.

'It must be quite a change from life in the city,' Seth continued.

'Oh, yes. It's darker here, even compared with a city in blackout. And it's much quieter. Have you ever lived in a city, Seth?'

'Oh no.' He seemed agitated by the idea. 'Beckindale born and bred. I was born here, I'll die here.'

'It's a nice place to live. A bit quiet.'

'Not many girls your age, eh?'

213

'There's a few. Like that Betty girl you're courting. And Rita Goldman.'

'They're both a bit old for you,' Seth suggested.

'Oh, don't worry, I know Betty's spoken for by you.'

'Aye,' Seth said.

'Are you waiting for her?'

'Not exactly.'

'More tea, Private Eagleton?'

'Thank you very much, Mrs Prendergast.'

Wally and her mother were getting on very well – it was almost unnatural.

'Do you like the scones, Private Eagleton?'

'I do, Mrs Prendergast. Did you make them?'

'I did.'

'We might go out later,' Betty suggested.

Wally actually looked disappointed at the idea. Somehow, Betty couldn't see Seth being such a mummy's boy. She wouldn't mind, but this wasn't even Wally's own mother.

'You should go out,' Mrs Prendergast agreed.

But Betty wasn't so keen any more.

Rita was waiting for Louise to finish her bath. She'd got used to the luxury of the Sullivans' house, and this was a rude awakening. Louise had got a sea-sponge from some-where, and was using it to pour water over her shoulders and neck. It ran down her in thick rivulets, and she was absorbed in watching it.

'Are you going to be long?' Rita asked.

Louise had been lost in thought. She looked up. 'No. I didn't think you were keen on baths.'

'What do you mean?'

'Well, it's something Alyson said – not that you're dirty,

just that you don't seem to have as many baths as we do.'

Rita smiled. 'The Sullivans have a nicer one. Jean let me use it. So what's been going on while I've been away?'

'Virginia's helping Annie do something in the village hall tonight. Oh, Alyson's got a letter from Taffy. It's over there if you want a read, in her drawer.'

'And you've read it?'

'Virginia and I both have. It's not very racy stuff, though. He likes her.'

'That's good, then.'

'It's the romance of the century.' Every word dripped with sarcasm.

Rita hesitated. 'Louise . . .'

Louise looked amused. 'That's a serious tone of voice.'

'Do you really not believe in romance?'

'No. The world doesn't work that way. It's a lie.'

'Wouldn't it be better if it was true?'

'It'd be better if there was a Father Christmas and an Easter Bunny, too.'

'Oh, I know they're not real.' Rita chuckled. 'I'm a good Jewish girl.'

'But why do parents tell kids they are?'

'It's comforting, makes the world seem a nicer place.'

'That's it exactly. And that's what romance is. A comfort. A way of dressing up the truth.'

'The truth?'

'That what the man really wants is to take you to bed, to get a good look at you naked, to have his way with you.' Louise pulled herself out of the bath, stood dripping for a moment. 'There you go. A naked body. Is it really worth the fuss?'

'Adam, the eldest boy staying at the shop would certainly seem to think so.'

'Keen is he?'

'He's fourteen. Far too young.'

'I usually go for the older man myself,' Louise agreed, 'but youth has its advantages.'

'I don't think of him like that. Although that's certainly how he sees me. It's sweet, I suppose.'

'What about Mr Sullivan?'

'No . . . I mean he's generous, nice to Jean. But . . . no. And married, of course.'

Louise was beautiful. Thin, but in a healthy way. She barely had hips or breasts, but managed to be feminine. It was her confidence, Rita realised. It wasn't what you were given, it was what you did with it.

But she found Louise too calculating, too sure of herself.

'You're very cynical,' she said, pulling off her nightshirt.

Louise smiled with just a hint of cruelty. 'Name one man you know who wouldn't kill to be in this room. Two young women, no clothes. You can't do it, can you?' Rita tried to think. She didn't know many men. Louise was pulling on her robe, and found her cigarettes. 'If they could get away with it, any man would sleep with any woman who let them. Doesn't matter whether they're married, doesn't matter how shy, or what they do for a living, or where they were born. If there weren't consequences, they'd do it.'

'You probably think you're being realistic, but the world you live in sounds horrid.'

'No, it's nice. Uncomplicated. I meet a man I like, we have sex.'

'Straight away?'

Louise laughed. 'Roland and I did it before he knew my name. We were in such a rush he forgot to ask.'

Rita looked at her. There was no hint that Louise was only saying it to make her point, she seemed to mean it. And she didn't seem guilty or embarrassed.

'I bet Mr Sullivan fancies you,' Louise went on. 'And I bet that fourteen-year-old has a massive crush on you.'

216

'But that doesn't mean I should let them have their way with me.'

'Of course not. But you've got something they want, and romance is their way of getting it. Little gifts, nights on the town, getting you all alone and a bit drunk, it's a strategy, just like fighting a battle.'

'Paul wasn't like that.'

'He was,' Louise assured her.

'You never met him.'

'No. And I'm sure he loved you. But that's got nothing to do with romance. That's friendship. He wanted to have sex with you, but he knew that it would be better if you waited until you were both ready.'

'And now we never will.'

'No. But that doesn't mean you were wrong.'

'You think I was.'

'I think there's a lot of nonsense talked about sex. There's a lot of hypocrisy. People dress it up, make it seem like some mystical process. It's what our bodies do. It's like sneezing, or needing to wear thick socks when it's a cold day.'

'You really think so?'

'Yes. It can be a wonderful experience, it usually is, but that's all it is. People shouldn't get so guilty about it. And they shouldn't pretend that getting married means everything's fine. It's all an illusion, Rita. It should be about two people, and how they feel about each other. Everything else . . . well, everything else is nonsense.'

'I think you're right,' Rita said slowly.

Ron was moving around the shop, but Jean could already see he was here to moan, not to buy. 'Nothing like this happened until those airmen came along,' he told her.

'Nothing like what?' Jean asked, hoping to convey at least some of her lack of interest in the answer.

217

Ron wasn't discouraged. 'Sex,' he muttered, going bright red.

'Speak for yourself,' Jean laughed.

'I don't mean . . . you know. In wedlock.'

'Ron, I daresay it was going on before the war.'

'It's wrong.'

'Why?' Jean really wasn't listening.

'It's not right. It's immoral. I wouldn't expect you to understand.'

Jean bristled. 'No?'

'Well, you know.' Jean did know, and she didn't want him to make it worse by spelling it out. 'I know it's different for your lot.'

'Not that different.'

'Well, no. You've got the Ten Commandments. Do those girls even know they could get pregnant? Or, worse, that they could catch something and spread it around? It's not healthy.'

'They meet up in the Woolpack, don't they?'

'Aye, but . . .'

'It must be good business for you.'

'I didn't think you'd understand.'

And with that, Ron left.

Annie arrived home late.

'Jacob?'

'Did you have a nice time?'

'I did, yes.'

'I missed you.'

She hugged him. 'I missed you.'

'How were your posh new friends?'

'It was like a dream,' Annie told him, 'like being in a movie, and no substitute for real life.'

'I'm not sure I like real life,' he told her. 'And in the movies the British ships don't get sunk.'

'Edward died trying to keep the convoy routes clear. He died so that we could carry on. He wouldn't want us to give up.'

'No, he wouldn't. So we won't. I won't.' Jacob hugged her. 'Life goes on, doesn't it?'

CHAPTER NINETEEN:

Act of Revenge

There was a man in the front room with Mother. Betty hesitated at the door. It was rude to listen in, but it was just as rude to interrupt, especially when she didn't know who her visitor was.

'You're the same age as me, give or take. You're still young,' the man assured her. Betty didn't need to look to tell it was Brian Sullivan.

'My daughters aren't much younger than your wife.'

'Jean's more than ten years older,' Mr Sullivan objected, 'and those evacuees are making us feel our age, I can tell you. They aren't much younger than Betty and Margaret.'

'I suppose not. My girls seem so much older. They're both growing up so fast.'

'Oh, you wait a few years. One of the Land Girls has got friendly with Jean, and by the sound of it – well, the things those Land Girls get up to. She's a good girl, is Rita, but the others . . .'

'Girls today.' Betty's mother sighed. 'I despair for mine sometimes. Always talking about boys and courting.'

Betty was very surprised when Mr Sullivan laughed. 'If they're only talking about it, then they're late developers compared with our generation.'

Betty wanted to run into the room and interrogate them. What was that supposed to mean? Instead she stood perfectly still, with her ear pressed to the door.

'That's what I'm afraid of!' Her mother chuckled. 'I remember what I used to get up to.'

Well, go on, tell him what you mean, Betty thought, exasperated.

'I suppose it's what life's all about,' Mr Sullivan said. 'Young people doing things that shock their parents. Then growing up and being shocked by their own children. What they do when they're young doesn't really change, though.'

'I hope I'm not like my mother,' she said quietly. 'She was a right dragon.'

They heard what sounded like a muffled giggle from the other side of the door, but by the time Mrs Prendergast had opened the door to investigate, no one was there.

'I've got a doctor's appointment in Hotten. I want to check . . . well, you know, I want to be sure. I'll be back at two,' Jean told her.

'Doesn't that mean you'll miss the opening ceremony?' Rita asked.

'Yes. Could you take Joe and Adam up there? They'd love to explore, I'm sure. Brian will be minding the shop.'

'It's the least I could do,' Rita said happily.

Jean smiled. 'You're a lot . . . calmer, now.'

'Paul's death has sunk in. I've come to terms with it. For a while, I lost my bearings, you know.'

Jean smiled, then went upstairs.

Adam was sitting on the landing.

'Are you going to the opening ceremony?' Rita asked him.

'Joe wants to. But Mrs Sullivan's not going, and Mr Sullivan's got to mind the shop.'

'You don't need them, do you? You spend half your time playing up there.'

'Not playing,' Adam objected. 'Watching them open the aerodrome.'

'But you're not going?'

'I told you, Joe's going, I'm not.'

'What are you going to do instead?'

'Stay in.'

Rita took a deep breath. 'Stay in?' she repeated.

'Yes.'

'Would you like to go out?'

'No, I told you, I—'

'I mean with me.'

'You?'

'Yes.' She handed him her packet of cigarettes.

'I don't smoke.'

'I'll teach you how. I'll meet you there at two. But I need you to make yourself scarce until then.'

She had barely finished the sentence before he was out of the door.

There was usually a small opening ceremony and dedication when an airfield was opened. Often they were small, private affairs but, at Roland's suggestion, the villagers had been invited to the opening of RAF Emmerdale and almost everyone turned up.

George Verney looked proud, as well he might. This place was a model of co-operation with the locals and efficient working practices, completed ahead of time. And it was the point at which he stopped being lord of the manor, and became a full-time RAF officer. He had a desk job, but an important one: he was to be second-in-command on the ground, below the wing commander. George would keep the station ticking over but he wouldn't be involved in the fighting.

Annie Pearson was there with Jacob and their fathers. Jacob had his arm around Annie, which struck Roland as demonstrative, a trait he'd not seen in the farmer before. His brother's death must have brought them closer together. Sam Pearson had come too – he must have put aside his objections to the airfield at least for the ceremony. Roland had seen Joseph Sugden around Home Farm a lot, and in the weeks since his son's death, he'd looked older, pale and drawn. He made a mental note to phone his own father that evening, before Louise arrived.

The Land Girls stood in a group close to the Sugdens. Louise stood with them demurely, knowing that a public display of affection, or even familiarity, towards him would be inappropriate. She also knew that her presence would make it difficult for him to keep his mind on the job. The Jewish girl – Rita? – wasn't there, but Virginia was. Most interesting of all, Alyson was clearly making eyes at Taffy, and it was all Taffy could do to keep a straight face. Something was going on there, Roland thought.

Ron was there, but Colin wasn't – the pub couldn't close. Ron had typed up an invitation for the men serving here to visit the Woolpack, and had made several carbon copies. Roland admired his nerve, and directed him over to George Verney for permission to put them up. It would do morale good if the lads posted here felt they were part of a community, and there were worse places they could end up on a night out than the Woolpack.

A delegation of Dingles was there, trying to look their smartest.

So, who wasn't? The Sullivans were presumably running the shop. The youngest of the evacuees was here, so his brother couldn't be far away. The only notable absentee was Seth Armstrong. He must have something special on that was keeping him from hobnobbing with the airmen, and taking advantage of the free drink.

'Rita?'

She'd come into the shop from the back room, wearing a short dress. She was a good-looking young woman.

'Jean's in Hotten,' Brian told her.

'I know. I came to see you. Do you want to come into the back? We could talk.'

He was a little bewildered, but he'd not had a customer for an hour, thanks to the ceremony up at the airfield. He followed Rita through.

'Can I get you a drink?' he asked

'Whisky?' she asked.

He looked at her, surprised. 'I meant tea or coffee, but if you want something stronger . . .' He went over to the sideboard, fished out a bottle and a couple of glasses.

She was sitting on the sofa. 'I thought you'd moved back up to Emmerdale,' he said, and sat next to her. He expected her to shift over, and she did, but towards him, not away.

'I wanted to say thank you.'

'Oh, right. No problem. I know you had a difficult time and needed Jean's support.'

'You helped me, too. I don't know very much about you. I spend a lot of time with Jean, and she talks about you, but that's all.' She sniffed her whisky, took a swig – a little too much. She covered well, pretending she had expected the jolt. 'Would you have liked to see more of me?' she asked.

'Well, yes. You said Jean talks about me? What sort of things does she say?' Brian asked.

'What do you think?'

'She's so beautiful.' He hesitated. 'You look a lot like her.'

224

Rita looked straight at him, almost straight through him. 'Are you saying I'm your type?'

He looked away. 'Well, you're an attractive woman, yes.' He felt guilty admitting even that much, although it was obvious.

'I think Jena's a very lucky woman,' Rita told him.

'Do you?'

'You've got your own business, this is a good life for her.'

'I sometimes think she deserves better. This is a small village, there aren't many opportunities. She runs the shop, you know. If we lived in Manchester or Leeds, I'm sure she'd have a chain of shops by now. I'm holding her back. I don't grab the nettle. Do you know what I mean? I play it safe.'

'You find me attractive?'

'Yes.'

'I like you, too.'

Brian stared at her. She was smiling at him. It looked as though she meant it.

'Take me upstairs,' she said.

Brian swallowed. 'What?'

'I want you to take me to bed. To say thank you.'

'But my wife . . .'

Rita leant in. 'You're playing it safe again. I've seen you looking at me. You want to do it. She won't be back until four.'

'Four?'

'She's in Hotten, you know that. We won't be disturbed.'

He'd thought about it, idly but he'd never considered that it might be possible.

'Haven't you seen me looking at you the same way?'

'I . . . thought I did. But I'm nothing special.'

'You must be.'

'No, I . . . Jean and I, the physical side's never been that important. We both like it that way.'

'You don't.'

'What?'

'You don't. You like to play it safe, but really you wish you could do more, you wish it wasn't a problem. You find her beautiful, but you can't express that in the way you want to.'

'She told you this?'

'Of course not. But I can tell.'

He leant in, kissed her, found himself grabbing at her breast.

After a few moments of that, she pulled away. 'Not here. Bedroom.'

Seth stood a little nervously at the foot of Betty's bed. She came into the room, looked down at him. 'There's nowhere to sit,' he said.

'I've locked the front door,' Betty told him. She went over to the window. 'It's a bit stuffy.' She opened the windows then closed the curtains. If this was her idea of stuffy, Seth was glad he hadn't invited her into his room.

'Er . . . and your mother and Maggie are at the opening ceremony?'

'That's right.' She sat on the end of the bed. Betty patted the mattress. 'Come here, Seth love.'

It was softer than he was used to. Sitting down next to Betty made a V-shape in it, which made her slide towards him. He had to hold her to keep her steady.

'What about Wally?'

'Wally's boring.'

He kissed her cheek. She kissed him back.

Seth risked a kiss on her mouth. She responded, and they spent a little while kissing like they did in the movies. He wondered what he'd do next, what Betty would let him get away with.

She pulled away. That was his ration for the day, Seth

thought. Well, it was a good start, and better than he'd
dared hope for. Certainly not a disappointment. He smiled
down at her.

'That moustache itches,' she complained, shifting away
from him. 'It's nice. A bit small, though.'

'Give it time. I'm going to grow one like some of those
RAF types have.'

It took him a moment to register that Betty was undo-
ing one of her blouse buttons, about half-way down. Then
she took his hand and guided it into the gap.

'Everyone's at it,' she explained. 'Even them that says
no one should be. I thought we could give it a go, too.'

Seth gulped. 'Well, if you like.'

'You know what you're doing?'

'Er . . . aye, yes.'

'But you've not done it before?'

'No. No. You're the only lass I've so much as kissed.
Only one I've ever wanted to kiss.'

'Good. Carry on.'

As his fingers made their way in, they cupped themselves against the lace of her brassière, and his thumb
found itself stroking surprisingly soft skin. He moved
his hand in a tiny circle, fascinated. Betty gave a little
moan. The sound shocked them both. Betty looked up at
him, a little embarrassed. 'It's nice, is that,' she admitted, holding his wrist so that he couldn't withdraw his
hand. 'You know what you're doing? Lads know, don't
they?'

But Seth wasn't listening. 'Can you smell burning?'

'Burning?'

'Aye.'

Seth pulled back, sniffing the air. 'Burning,' he
repeated.

Betty held out a hand. 'Come on, don't worry about
that. Someone else will—'

But Seth had reached for his helmet. 'No. It's me job.' He got up, hurried to the window. 'It's the pavilion,' he said. 'It's going up in smoke. I have to get over there.'

CHAPTER TWENTY:
Emergency Conditions

The base would have its own chaplain, but for the moment the local vicar, Mr Summerfield, was filling in. The villagers and men present bowed their heads and prayed that the airmen here would be kept safe, and that they would help to bring a swift victory.

Roland could imagine Louise laughing at that, pointing out that German vicars, or whatever they had instead of vicars, would be praying to the same God, asking for *their* boys to win. He looked over at her for confirmation. Perhaps he had misjudged her – her expression was as serious as he'd ever seen it. Maybe he was ascribing his own doubts to her. The Germans worshipped the same God as he did. They were building bases like this, in villages like this. And within a few days, he'd be over those bases and villages, and he'd be dropping thousand-pound bombs on them. He'd seen some of the latest bombs, so heavy the planes' runways had had to be modified to carry them. Some were designed to bury themselves fifty feet below ground. Most of the nearby buildings would collapse from the shockwave alone, but then the bomb would explode, destroying foundations and water pipes, gas lines and cellars. He'd attended a briefing at which the boffins had him told enthusistically that there wasn't a building in Germany or the occupied territories that they couldn't destroy. Presumably Roland's German counterparts had been shown a bomb capable of doing the same to British buildings.

No one was safe in this war. For the first time in centuries, ordinary British civilians were in as much danger as the soldiers. There had been Zeppelin raids last time, but not many. Now, as a matter of routine, both sides targeted cities and factories, because in a total war, with the whole economy geared to making tanks and planes, there was no such thing as an 'innocent bystander'. The RAF's *Instructions Governing Air Bombardment* had been changed to make it legal and all right, but five years ago it would have been seen as the most heinous war crime. When Annie Pearson had handed in her old saucepans so that they could be melted down and made into Spitfires, she became part of the war machine. Beckindale was a tiny village, but it had produced dozens of soldiers and workers, and would continue to do so.

Roland shuddered.

How would this war end? With the destruction of Germany, or of Britain. That was the only way. He imagined himself as an old man, fighting with an ancient German, the last two men alive. Europe had been ravaged by the last war; it had taken almost until now to recover from it. This time, the destruction would be even more comprehensive. Afterwards, would anything be be left? Or would America and Russia just divide the continent between them?

Such thoughts left him feeling cold inside. He made an effort to concentrate on the here and now. The chapel was just a Nissen hut, with a semicircular corrugated tin roof. The chairs were ordinary wooden ones, without cushions. The hymn books looked new – they had the thin paper and soft leatherette covers that they'd come to expect in wartime. One nice touch was that the crucifix had been made from an old wooden propeller, or had been carved to look like it had. At the moment, though, this chapel was cold, impersonal – there were no flowers, no colourful hassocks to kneel on. Even here he couldn't take his mind off his job. The chapel needed a few home comforts before the lads would – except for the devout ones – use it.

The short service ended with a speech from the regional commander, an air vice marshal. He stressed the importance of the airfield, and how it would be a valuable part of the war effort. He said nothing new, and Roland thought he detected an increase in the rate at which people were shuffling their feet. It was counterproductive, someone from outside coming in and telling them what they already knew. The top brass liked to think that showing their faces boosted morale, but in Roland's experience it did the opposite: it reminded the men of how far away their superiors were on all the other days, how little they knew about what was happening locally.

They shuffled out of the chapel into a cold winter day. The villagers were getting ready to set off down the lane back to Beckindale. As they chatted among themselves, it started to snow. Just the odd flake, so little that it took a moment to confirm that it was actually snow. The congregation broke up into small groups.

'Pilgrim, this is Wing Commander Harrow. He'll be in charge here.'

Roland saluted.

'I've seen the results of your work, Pilgrim. Good show.'

Roland's heart sank. First impressions were important and his first impression of his new CO was that he was another Colonel Blimp. He'd never heard of him. 'I could conduct a tour for you,' he offered.

'Later,' Harrow said, marching off, barely acknowledging the villagers who wanted to greet him.

Louise stepped over to Taffy. 'You were looking at me during the service,' she said sternly.

'No,' Taffy insisted. 'I was looking at Alyson.'

Alyson almost shoved Louise out of the way. 'I got your letter,' she told him.

He was bright red. 'I'm on duty, love.'

Louise had to stop herself smiling.

'Are there enough hangars for the planes?' Ron asked.

'Not every plane gets a hangar. Far from it. We'll be parking them up around the perimeter track,' Roland explained.

'Will they be Lancasters?' the evacuee asked. Like most boys, he'd have taken a keen interest in military vehicles and other equipment and paraphernalia, Roland decided. He'd know better than half the new recruits how many stripes a squadron leader had, and how to identify different planes.

'Halifaxes,' Roland told him, hoping he wasn't breaking the Official Secrets Act.

'They're better, aren't they?'

Roland grinned. 'That's what those of us who fly them think. The chaps who fly Lancasters think differently, though. The Halifax is harder to fly, but it gets you home more often.'

'I want to fly Halifaxes.'

'Well, I'm afraid the war will be over before you're old enough.'

'I hope not.'

Roland winced. 'It will be,' he said. 'I promise.'

'They all gave me their ties,' Ron told Mrs Prendergast.

'Their ties?' she repeated.

232

'Last night at the Woolpack. All the airmen who were there. I don't know how it started, but one handed me his tie, and said he'd be coming back for it. Then all of them took their ties off, and said the same.'

'For good luck?'

'That's it, yes. It was like that in the trenches. If you said you were coming back, it was like you'd made a promise. Soldiers are superstitious.'

'Miss Pearson,' George Verney said.

'Lieutenant.'

They smiled at a private joke.

'I've not seen you since London.'

'No.'

'You and Jacob look happy together.'

'We are. We always were. He's getting over Edward's death now, talking about the future again.'

'That's good.'

Louise caught up with Roland, looked as casual as possible so that no one would be suspicious. She wouldn't commit the same *faux pas* as Alyson. 'This place is very impressive.'

'Thank you,' he replied.

'Will the snow slow things down?'

And before Roland could answer, he didn't need to.

They all heard the droning, and looked around, a little concerned. The Germans occasionally launched daylight raids, and it was quite common to hear fighters, either the RAF on patrol or perhaps a Luftwaffe reconnaissance aircraft. But these were heavy bombers, great four-engined things. A couple of the villagers looked as if they might panic, but their nerves were steadied by the calm manner of the base personnel.

The first plane appeared over the horizon barely above

the treetops, and swept down, a perfect landing. Its tyres squeaked against the concrete of the runway. Within minutes, as they watched, more and more planes appeared, until there were ten altogether, all parked or parking.

Roland worked with these planes, but they were still a marvel to him. They were great big things, with four engines, each of which was the size of his Bugatti. They looked too solid, too massive to fly. But they were made of metal struts, paint and glass – they were flimsy things. The men called them 'kites', and that's all they were, really: the biggest, most powerful bomber was just a couple of generations away from a box kite.

'So soon?' Louise asked, watching the ground crews go about their business, guiding the planes in, shepherding them into their vast hangars.

'Why wait?'

'When will you be flying?'

'Not for a few days. We need to check the planes, get to know the crews, prepare for orders, get in some last minute training. I think the plan is that we fly out on Thursday.'

Louise gazed at the planes, silent.

There weren't blackout curtains at the pavilion. No one used the place at night, so they'd just taken the lightbulb out of the socket to prevent it being left on accidentally. Now Seth could see smoke drifting out under the door. As he approached, it was getting warmer. Seth could hear something burning. He could smell it, too. An unusual smell: fires smelt of coal or wood, as a rule, but this was different – the smell of cloth, the smell of paper. He pictured all those cricket bats and jumpers going up in smoke.

The pavilion was a hut, really, a large wooden shed

with a little open porch at the front where players sat watching the game. Seth played on the Beckindale team, he knew the inside of the building – there wasn't even room to get changed. There was some expensive equipment in there.

He peered in. The smoke was thick and everything had fallen over. And, right at the back of the room, was a figure. A boy, by the look of it. It was Adam. He was unconscious.

'Seth!' Betty was calling twenty or thirty yards behind him.

But Seth ignored her, concentrated on the pavilion.

'Get help,' he told her. 'Then get my stirrup pump.'

If the fire broke out, it would be a beacon – it would light up the village, make it a target. If German bombers spotted it they might head this way, and if that happened, they might even see the airfield as they circled over.

Right on cue, Seth heard planes.

A moment of panic. A trapped boy, a German invasion, and everyone was up at the airfield. Had the Nazis heard about the airfield? Were they trying to put it out of commission before it even opened?

Seth stopped himself, remembered his training, and that he should think things through.

It was daylight, so those were RAF planes.

His priority was to rescue the boy.

He heard glass tinkle and shatter in there. All those pictures of teams from years gone by, they'd be curling and burning now. They went back years, the oldest to the very early days of photography. In there, somewhere, was the Butterworth Ball, the trophy fought for every year between Robblesfield and Beckindale.

But none of that mattered.

Open the door, and he'd feed the flame with oxygen. Go in there, and he risked being overcome by fumes.

He remembered his gas-mask, and got it out of the box, then pulled the elasticated straps over his head. It wasn't a very good fit, but a couple of deep breaths and he couldn't smell smoke any more.

Seth kicked the door, right on the lock. It budged, but not enough. He kicked it again, and this time the door gave way, flying open.

There was a wave of hot air, and then a burst of flames. The heat was ferocious. Seth remembered something in his ARP book: it wasn't the flames that killed people in a house fire, it was inhaling the smoke or just the hot air.

It looked like a furnace in there. Opening the door had the same effect as opening the door on a wood-burner – the flames were getting higher, and brighter.

Seth stood on the doorstep, knowing that if the boy was alive he had just seconds to save him. He couldn't see him now for the smoke.

He launched in, heading straight for the back of the hut. It wasn't a big place, and it was full of flames. There wasn't anywhere else the boy could be.

He was trapped under a table. Seth grabbed him, tugged him out, picked him up, then bore out the way he'd come in, through the flames.

Betty was at the front of a group of villagers hurrying towards him. Lazarus Dingle and Colin from the Woolpack both had a couple of buckets.

Betty pulled off Seth's mask, and he sucked in the cold air.

'Anyone else in there?' Seth coughed. It hurt to speak.

'I don't know what happened,' the boy said quietly.

'Anyone else?' Seth repeated.

'No.'

Seth nodded, satisfied. Everything was going dark.

Brian closed the bedroom door behind them. 'Here we are,' he said, a little nervously.

Rita nodded, just wanting to get it over with.

He opened a drawer, rummaged around, and finally held up a flimsy white sliver of material. 'It's a slip. French lace. I bought it for her, but she never wore it for me. You're about the same size, I wonder if you might . . .'

'I'll wear it for you,' Rita heard herself say.

His eyes lit up.

'I'll get changed into it. Don't look.'

He turned away. But even so, Rita found herself opening the wardrobe door, using it as a screen. She undressed quickly, keeping her eyes on Brian the whole time. It was stupid, but she didn't want him to see her like this, not for a second longer than was necessary. He didn't even try to turn round.

She slipped on the lingerie, which made her feel exposed, foolish, rather than seductive. How he could ever have thought Jean would wear it baffled her.

'You can look now,' she told him.

He leered at her as she crossed the room, climbed into his bed and covered herself with the sheets. 'I've never cheated on Jean before,' he told her.

'Don't think of it like that,' she told him, trying to sound reassuring.

A sneeze, Rita thought, remembering what Louise had said. Something everyone did or wanted to do. There was nothing wrong. She was doing this to prove a point.

He began tugging off his clothes. Underneath them, he was fat, already sweating. Rita found herself watching, fascinated. He was naked, now. Everything seemed to hang and sag.

He clambered into bed, started pawing at her, kissing her. She did nothing to stop him. Before he'd really looked at her in it, the slip was in a pile on the floor. Wearing nothing was better than wearing that, she thought.

Not everything he was doing was unpleasant, but Rita

felt detached from events, as if she wasn't really there.

Brian didn't seem to notice her diffidence: he had clambered on top of her now. He was heavy, a solid, unfamiliar weight. It didn't hurt as much as she'd been expecting, it wasn't as clumsy. It was almost reassuring, and the totality of his devotion to her, or at least to the task at hand, was rather satisfying. He was giving himself to her, just as much as she was giving herself to him. She followed his lead, clutching at him, planting kisses all over his face.

It was clear when it was over, despite his hugging and holding. Rita found herself a little disappointed that there hadn't been more to it, and surprised at what a messy process it was.

Brian was red-faced, out of breath. 'That was fantastic,' he told her. 'The best I've ever—' He stopped himself.

She felt sorry for him. Was that really as good as it got for him?

'We ought to get up,' he told her, meaning it. They hadn't even caught their breath. They had been upstairs for a couple of minutes, no more.

'No. Stay . . .'

'But my wife—'

'Won't be back for hours.' She nodded towards the clock.

He looked at the clock, then at her, then sank back into the bed.

'There's a doctor on the way,' someone assured Betty. She'd been clutching Seth's hand.

Lazarus Dingle had his head on Seth's chest. 'I'm sorry, love, I think it's too late. I can't hear his heart.'

Betty started sobbing.

Then Seth's chest shook, and he gave a huge cough.

'Aye, well, I could be wrong,' Lazarus admitted.

'Help's on its way,' Betty whispered to Seth.

Colin and Lazarus had thrown the buckets of sand

they'd brought onto the fire, but it hadn't made any difference.

⸳ 'There's a fire engine coming from the airfield,' someone said. 'They've got three or four of them there in case the planes crash. Mr Pilgrim said he'll make sure there's a doctor on it.'

'How's the boy?'

Adam had come round and was sitting on the pitch, looking terrible. 'It's my fault.'

'What happened?' Colin asked.

'I was – I was smoking, and I must have dropped a match. The fumes . . .'

They could hear the fire engine now.

Mr Sullivan and Rita lay there for a few minutes. He made a show of cuddling her a little, kissing her cheek. But a few minutes after that he was asleep.

Rita couldn't relax. She kept glancing at the bedside clock, waiting. It was twenty to two. She just thought it took longer than it did. The plan was that Jean was going to come home and find them in the middle of it. Jean thought she could rely on her husband. But Louise had been right. It had been so easy. Stupidly easy. Was every marriage like this? Why would Jean want to cling to this?

For twenty minutes, she didn't dare move, for fear of waking Brian. He wasn't sweaty, so that was something.

There were bells – it sounded like a police car. She thought that the noise had woken Brian, but his shift towards her, and a new source of warmth, seemed entirely unconscious.

She had time to consider what she had done.

Slept with her friend's husband, made him cheat on her for the first time. Rita wanted Jean to know that it was possible, that there was no stability here, it was an illusion, just like Louise had said. Carefully, Rita pulled back the sheet until it was around their knees. There shouldn't be any doubt, she thought. No room for the slightest doubt.

She was lying flat on the bed and he was pressed alongside her, his arm draped on her stomach. Brian was snoring now, ever so softly. His hand moved up until it was resting on her breast – his hands had barely left her breasts since he'd first made his move.

He was a tender man, gentle. A good husband. Someone who looked after the boys as well as they could hope for.

For the first time, Rita felt guilty, selfish. How dare she intrude on this marriage? He had cheated on Jean, just as Louise had predicted, but what did that prove? He hadn't ever done it before, he wouldn't do it again.

Downstairs. The back door opened and there was a noise on the stairs. Rita looked over at Mr Sullivan. He was still fast asleep, a loose smile on his face.

No. She thought. I have to go through with this.

There was a knock at the bedroom door, just a faint one.

Rita lay back, pretended to be fast asleep.

She heard the door open, counted to ten, then made a great show of opening her eyes and stretching.

Adam was standing in the doorway, fixed to the spot. He was gaping, unsure whether to run away, or just stare. Rita couldn't do anything but play the part she had planned – let him look at her, let what they'd just been doing sink in. She felt her skin get warmer as she flushed with embarrassment.

Adam was pale, dirty.

'There was no one in the shop,' Adam explained. 'There are people downstairs. There's been an accident. I have to go to hospital. I told them to wait downstairs.'

His guardian was awake, now, aware of the problem or perhaps just the draught.

'Adam!'

The boy looked right at her. 'Rita, I thought we were . . .'

He turned on his heel.

'Wait!' Mr Sullivan called. He was climbing out over Rita, reaching for his dressing gown.

The boy was already downstairs. 'Leave me alone!' Rita heard him shout. And there were other voices – one sounded like an astonished Betty Prendergast, another like the barman from the Woolpack.

What was going on?

Rita got up, and quickly got dressed. What happened next? Would Adam tell the villagers down there? Would they be able to work it out? She didn't want to humiliate Jean – this was between them. It wasn't what she'd planned, she'd hoped for instant . . . well, instant revenge. Louise had told her it would all be so simple. The act itself had been easy. It was supposed to be Jean who found them. Then that was supposed to be the end of it. Conclusive proof that Jean was wrong. What sort of plan was that? All the doubts, all the guilt Rita had managed to keep in check surfaced like a great wave.

She found herself sitting up, struggling for breath.

She'd done something terribly wrong.

CHAPTER TWENTY-ONE:

Marching Orders

Wing Commander Harrow was pacing around his office, trying to get the feel of it. There was already a great pile of reports and forms on his desk.

'First operation on Thursday night, Pilgrim. That won't be a problem, will it?'

'No, sir. Can I ask—'

'Not yet, we're still finalising it. Until then, you and your men enjoy yourselves. Do what you can to relax. I want you all in and ready at noon on Thursday.'

'Sir. Thank you.'

As Roland left the office, one of the CO's assistants, a pretty WAAF (they were all pretty, Roland had noticed), was shuffling with some papers on her desk.

'Have you made a will, Squadron Leader Pilgrim?'

There was a nugget of cold in his stomach. 'No,' he told her.

She handed him a couple of pieces of paper. 'We've got forms. Just a few boxes to fill. We can get it witnessed here.'

Death. He could accept death. It came with the job. He didn't want to die, of course he didn't, but he knew there was a chance of it. The Ministry was keeping a tight lid on casualty figures, and that was always a sign that things were bad. Roland had talked to colleagues, and being in a bomber crew would be risky. Alone over enemy territory, at the mercy of the weather and mechanical failure. Those were the real killers – the anti-aircraft guns and fighter planes took their toll, but at 2,500 feet up it didn't take much to kill a man. As the commander-in-chief of Bomber Command said, the army fought six battles a year, the navy fought six battles a war, and bombers fought six battles every night.

But if it came, it would be quick, in the thick of it. A hero's death.

And death had never bothered him until he'd been handed this piece of paper. He filled in the details quickly, thinking that it was making his death inevitable – official.

He shook himself. He should have thought of this for himself. It was a necessary piece of business, not a death warrant.

He had thought he had few possessions, but as he came to list them, he was surprised by just how much he had: the Bugatti, bits of furniture, books, a couple of rather expensive watches, a few heirlooms. But what really surprised him was that he'd bequeathed it all to Louise. He'd written her name on the form without even thinking about it. There weren't many other candidates – no close family still alive, only a handful of friends, most of them in the forces.

Louise it was.

And then he signed the form. The WAAF and her colleague witnessed it, and it was official.

Jean Sullivan didn't recognise Adam in the waiting room at first – why would he be there? 'What's going on?' she asked.

'I went off. I'm sorry.'

'What's the matter?'

'I was in a fire.'

'A fire?'

'Yes. Seth Armstrong rescued me. He's here, too. They don't know if he's going to be all right.'

'This was at the shop?'

'No, the pavilion. The cricket pavilion.'

'Where's Brian?'

He looked away.

'He's all right, isn't he?' Jean asked.

Adam was crying.

'Adam?'

'Before they brought me here, they took me back to the shop to tell you where I was. But . . . he wasn't in the shop, so I went upstairs, and he wasn't anywhere else, and I knocked on the bedroom door. And he was in there with Rita.'

'Doing what?' she asked, although she knew she didn't have to.

'They were asleep together. They weren't wearing any clothes.'

'I see. You know what they had been doing?'

Adam went bright red. 'They were having it off.'

'That's not a polite expression.'

'But that's what they'd been doing.'

'Yes.'

He hesitated. 'You're not angry?'

'Why would I be angry with you?'

'With . . . him.'

She sighed. 'I'm disappointed.'

'I am too,' Adam said.

She frowned. 'You are? Why?'

'I . . . like Rita. And I like Mr Sullivan, too, of course.'

'You fancy her?'

Adam squirmed. 'A bit,' he admitted. 'So what happens now?'

Jean sighed. 'What indeed?'

'Are you all right, Rita?'

'Alyson. Hi.'

Alyson had been cleaning her teeth at the sink by the door, and had heard Rita coming in and sitting on the stairs. When Alyson opened the door, she saw that the other girl had been crying. 'What's the matter?'

'It's gone wrong,' Rita told her. 'Everything's gone wrong.'

'Paul?'

'Not just that, but . . . I wish I'd slept with Paul. Well, I think I do. He would still have died, it wouldn't have changed that, but I . . . I didn't realise what it meant. You love Taffy, don't you? Just don't wait if you do.'

'Well, now you mention it . . .' Alyson took her hand and led her to the door, which she pushed open. Taffy was lying face down on Alyson's bed, fast asleep and quite naked.

'I've worn him out,' she said cheerfully. 'He was so eager. Your first time isn't meant to be any good, is it? But he really knew what he was doing. You don't mind me bringing him back? It's just that everyone else was at the airfield, so straight after the service was over we hurried back here.'

'Of course I don't mind,' Rita said. 'I – I need to go for a walk.'

'Don't do anything I wouldn't do.' Alyson grinned, and disappeared back into the bedroom.

Everything was very white, Seth thought. He couldn't remember Mr Summerfield ever saying that heaven smelt of carbolic soap, though. He was awake, Seth realised. He was alive.

Hospital.

He couldn't remember the last time he'd been in the

cottage hospital in Hotten, but he recognised the place. A green curtain was drawn around the bed, but Seth thought he must be in quite a large ward. He could hear hustle and bustle around him from outside the curtain.

Betty was sitting at the side of the bed. 'His eyes are open,' she said.

Whatever medicine he was on was working, because it took him a few seconds to work out who she was talking about. The world was a bit of a blur.

He flexed his fingers and toes, making sure they were all still there. He couldn't feel any bandages on his body, but there was a smallish one on his cheek, one of those ones where they used cotton wool. It was a bit uncomfortable to breathe.

He felt sore all over, like he'd been in a fight.

'The boy,' he remembered. 'How's Adam?'

'He's fine,' said a male voice.

'Wally?' Seth asked.

'That's right. The doctors say he'll be discharged tomorrow. You saved his life. You're a hero.'

Betty and Wally were smiling down at him. Wally had a comforting arm around Betty's shoulder. He looked smart in his army uniform.

Seth opened his mouth to say something, but couldn't think of the right words.

'You need your rest,' Betty told him. 'Come on, Wally.'

Jean Sullivan found her husband sitting by the remains of the cricket pavilion. He was hunched up, hands on his knees. 'You must be cold,' she said.

'You know?' he asked.

'I know.'

'I'm sorry,' he said. 'I don't know why I—'

She put a finger on his lips. 'You made a mistake.'

'I slept with your best friend.'

246

'And I'm not happy about it, I certainly don't forgive you.'

He gazed off into the distance. 'You can have the shop and anything else you want. I won't make it difficult for you.'

She laughed. 'Oh, no, you don't get away with it that easily.'

He turned to look at her. 'You don't want a divorce?'

'No.'

'What do you want?'

'To be with you.'

'Really?'

'Of course. I'm pregnant, Brian.'

His mouth did funny things. 'Really? I mean, we weren't . . .'

'I love you.'

'But I—'

'You had . . . an indiscretion. I'm sure it happens a lot. I found out about it. It doesn't mean you don't love me. Rita's a pretty girl, you fell for her. Got carried away. In your position, I'd have done the same thing.'

'How can you be so understanding? How do you know I won't do it again? I don't understand why I did it,' he confessed. 'You're so much more beautiful.'

Jean smiled. 'That's the spirit. Come on, we should get inside, where it's warm.'

Roland clung to Louise, falling and rising, falling and rising, losing himself, as if it was the last time they'd ever do this.

It might be, of course. They both knew it. For the moment, it was possible to obliterate the thought. It was like getting drunk, or immersing yourself in work, or playing the wireless really loudly and just dancing. It stopped you thinking.

Only them.

The war, his mission, the airfield, Home Farm, Roland's room, even the edges of the bed, they all seemed so far away, so unimportant.

Only them.

And then Louise cried out, and Roland gasped, and Louise cried out again, and Roland fell onto her for the last time, and they held each other and the rest of the world existed again, and they were both scared by it.

'I love you,' Louise said.

She felt him shake as he laughed. 'Be careful. I've got pals who've proposed before they've got their breath back, and ended up regretting it.'

She squeezed him. 'No. I mean it, I love you.'

He was looking down at her. 'You do mean it.' He hesitated. 'I . . . love you, too.'

'I'm so scared.'

Roland was sitting up. He ran his fingers over her stomach, tickling her a little. 'It's not you who's going.'

'No. I don't think I could.'

'If you could, you would. I could have chosen to join some other service. We're only people . . . but that's enough, isn't it?'

'I don't doubt *you*, or your crew, but those planes are just machines. Like tractors. They go wrong, you said yourself they have their limits. And you're out there on your own, actually over Germany, over all those millions of soldiers.'

'Yes. But I have a good incentive to get home.'

She was sitting up now, stroking his face. 'I don't think I can bear to see you off,' she told him. 'I just don't think I could stand there and watch your plane leave.'

'I understand,' Roland said, hugging her. 'I'd rather think of you here, waiting for me to come back. Keeping warm.'

'I can't stay *here*,' she reminded him. 'Thanks to everything that's happened in the last few weeks, there's hardly been any work done on the farm. They need all hands on deck.'

Roland squeezed her hand. 'Stay here tonight, if you think you can.'

Louise glanced around at her luxurious surroundings. 'This isn't your room any more. You've moved into that draughty hut.'

Roland grimaced. 'Don't remind me. But I want to know where you are.'

'Mr Verney . . .'

'Flight Lieutenant Verney will be in the control tower with other things on his mind. I'll ask him. He'll approve. Just for tonight.'

'I'll be here,' Louise told him.

'And I'll come back,' Roland promised.

As the years went on, it would become a familiar sight, a routine, just one more indication that night was falling. But that first night, those living at Emmerdale Farm sat on the wall facing Home Farm, and listened and watched as the bombers set off for Germany.

There were dozens, all taking off within a minute of each other. And they seemed larger at night than they had when they landed after the opening ceremony. The Land Girls and the Sugdens debated whether they'd be able to work out which Halifax Squadron Leader Pilgrim and Sergeant Jones were on, but in the event all the planes were silhouettes, anonymous in the night.

'Taffy might not come back,' Virginia told Alyson.

'No, but he's doing a job that needs doing,' Rita said.

'They all are,' Louise agreed.

Jacob was standing a little apart from the others and Annie went over to him. 'Edward?' she asked.

'He died for a reason,' Jacob said. 'He died to make sure all this carried on. Maybe more than that – so that all this gets better. He was brave, he did his duty. But the most important thing was that he was *right*. Places like Beckindale, Emmerdale, they've been here for centuries. The life here, not just the traditions, but the things people do, the way people go about their business . . . It's worth fighting for.'

Annie held him close, and together they watched the bombers head off into the night.